CHECK FOR CD IN BACK POCKET
ON ISSUE AND RETURN
19. MAR 10.
20. FEB 06
10. NOV 07
25. JUL 09
02. JAN 10

D0996400

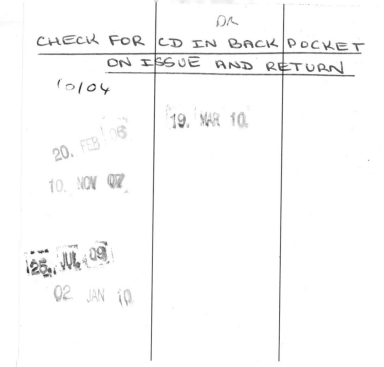

Abracadabra
CLARINET

The way to learn
through songs and tunes

Jonathan
Rutland

Second edition

A & C Black • London

Second edition 2002
A&C Black Publishers Ltd
37 Soho Square
London W1D 3QZ
© 2002, 1988 A&C Black Publishers Ltd
Book ISBN 0 7136 6199 2
Book/CD ISBN 0 7136 6200 X

Music setting by Jeanne Fisher
Illustrations by Caroline Glicksman
Fingering diagrams by Graham Pinder
Cover illustration by Dee Shulman
Text design by Jocelyn Lucas
Edited by Brian Hunt and Jane Sebba

Printed by Caligraving Ltd, Thetford, Norfolk

A&C Black uses paper produced with elemental
chlorine-free pulp, harvested from managed
sustainable forests.

Contents

D.C. al Fine

RH   LH

NEW NOTE

E

NEW NOTE

D

NEW NOTE

C

The first tunes in this book use three notes and three note-values:

O   semibreve — worth four beats

♩   minim — worth two beats

♩   crotchet — worth one beat

Music is divided into bars by vertical strokes called bar lines.

4/4   time signature — this time signature shows that there are four crotchet beats to the bar

,   breath mark — you may need to take extra breaths in other places at first. Choose the places carefully, and try not to interrupt the flow of the music.

1 EASY ①

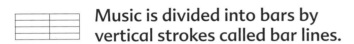

JS

Ea - sy, bree - zy, le - mon squee - zy.

2 EARWIG CRUNCH ②

JS

Hun - gry, hun - gry, what's for lunch? Eels and eggs and ear - wig crunch.

3 YES INDEED ③

AP

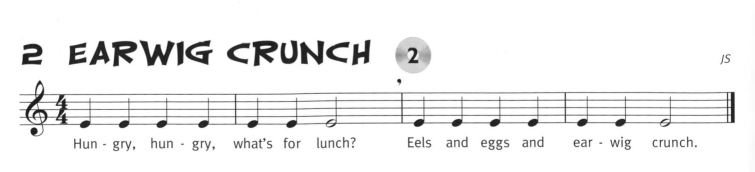

D   E   E   D,   Yes   in - deed.

4 KEEP ON RUNNING

JS

Ex - er - cise a bit, Keep on run - ning to get fit.

5 CURIOUS TORTOISE 5

AP

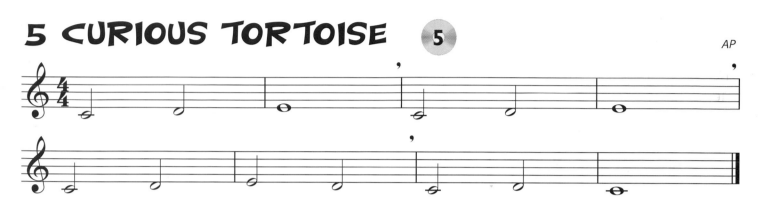

6 AU CLAIR DE LA LUNE 6

French

7 SETTING OUT 7

JR

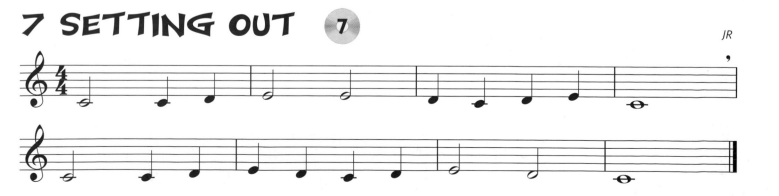

8 SUO-GÂN
8
words: Percy Dearmer
music: Welsh
Win - ter creeps, Na - ture sleeps, Birds are gone, Flowers are none.
9 THE OLD SHEPHERD
9
L H Page
10 IN PARIS
10
Dorothy Armstrong
(from a French song)
11 SALAD DAYS (duet)
JR arr. JS
You
Let - tuce leaves, let - tuce leaves, Ra - dish and to - ma - to,
Your teacher
5
Cu - cum - ber, gra - ted cheese, Egg and may - on - naise.

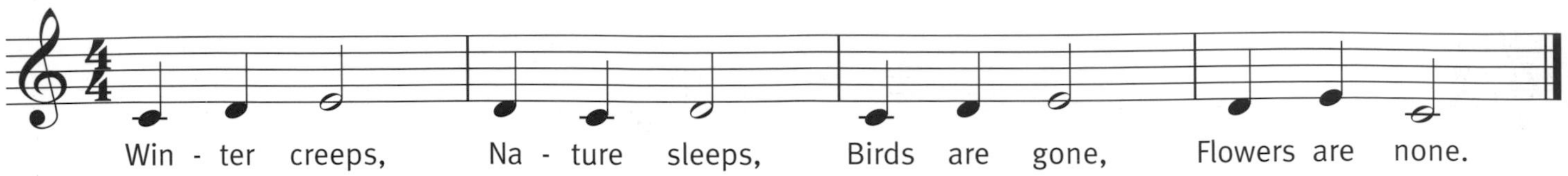

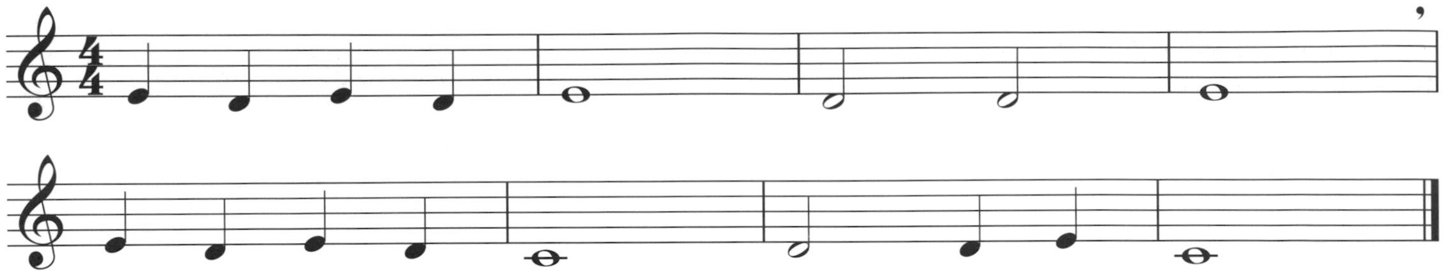

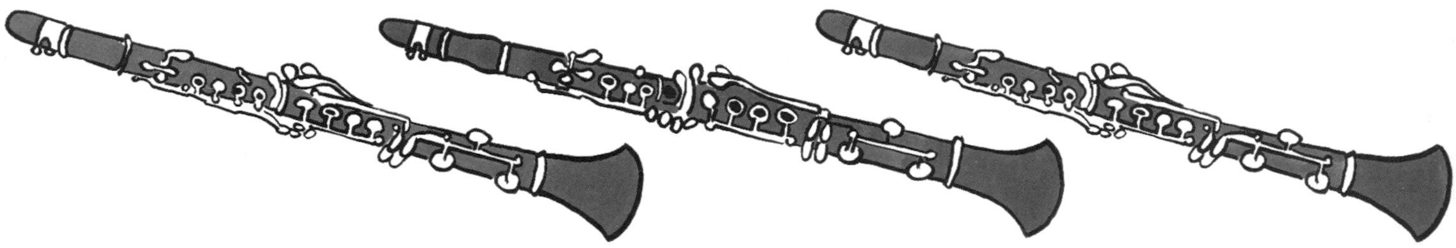

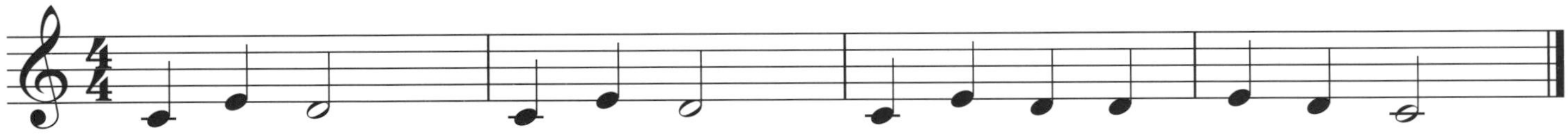

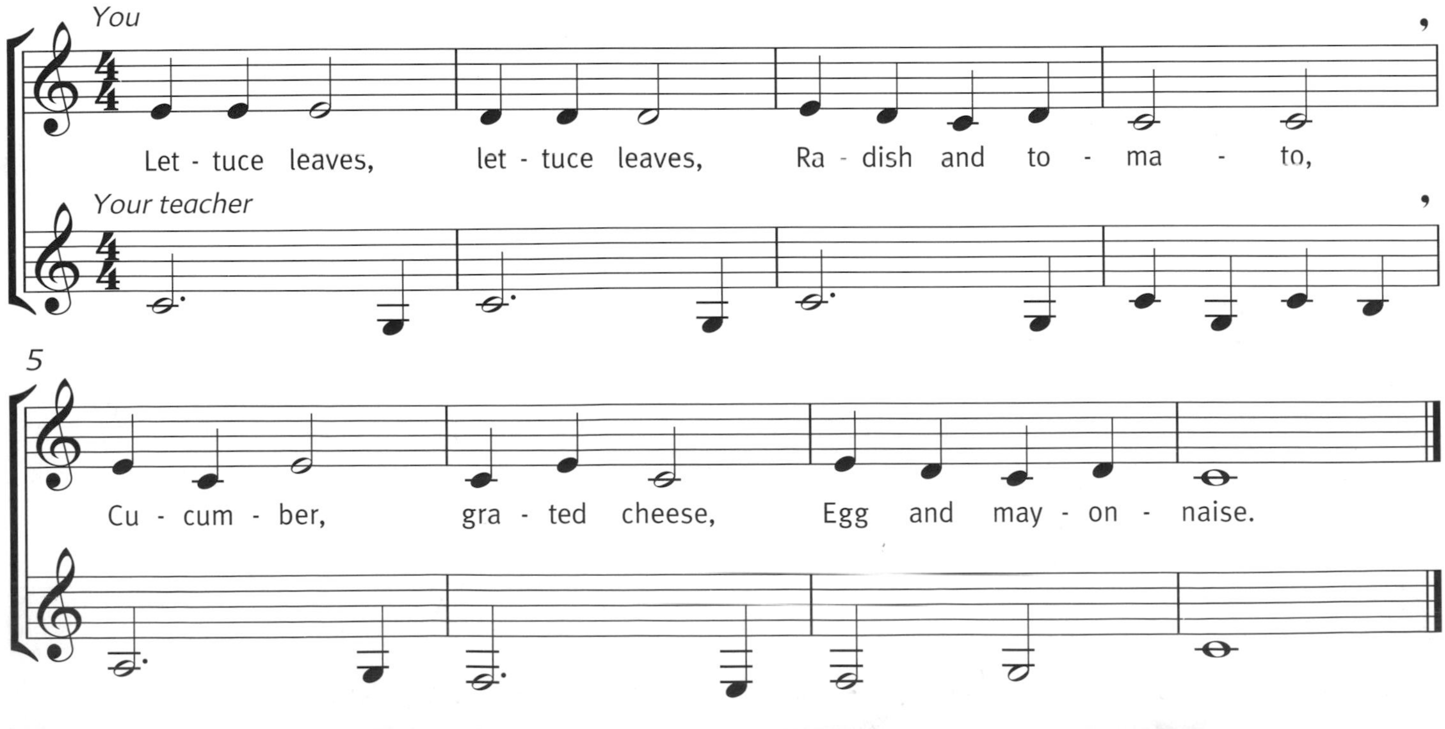

12 COOL 11
JR
NEW NOTE
F
NEW NOTE
G
13 ZIG-ZAG 12
AP
14 CLOWN DANCE 13
French
15 MERRILY 14
traditional
Briskly
Mer - ri - ly we roll a - long, roll a - long, roll a - long,
Mer - ri - ly we roll a - long, all the live - long day.

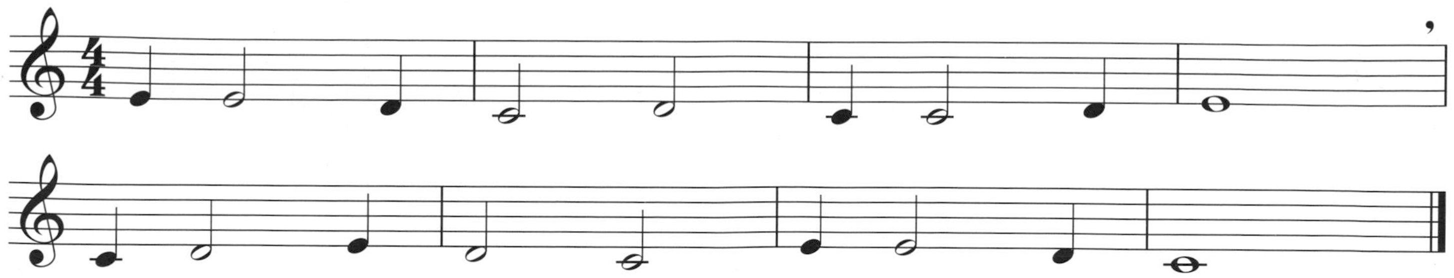

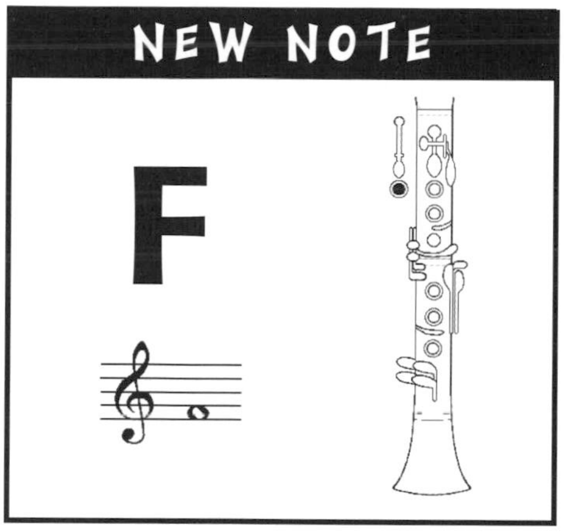

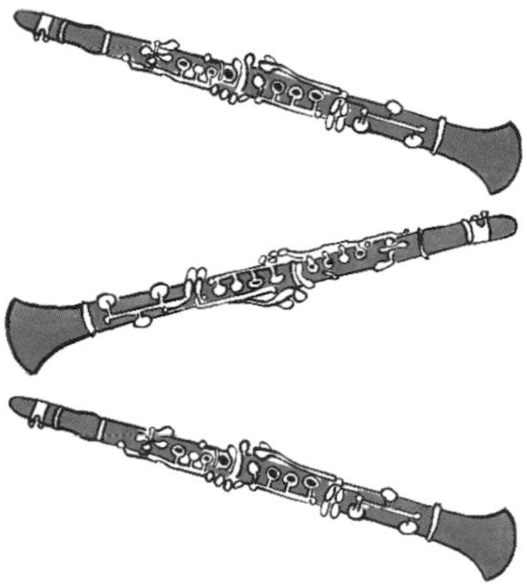

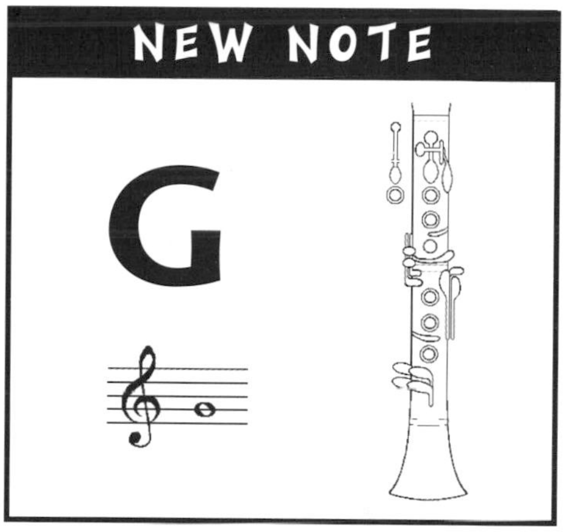

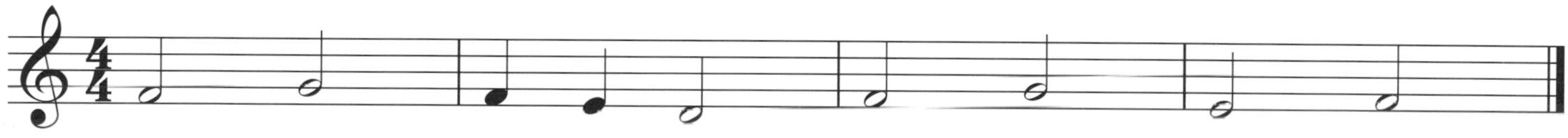

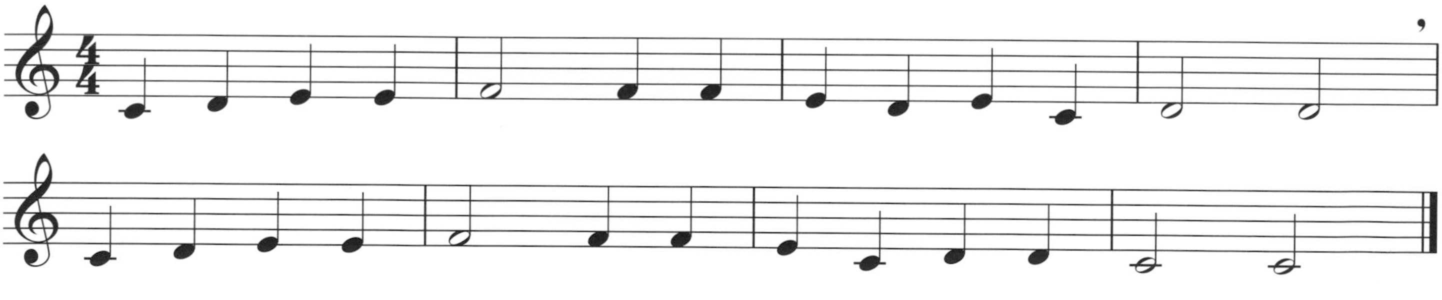

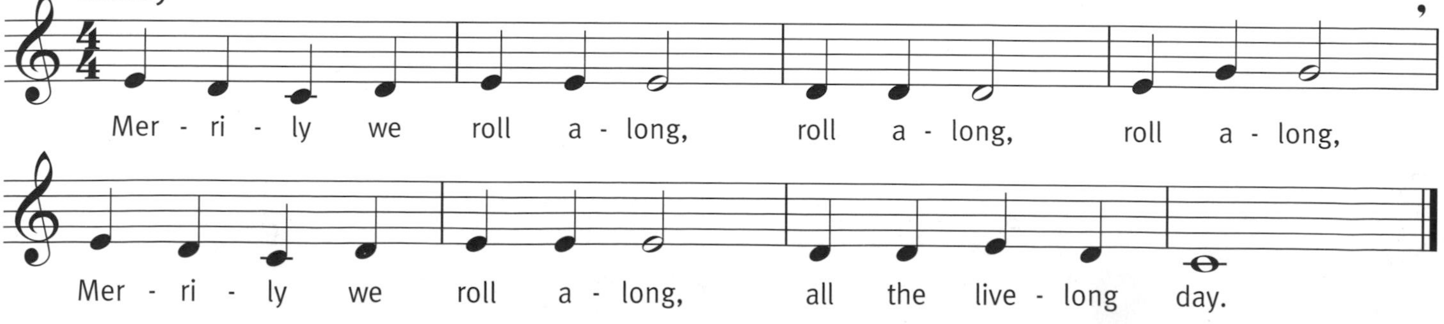

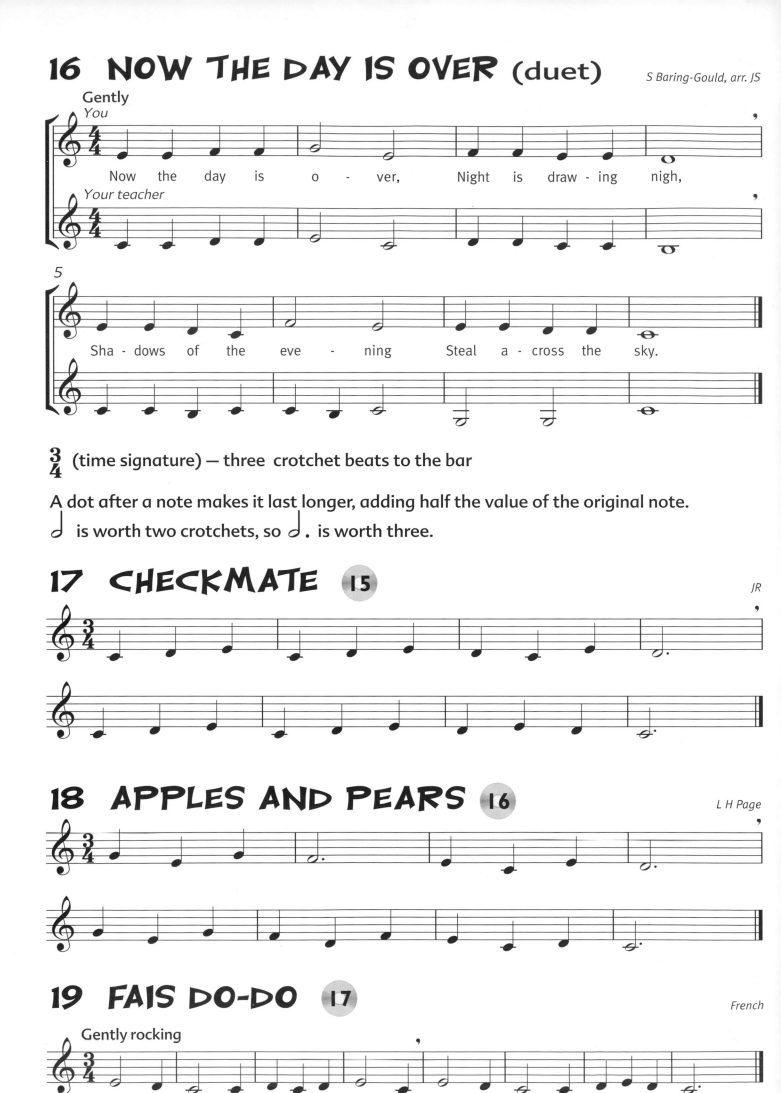

16 NOW THE DAY IS OVER (duet)

S Baring-Gould, arr. JS

Gently

Now the day is o - ver, Night is draw - ing nigh,

Sha - dows of the eve - ning Steal a - cross the sky.

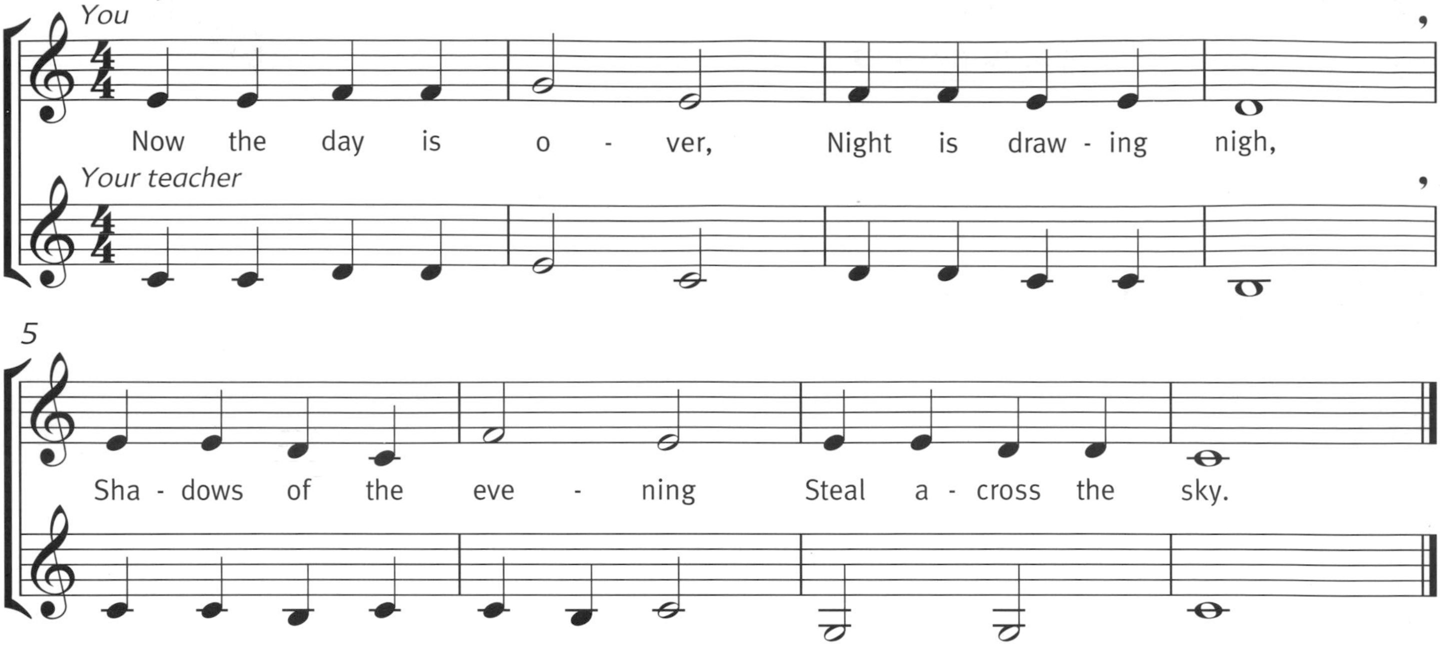

$\frac{3}{4}$ (time signature) — three crotchet beats to the bar

A dot after a note makes it last longer, adding half the value of the original note. ♩ is worth two crotchets, so ♩. is worth three.

17 CHECKMATE 15

JR

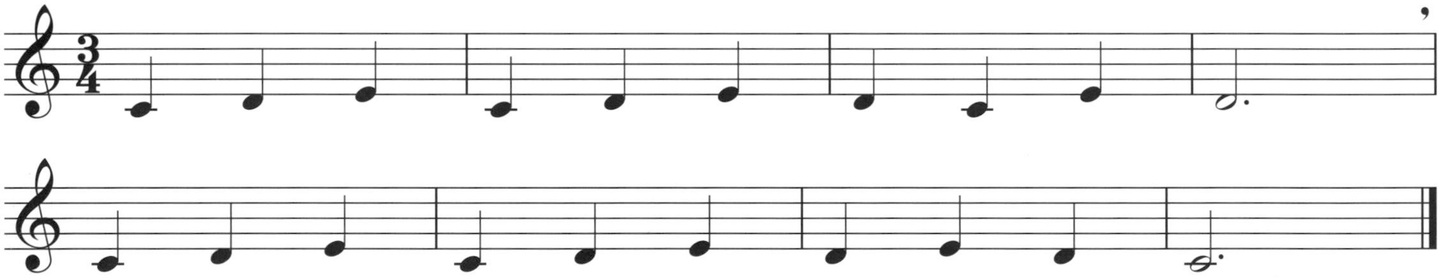

18 APPLES AND PEARS 16

L H Page

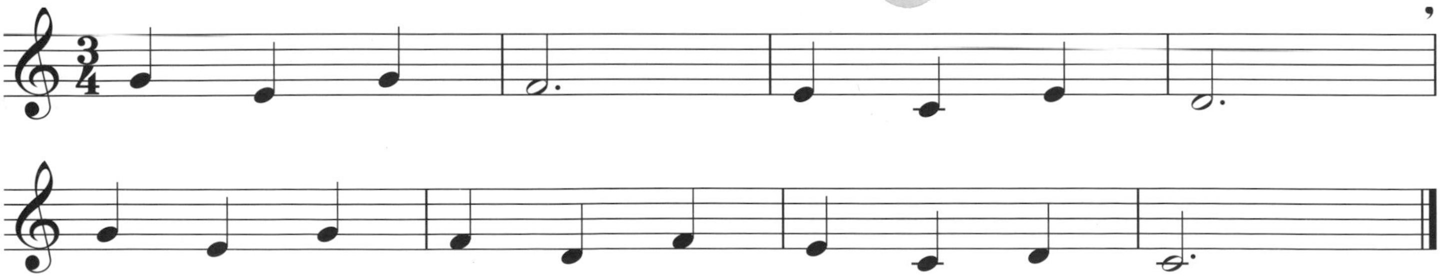

19 FAIS DO-DO 17

French

Gently rocking

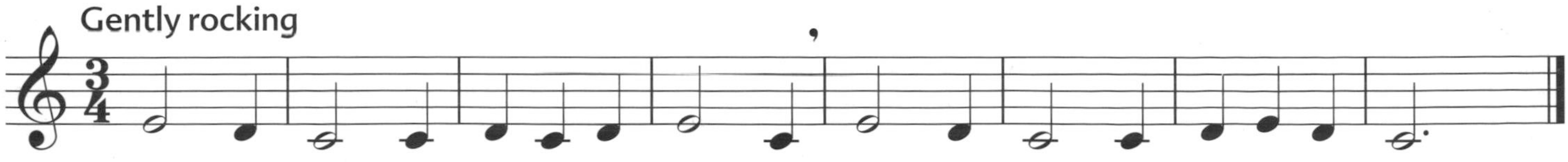

Sometimes music contains rests which are moments of silence. Every note-value has a rest of the same value, showing the length of silence to be held:

𝄽   crotchet rest — worth one beat

▬   minim rest — worth two beats

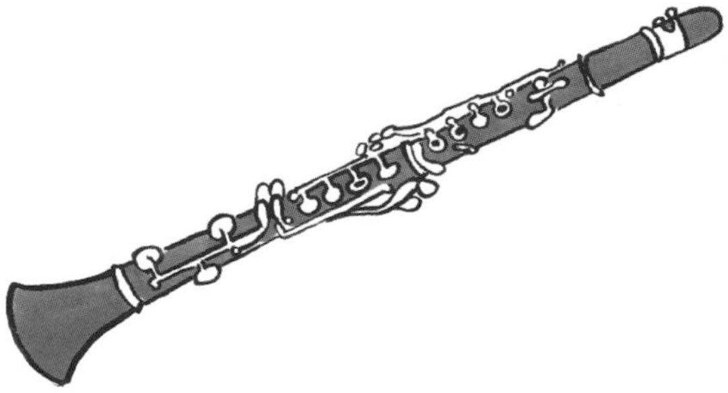

20 LITTLE JOHN   18

German

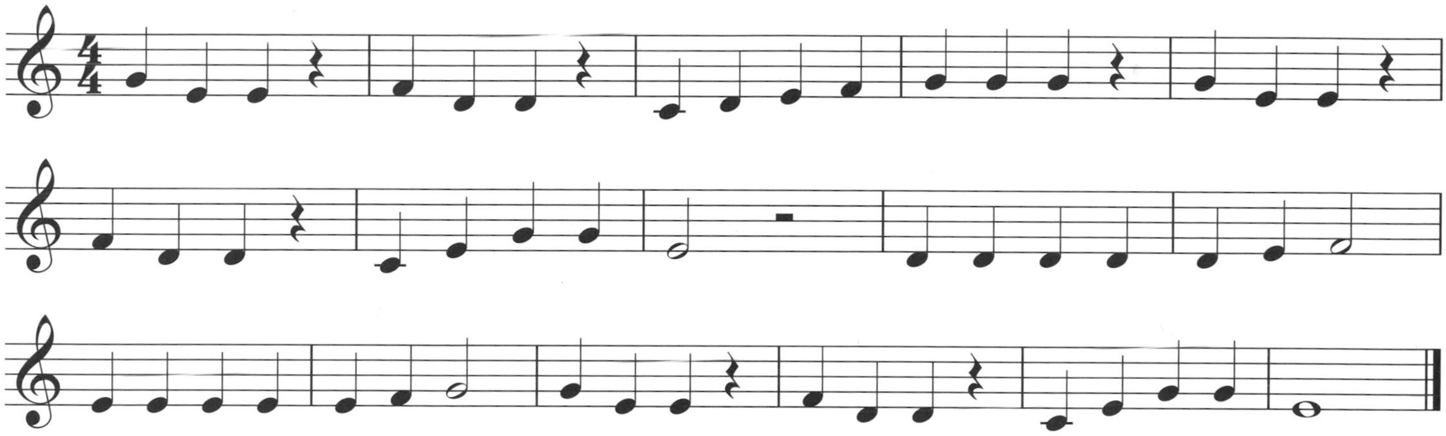

21 WHEN THE SAINTS GO MARCHING IN   19

spiritual

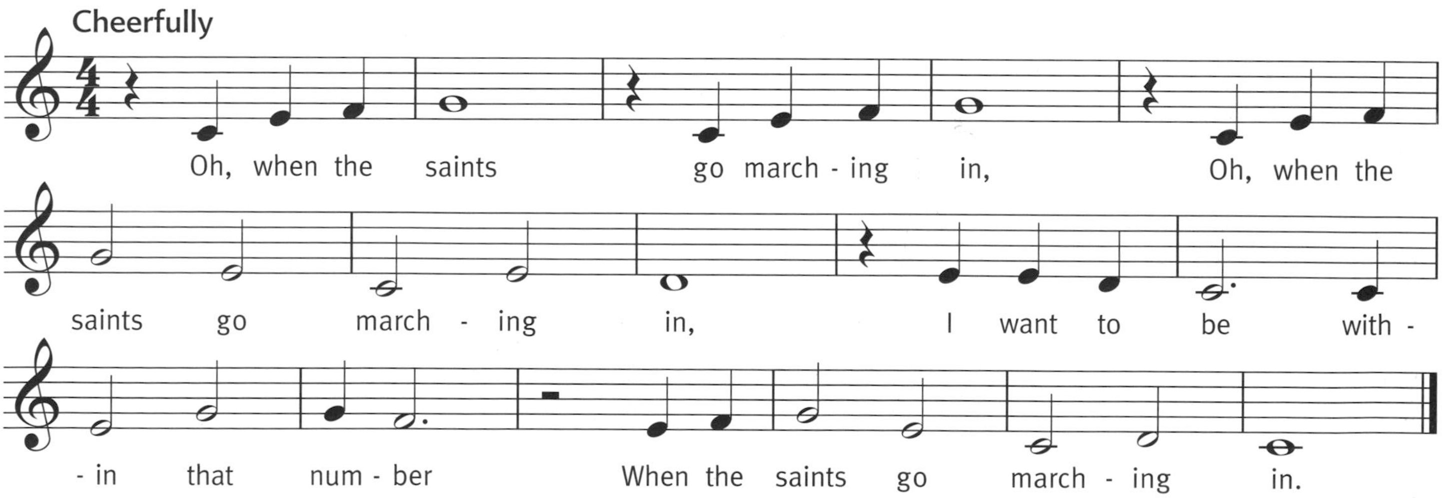

Cheerfully

Oh, when the saints   go march - ing   in,   Oh, when the

saints   go   march - ing   in,   I want to be with -

- in   that   num - ber   When the saints go march - ing in.

22 ONE-LEGGED CHICKEN   20

AP

With spirit

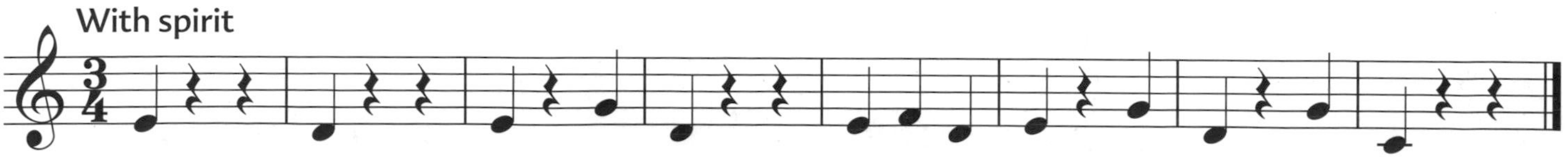

♪ quaver — worth half a crotchet beat. Two quavers ♫ are worth one crotchet beat.

23 PEASE PUDDING (21)

traditional

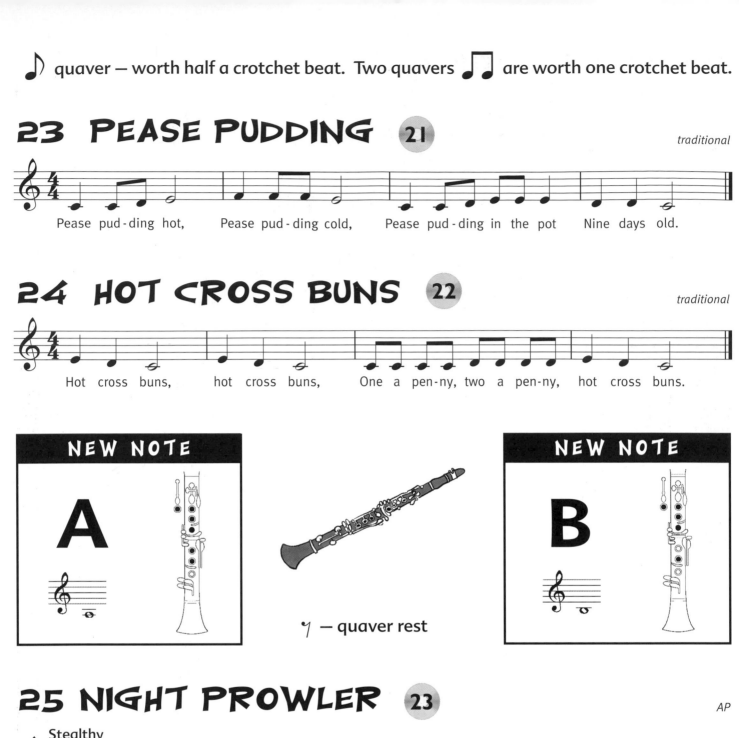

Pease pud-ding hot,   Pease pud-ding cold,   Pease pud-ding in the pot   Nine days old.

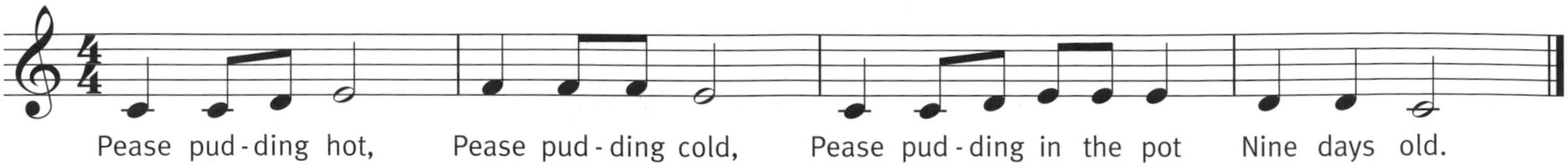

24 HOT CROSS BUNS (22)

traditional

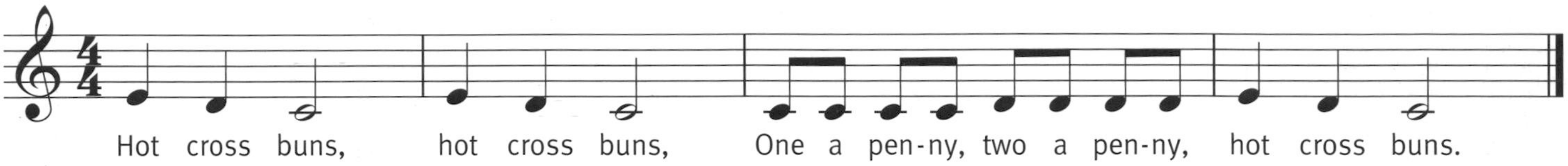

Hot cross buns,   hot cross buns,   One a pen-ny, two a pen-ny,   hot cross buns.

NEW NOTE

A

ɣ — quaver rest

NEW NOTE

B

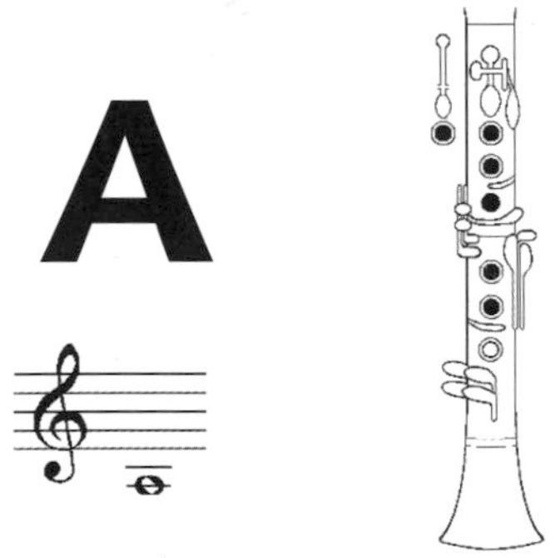

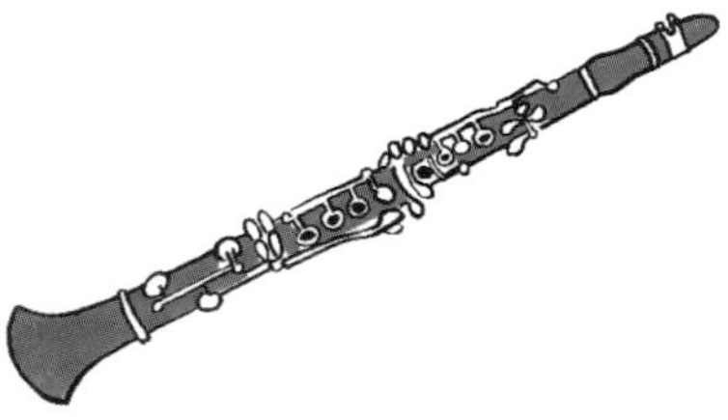

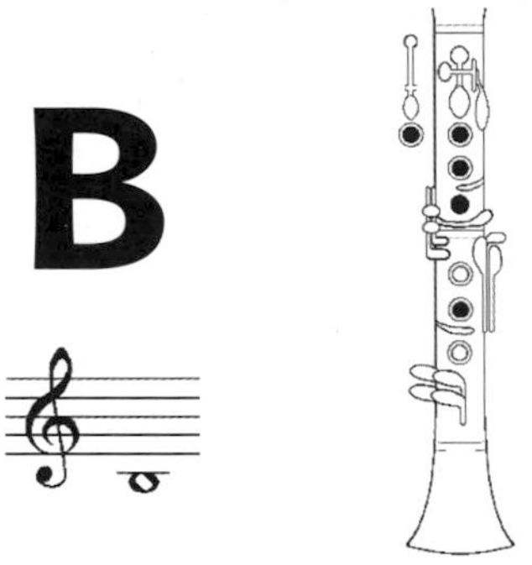

25 NIGHT PROWLER (23)

AP

Stealthy

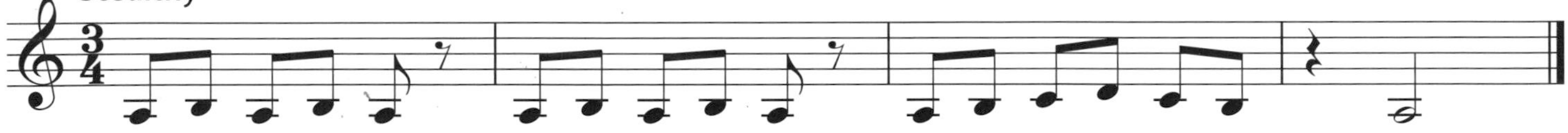

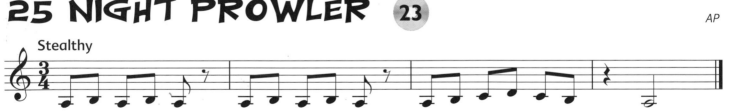

≕ semibreve rest — worth four beats

26 TAKE YOUR PARTNERS (duet)

AP

Lively

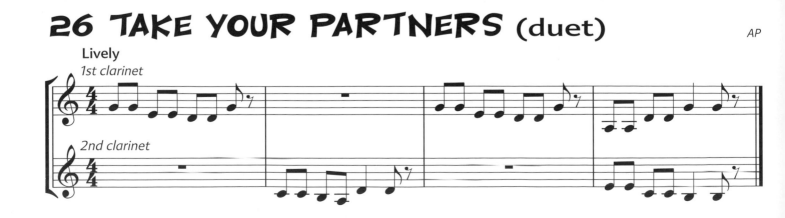

1st clarinet

2nd clarinet

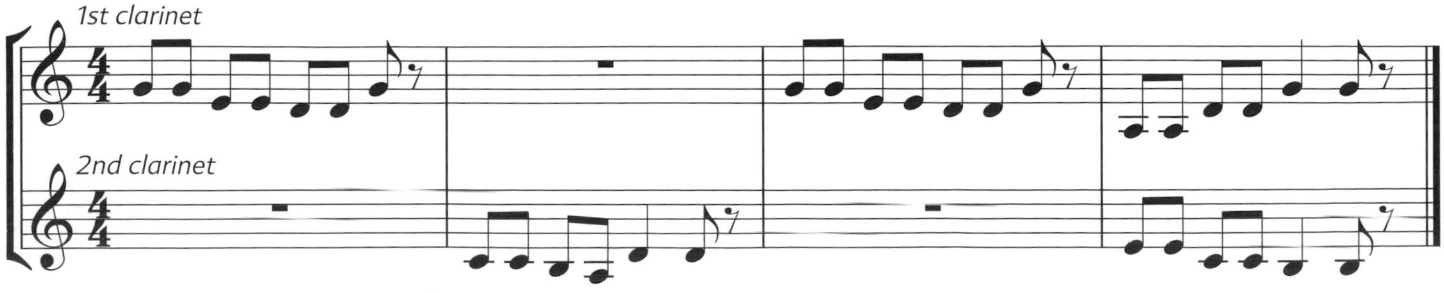

27 SHANTY TUNE (24)

traditional

Rhythmically

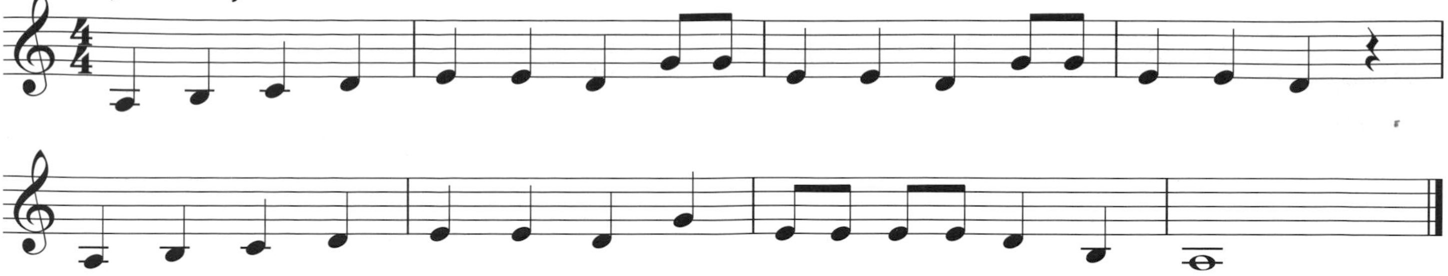

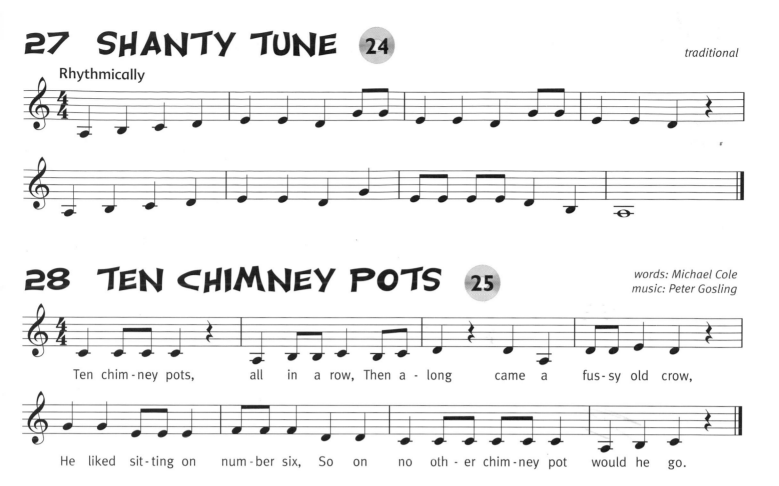

28 TEN CHIMNEY POTS (25)

words: Michael Cole
music: Peter Gosling

Ten chim-ney pots, all in a row, Then a - long came a fus-sy old crow,

He liked sit-ting on num-ber six, So on no oth-er chim-ney pot would he go.

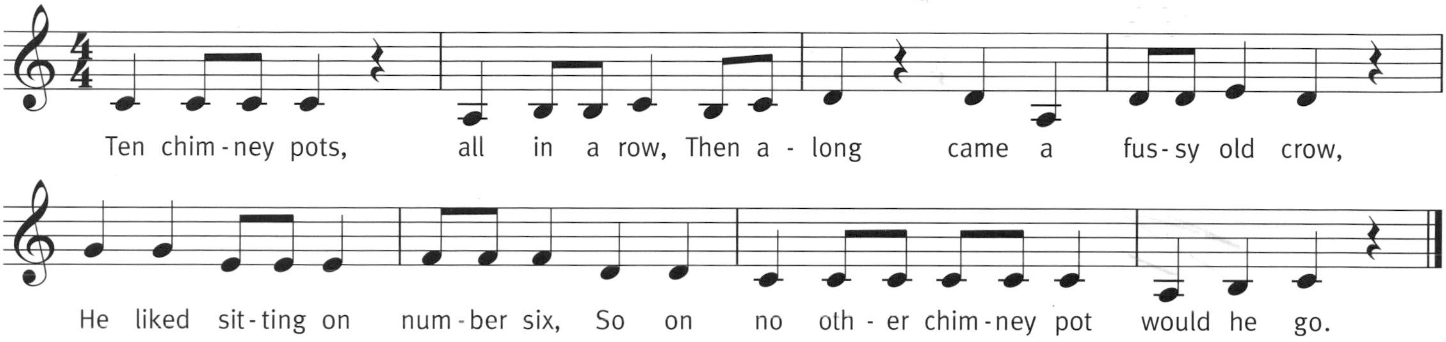

$\frac{2}{4}$ (time signature) — two crotchet beats to the bar

29 SOUTHWELL (26)

from Damon's Psalter

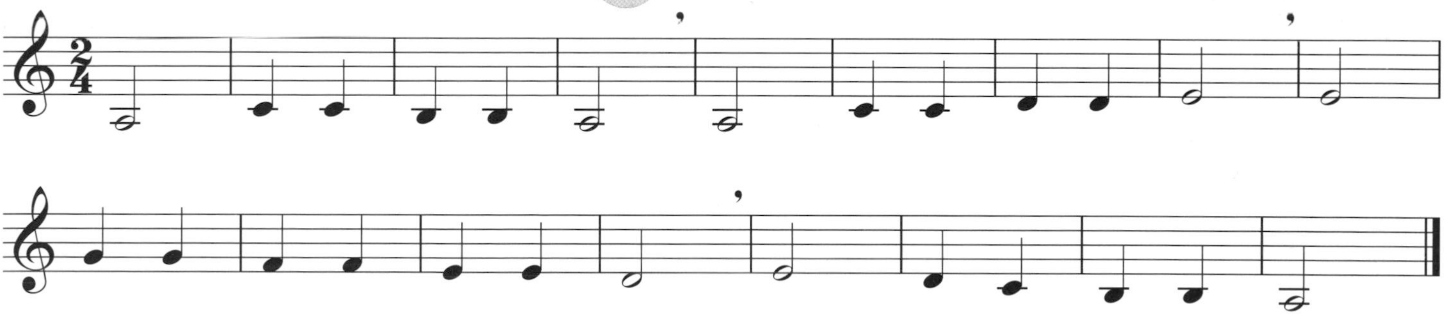

⌣ ⌢ slurs

When two different notes are joined by a slur, tongue only the first one, then keep blowing as your fingers move to the next note.

30 BUTTERCUP (27)

North American

All a - round the but - ter - cup, one, two, three.

If you want a pret - ty maid, just choose me.

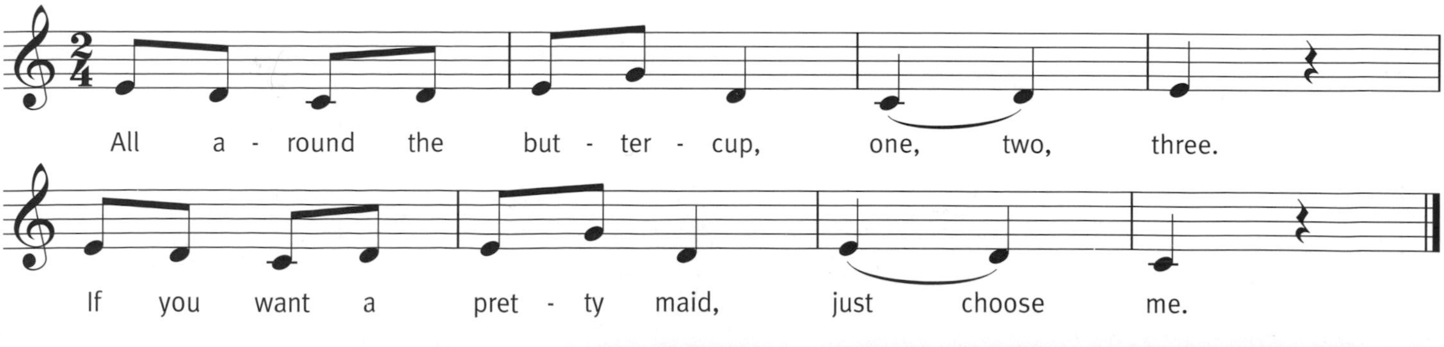

The breath mark is not used in the rest of this book. You will soon develop an instinct for where to breathe. Pencil in breath marks wherever you feel you need a reminder — even the most experienced players do this.

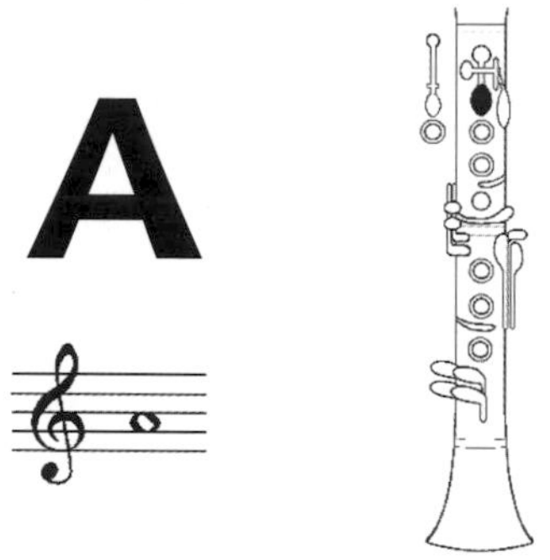

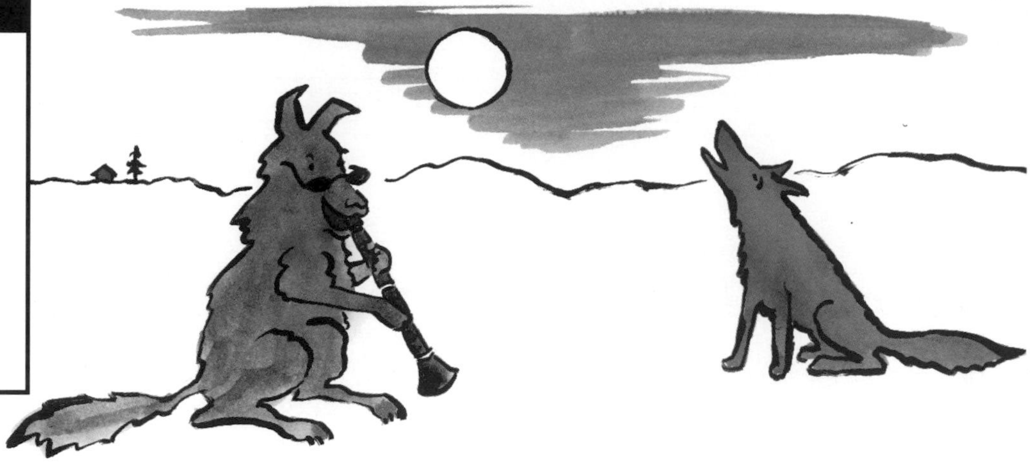

When moving to A from a lower note, lean your finger on to the key. Don't 'hop', or the open G will sound.

31 PRAIRIE CALL 28

AP

Haunting

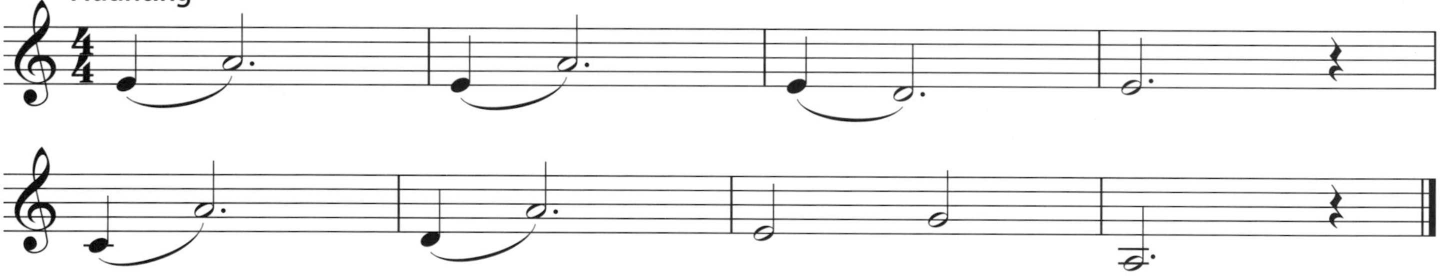

:‖ repeat sign — repeat the music from the beginning, or from ‖:

32 TWINKLE, TWINKLE LITTLE STAR 29

traditional

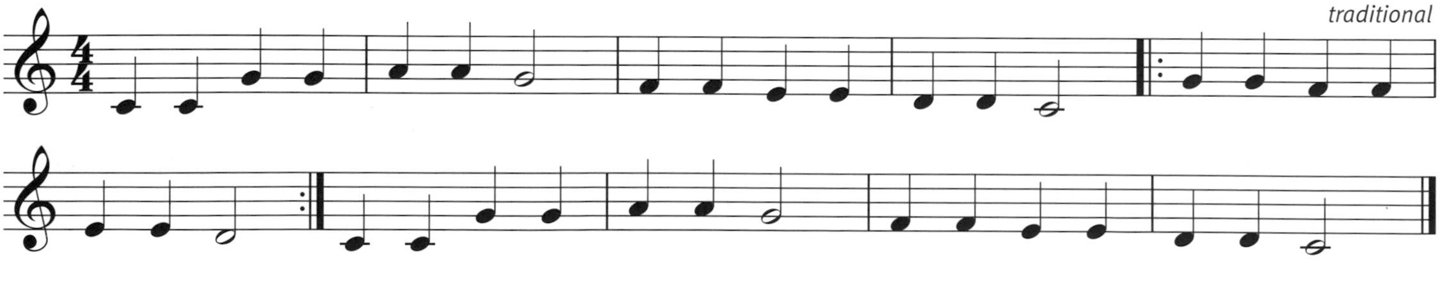

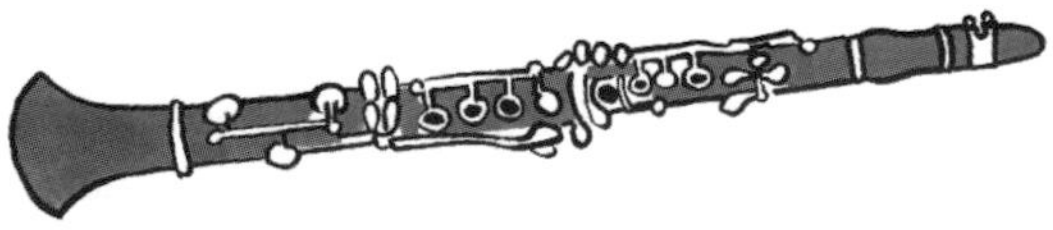

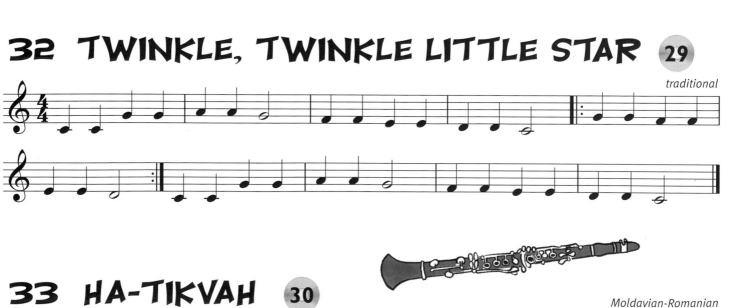

33 HA-TIKVAH 30

Moldavian-Romanian

With a full tone

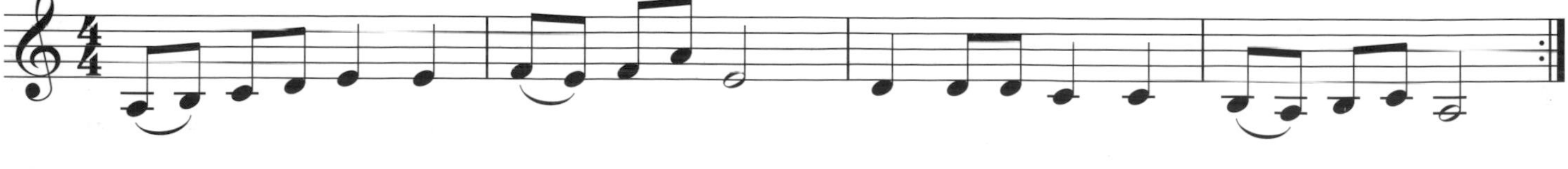

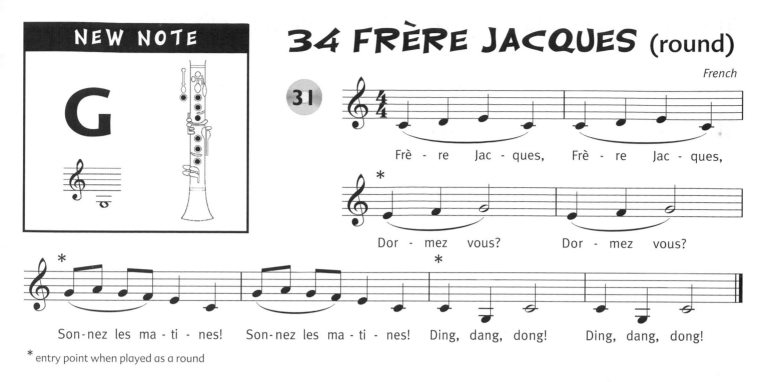

NEW NOTE

G

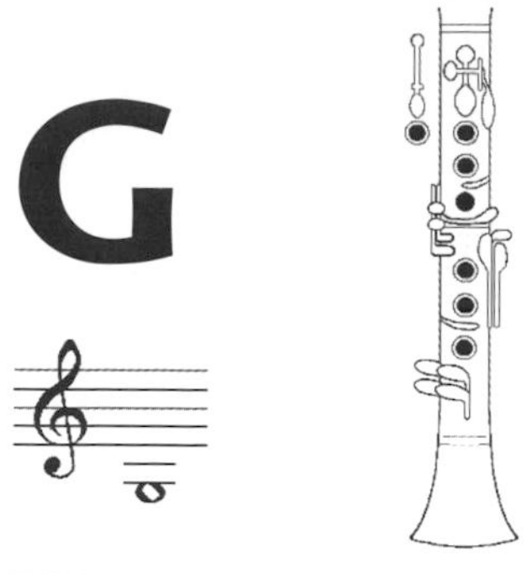

34 FRÈRE JACQUES (round)

French

31

Frè - re Jac - ques, Frè - re Jac - ques,

*

Dor - mez vous? Dor - mez vous?

Son - nez les ma - ti - nes! Son - nez les ma - ti - nes! Ding, dang, dong! Ding, dang, dong!

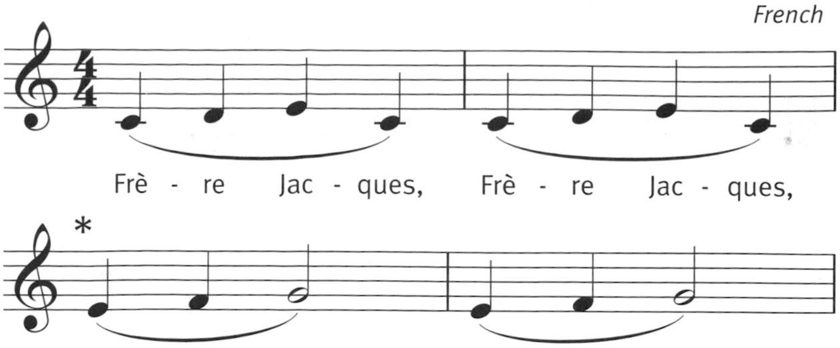

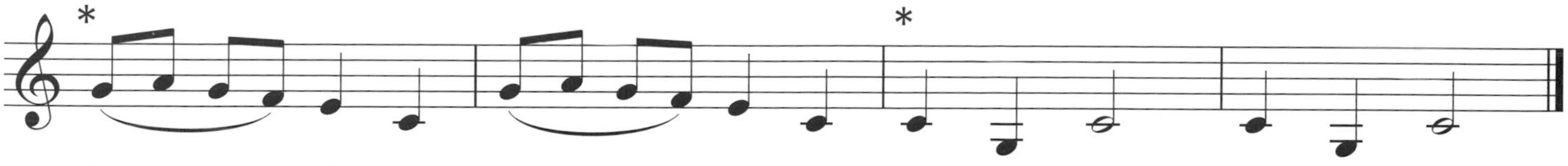

* entry point when played as a round

p   (piano) – quiet
f   (forte) – loud

The next piece starts on the third crotchet of the bar. This is called 'starting on the upbeat'. In order to have the correct number of beats in the piece, the last bar has only two crotchets.

35 AWAY IN A MANGER   **32**

W J Kirkpatrick

p   A - way in a___ man - ger, No___ crib for a bed, The___ lit - tle Lord

Je - sus Laid___ down His sweet head, The stars in the___ bright sky looked___

down where He lay, The___ lit - tle Lord Je - sus A - sleep on the hay.

36 COME AND SING TOGETHER (round)   **33**

Hungarian

p

f

p

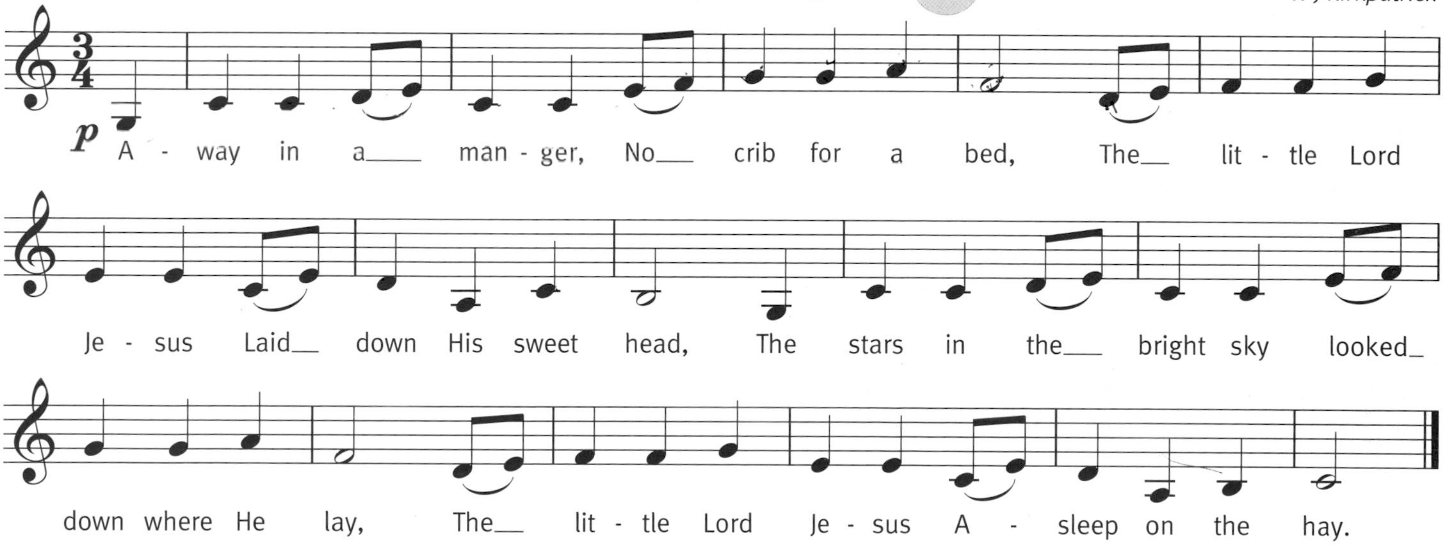

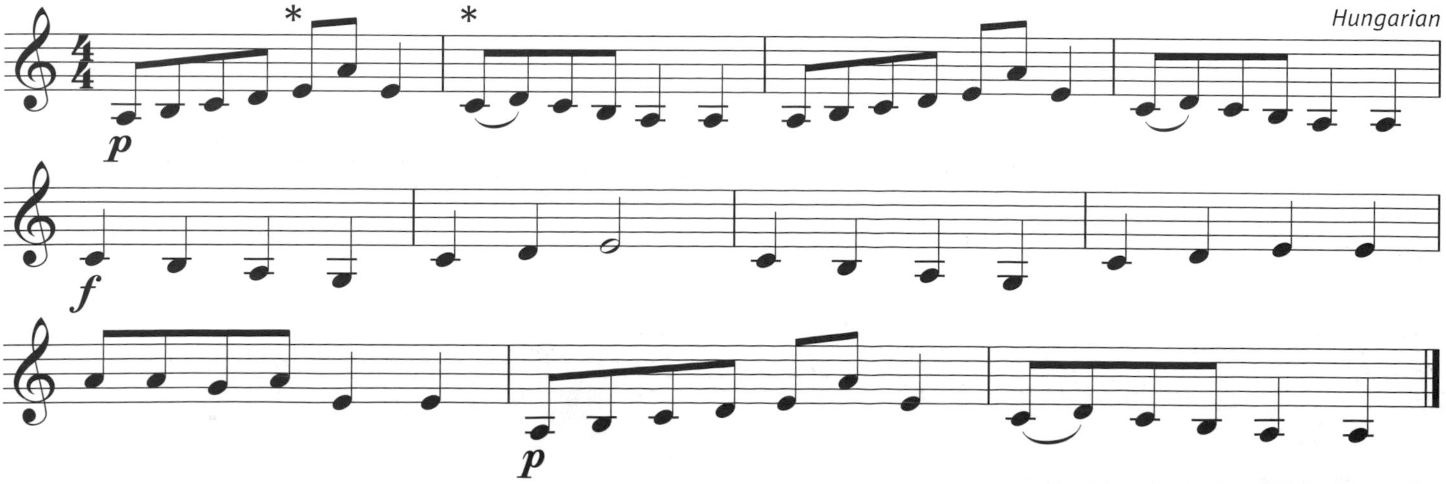

♩. dotted crotchet — worth one and a half crotchet beats

37 ONE MAN WENT TO MOW 34

traditional

♩ ⌣ ♩ tie — it joins two notes of the same pitch. Play tied notes as one long note.

38 ODE TO JOY 35

Beethoven

Lively and with feeling

39 CANON FROM 'MIKROKOSMOS' (duet)

Bartok arr. Suchoff

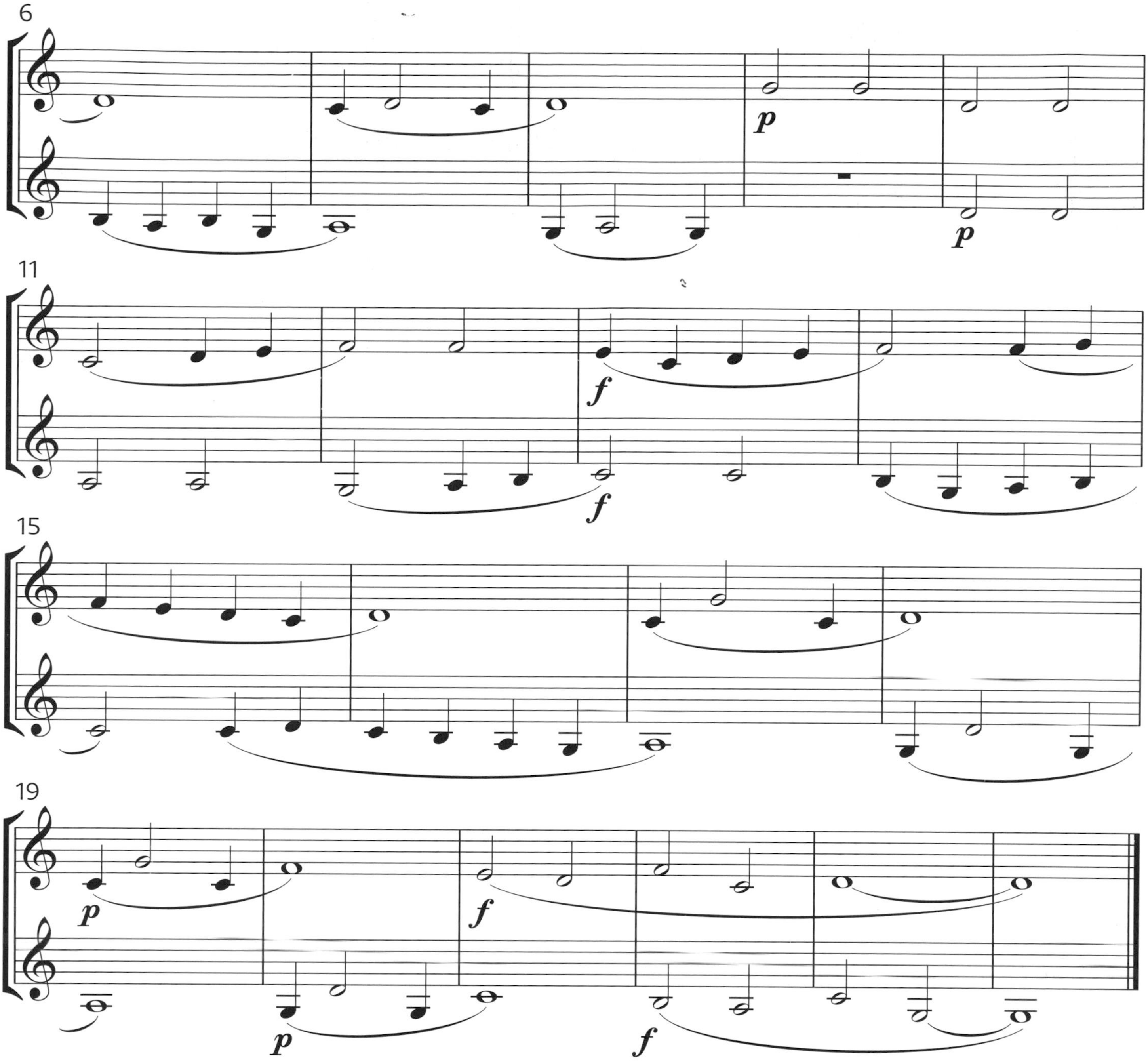

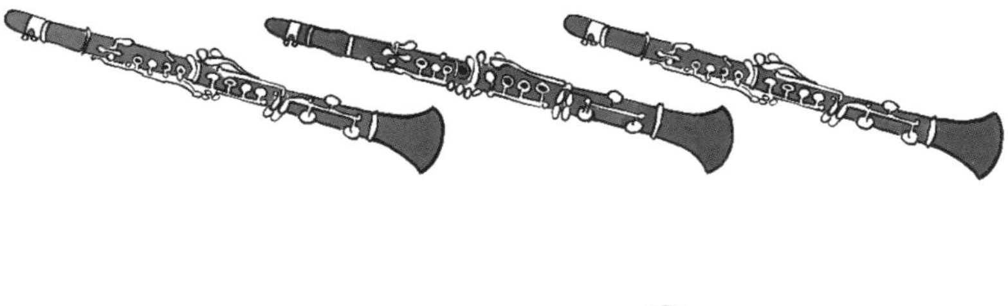

40 LOVE ME TENDER 36

traditional

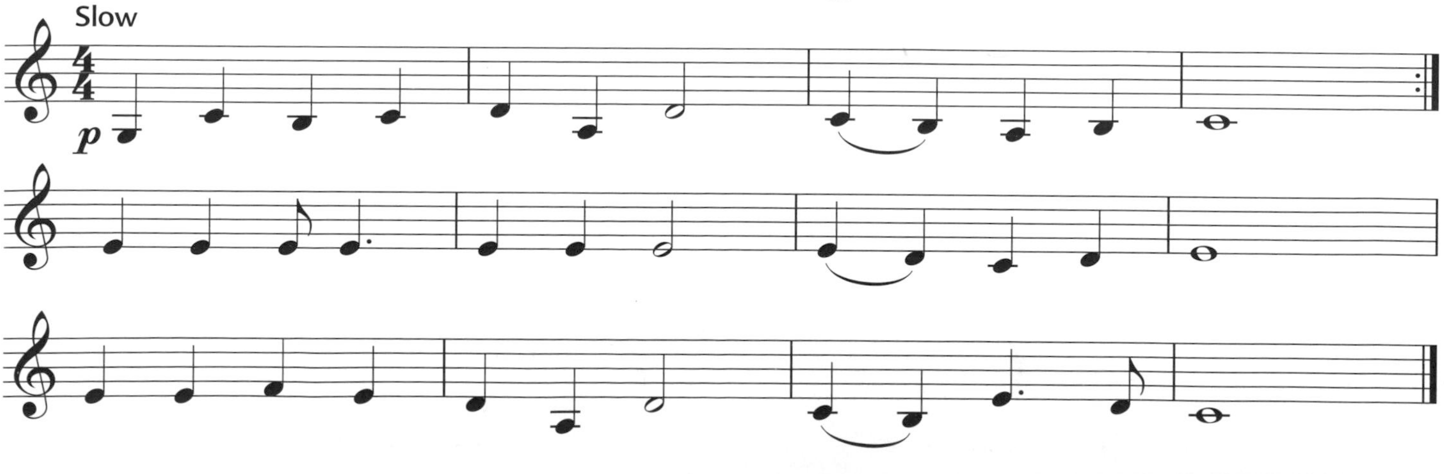

F#

sharp sign — it raises a note by a semitone.
Play F followed by F# and listen to the difference.

In *41 Morningtown Ride*, the sharp sign # is written on
the F line before the time signature. This is called the
key signature, and it sharpens the note F whenever it
appears in the tune.

In *42 Scarborough Fair*, the sharp sign # appears before
the note F in the course of the music. This is called an
accidental. Its influence lasts only until the next barline.

mp (mezzo piano) — moderately quiet

41 MORNINGTOWN RIDE (duet)

Malvina Reynolds, arr. L H Page

mf (mezzo forte) — moderately loud

42 SCARBOROUGH FAIR (37)

traditional

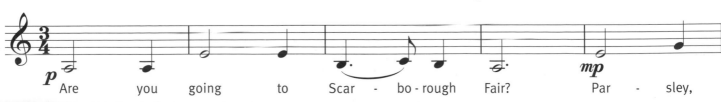

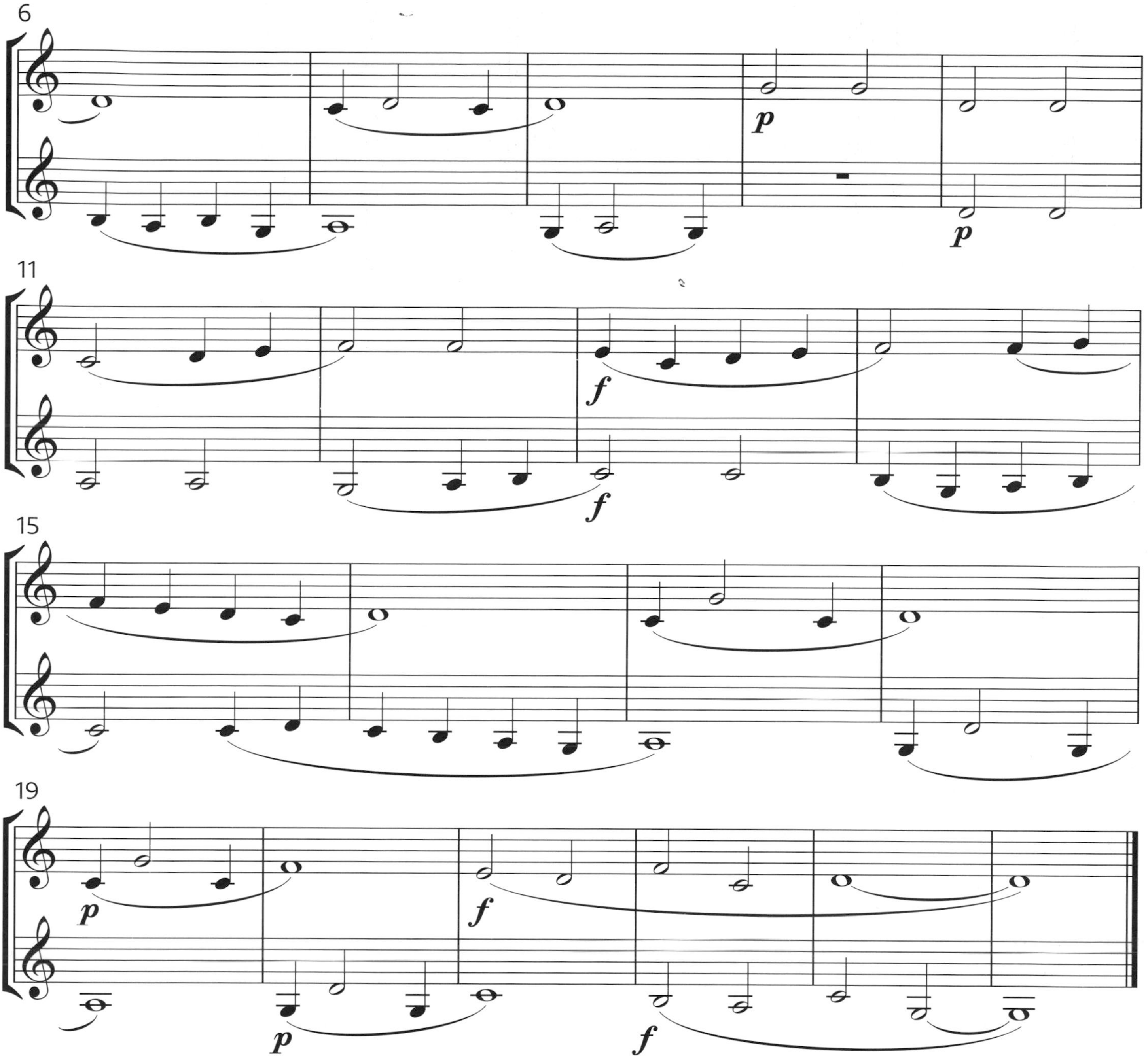

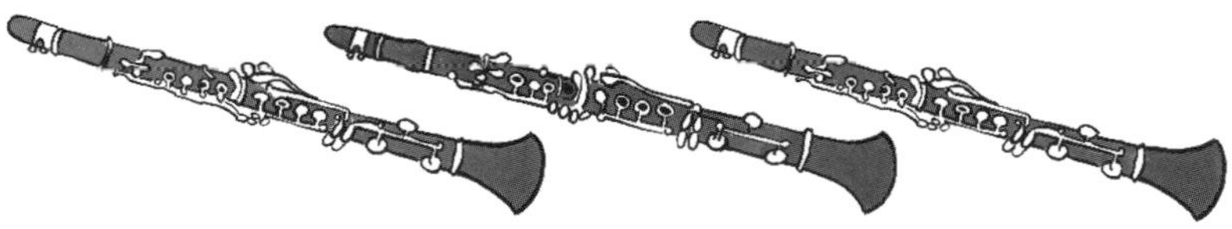

40 LOVE ME TENDER 36

traditional

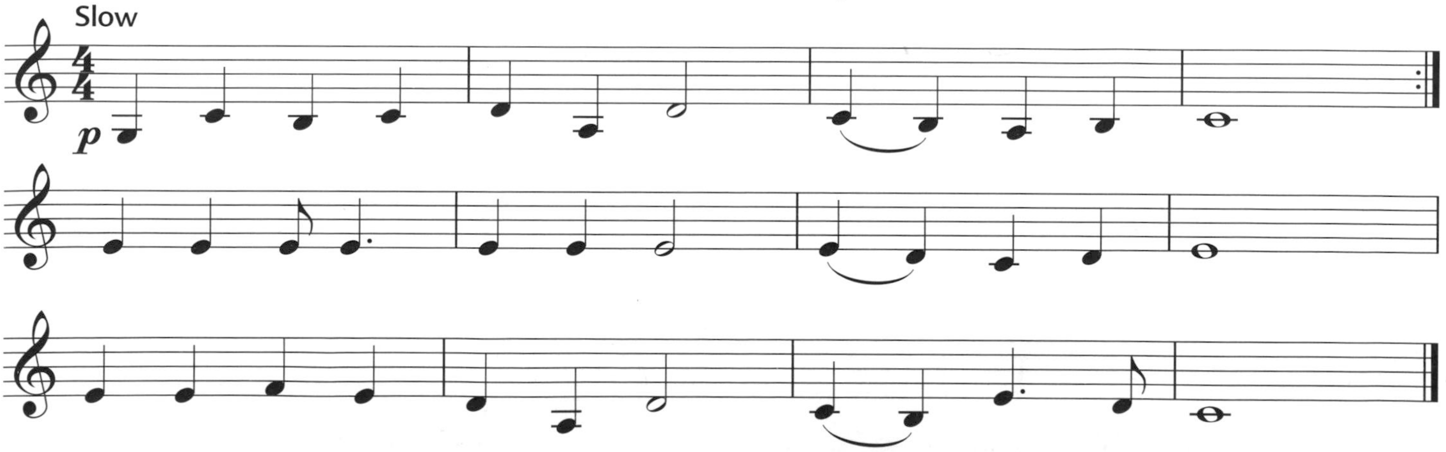

NEW NOTE

F#

♯ sharp sign — it raises a note by a semitone.
Play F followed by F♯ and listen to the difference.

In *41 Morningtown Ride*, the sharp sign ♯ is written on the F line before the time signature. This is called the **key signature**, and it sharpens the note F whenever it appears in the tune.

In *42 Scarborough Fair*, the sharp sign ♯ appears before the note F in the course of the music. This is called an accidental. Its influence lasts only until the next barline.

mp (mezzo piano) — moderately quiet

41 MORNINGTOWN RIDE (duet)

Malvina Reynolds, arr. L H Page

1st clarinet

mp

Train whis-tle blow-ing, makes a sleep-y noise; Un-der-neath their

2nd clarinet

mp

6

blan-kets Go all the girls and boys. Rock-ing, roll-ing, ri-ding,

11

Out a-long the bay, All bound for Morn-ing-town, Ma-ny miles a-way.

mf (mezzo forte) — moderately loud

42 SCARBOROUGH FAIR ③⑦

traditional

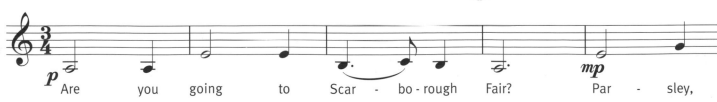

p
Are you going to Scar-bo-rough Fair? Par - sley,
mp

sage, rose - ma - ry and thyme. *mf* Re - mem - ber me to

one who lives there, *p* She once was a true love of mine.

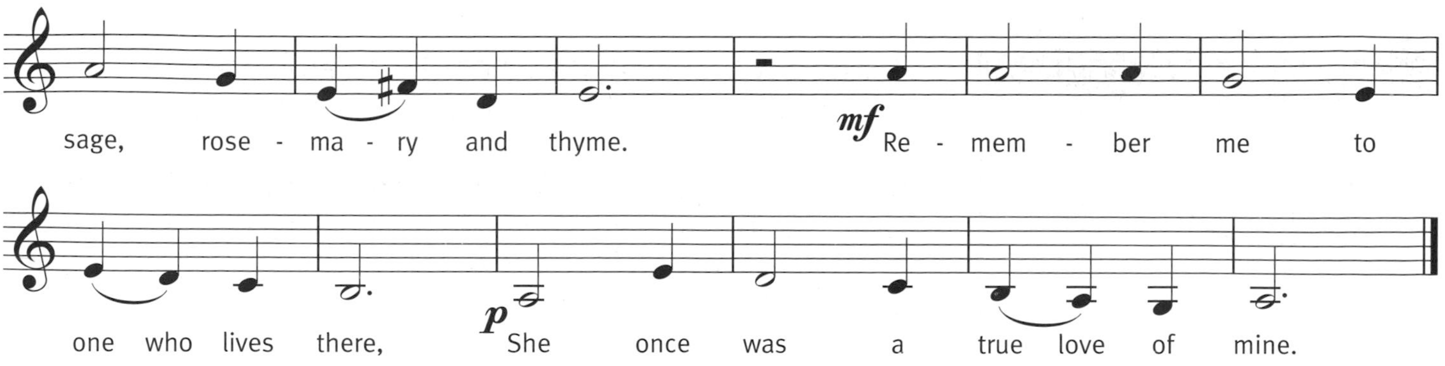

43 PUFF THE MAGIC DRAGON 38

*Peter Yarrow and
Leonard Upton*

mf Puff the ma - gic dra - gon lived by the sea, And

fro - licked in the au - tumn mist in a land called Hon - a - lee.

Lit - tle Jack - ie Pa - per loved that ras - cal Puff, And

brought him strings and seal - ing wax and oth - er fan - cy stuff.

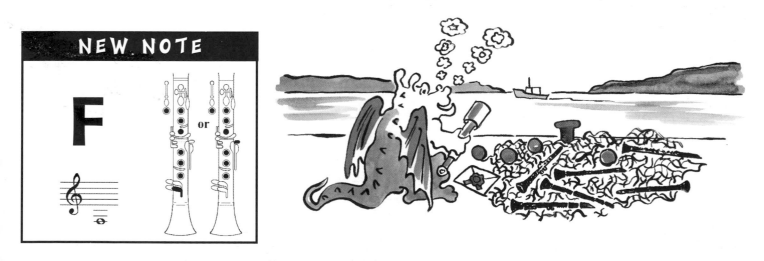

NEW NOTE

F

or

44 WOBBLY JELLY 39

AP

1° *mf*
2° *mp*

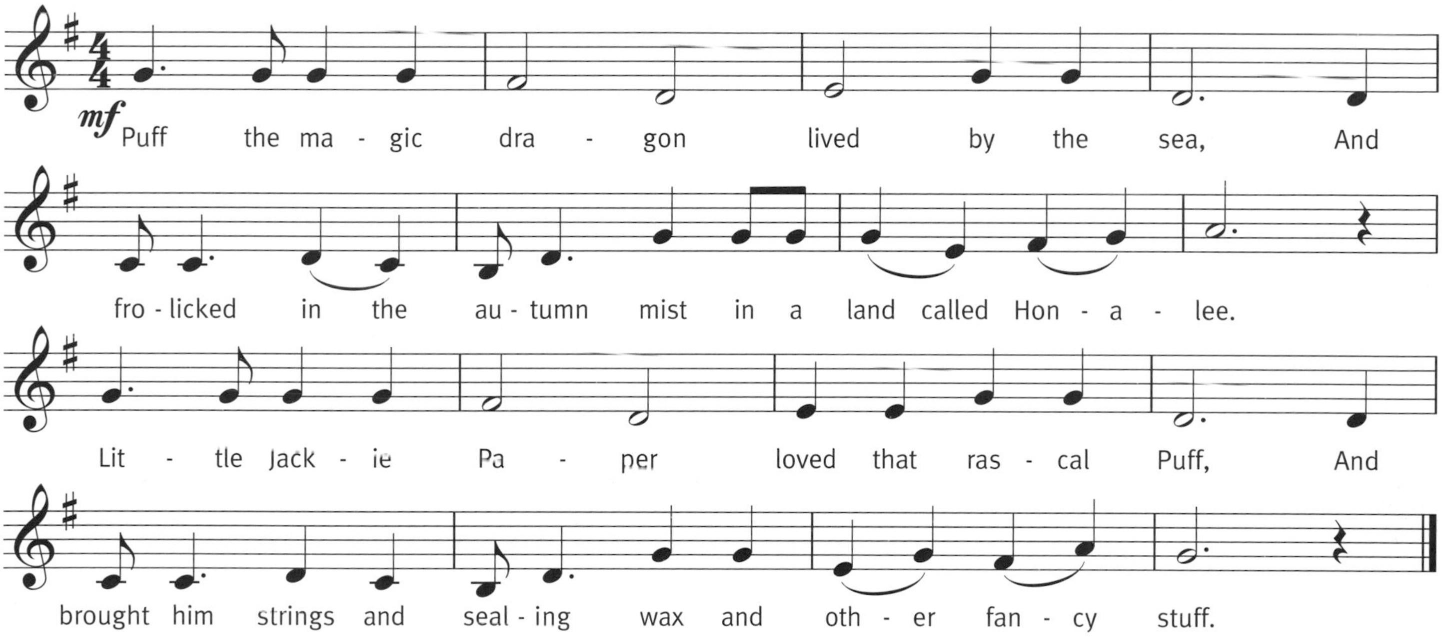

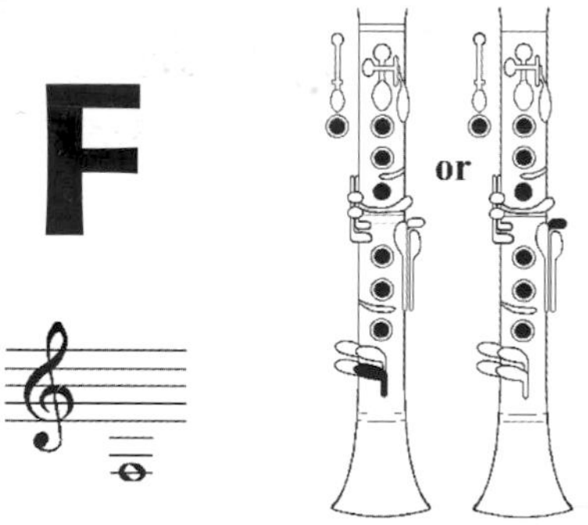

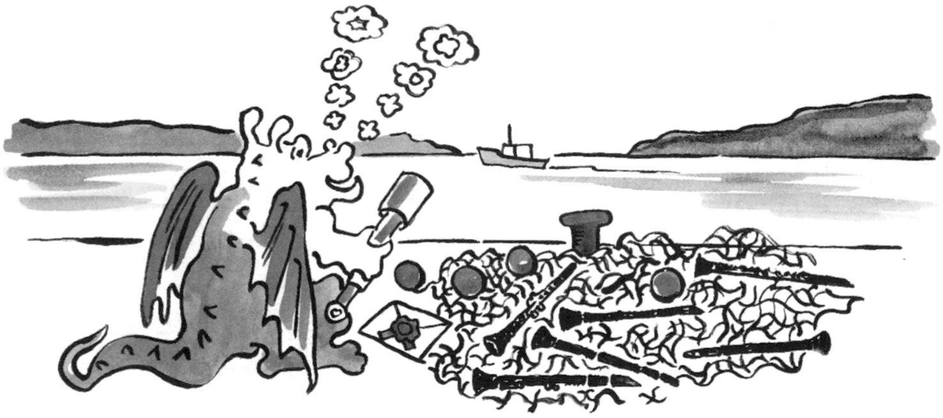

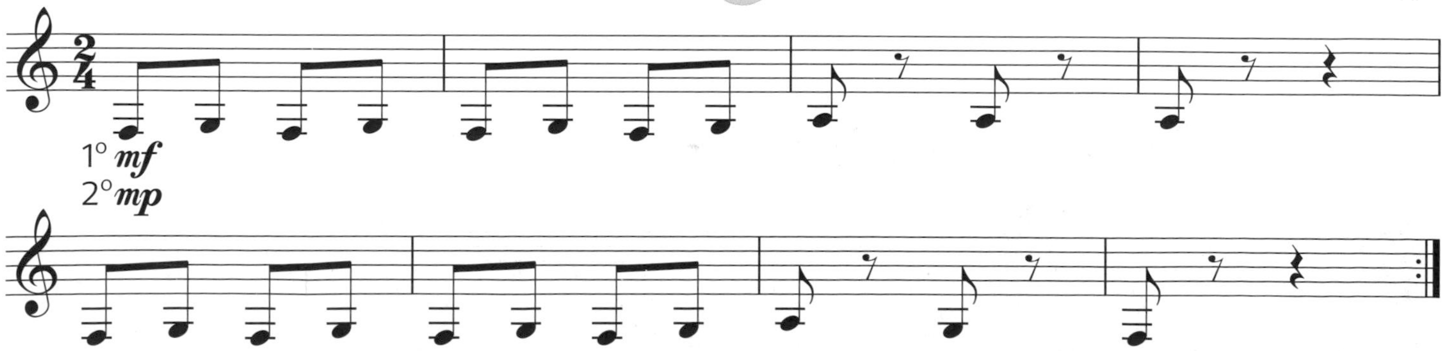

NEW NOTE

B♭

♭ flat sign — it lowers a note by a semitone.
Play B followed by B♭ and listen to the difference.

Within a key signature, the flat sign ♭ is placed on the middle line of the stave. The rules for key signatures and accidentals are the same as for sharps.

Notice the change of key signature in the next piece.

45 THANK U VERY MUCH 40

Michael McGear

46 BUSHES AND BRIARS 41

English

47 OLD MACDONALD (duet)

traditional arr. R H Page

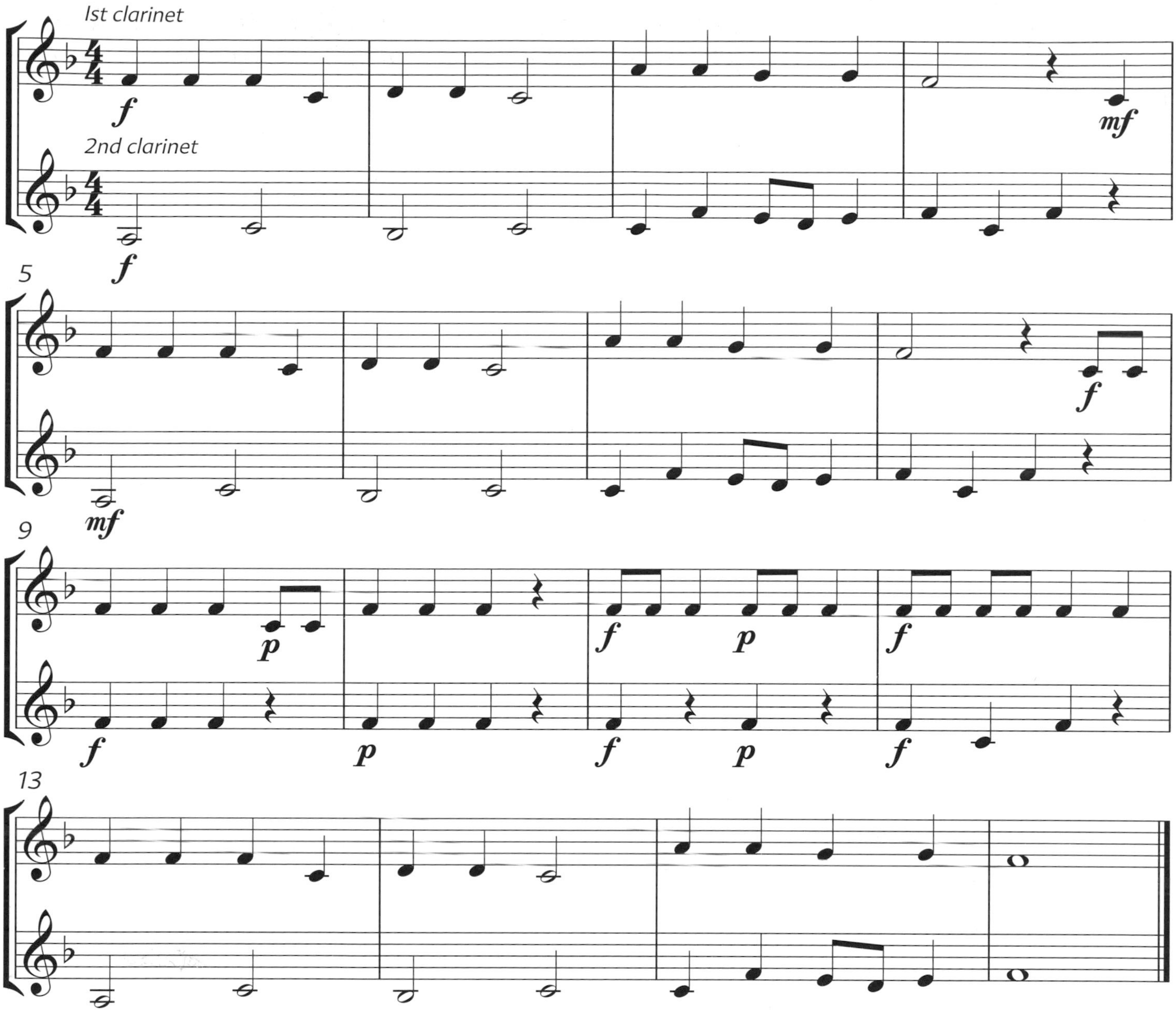

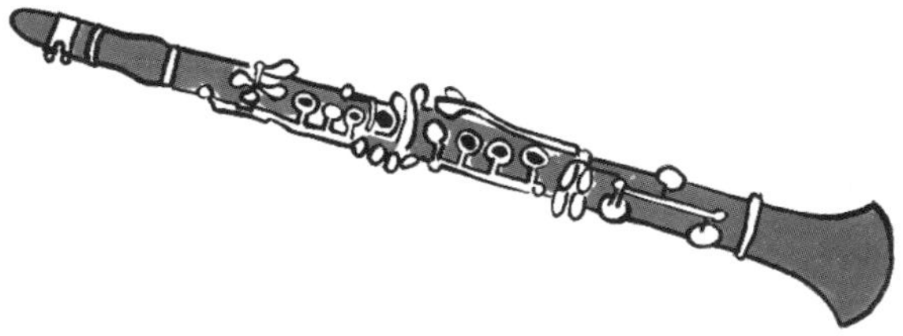

2/2 (time signature) — two minim beats to the bar

48 KOOKABURRA (round) 42

Australian

Koo - ka - bur - ra sits on an old gum tree___ Mer - ry mer - ry king of the bush is he;___

Laugh, koo - ka - bur - ra laugh, koo - ka - bur - ra, Gay your life must be.

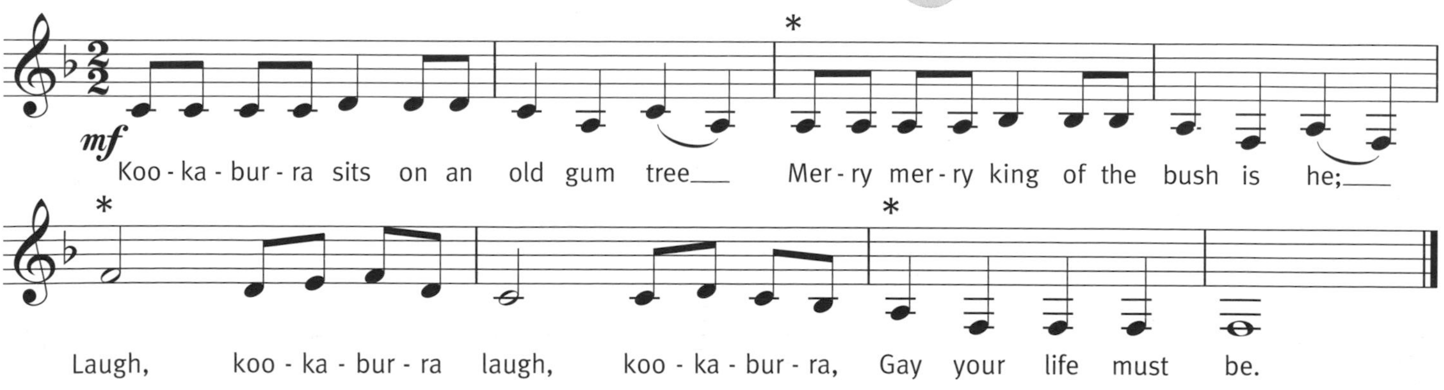

* entry point when played as a round

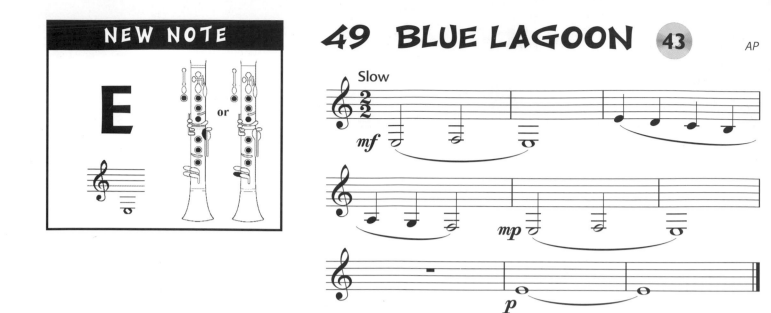

NEW NOTE
E

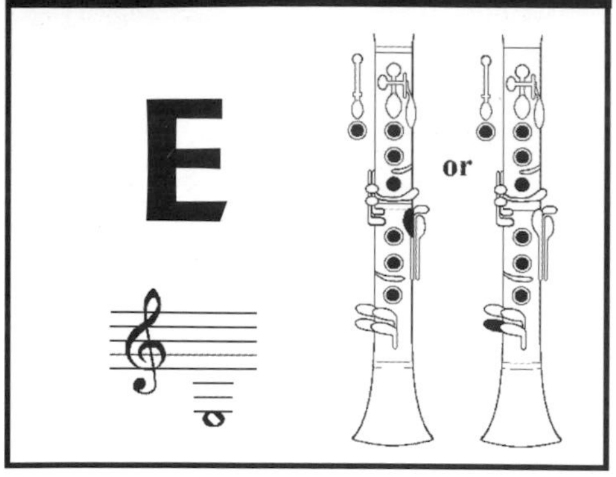

49 BLUE LAGOON 43

AP

Slow

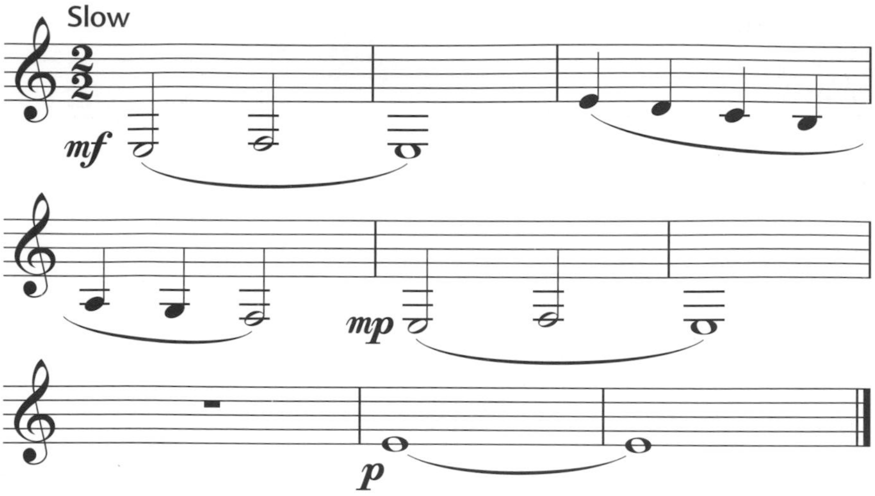

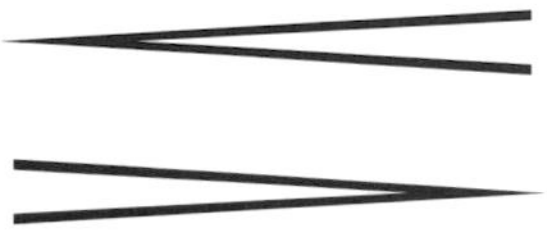

crescendo or cresc. — gradually becoming louder

diminuendo or dim. — gradually becoming quieter

50 TURPIN HERO 44

traditional

mf As Tur - pin rode a - cross the__ moor He saw a law - yer

ri - ding be - fore 'Kind__ sir', says he, 'aren't you a - fraid Of Tur - pin, that mis -

- chie - vous blade?'. O rare Tur - pin he - ro, O rare Tur - pin__ O.

51 SONG OF THE VOLGA BOATMEN 45

Russian

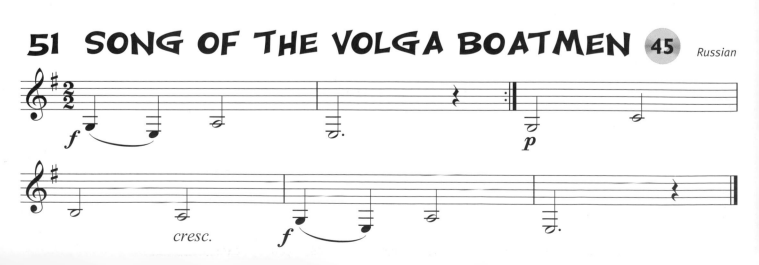

cresc.

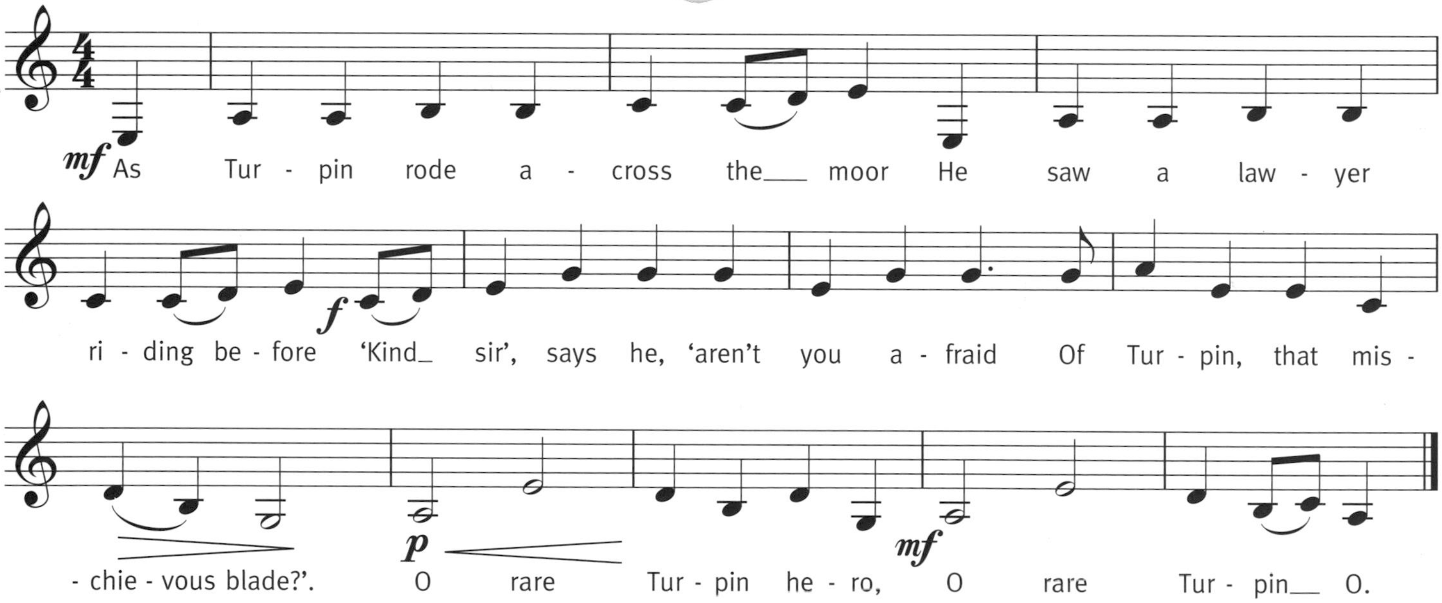

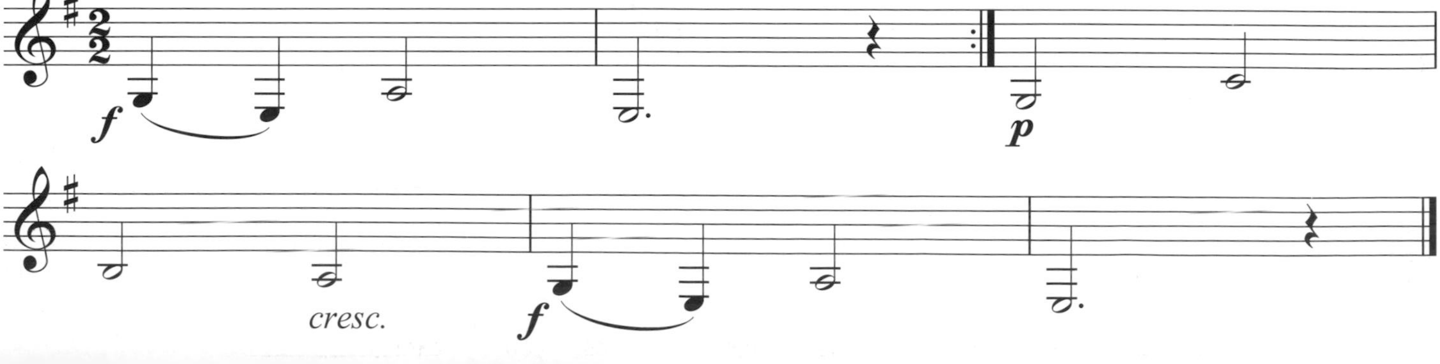

52 DAISY BELL (46)

Harry Dacre

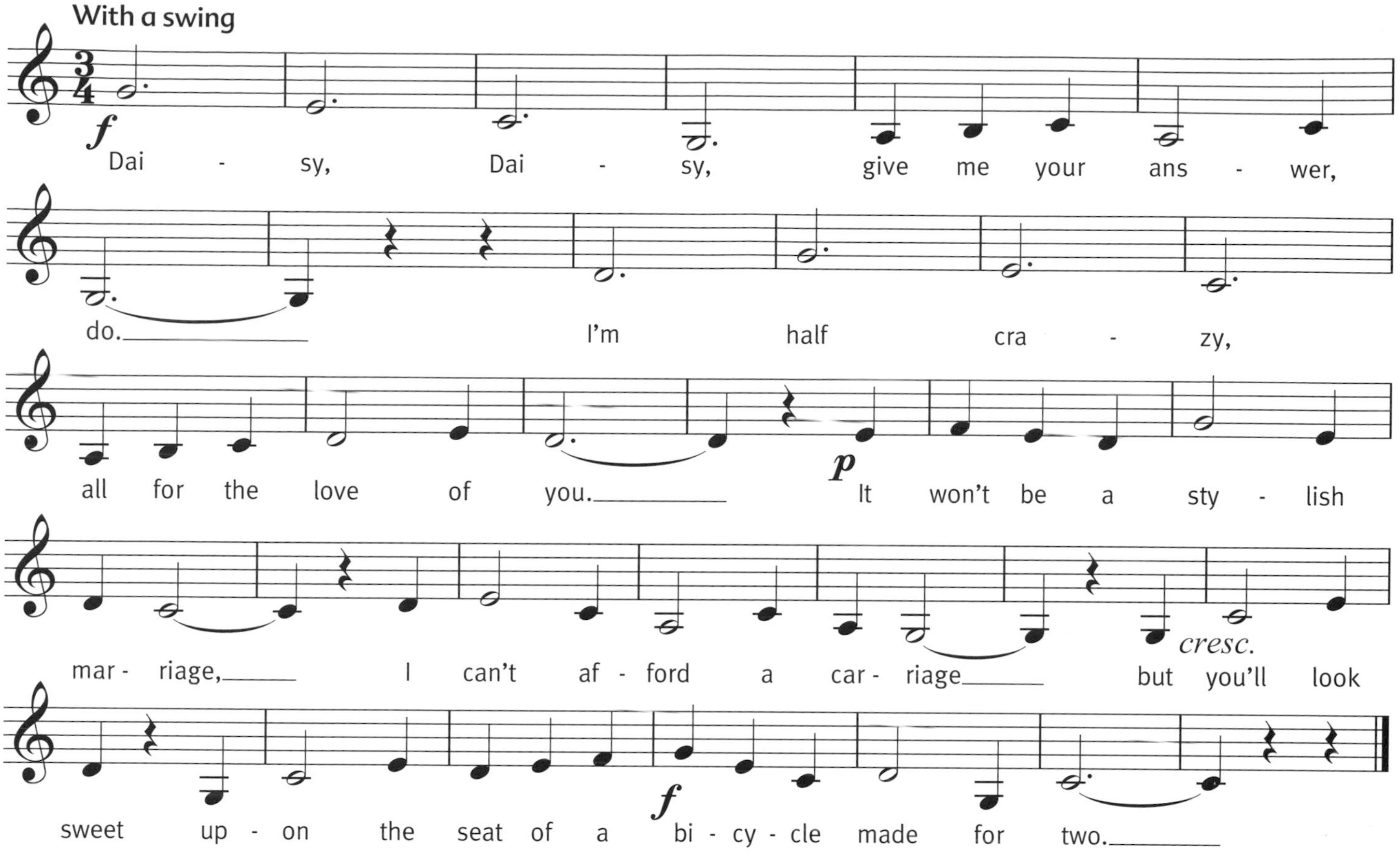

Dai - sy, Dai - sy, give me your ans - wer, do._____ I'm half cra - zy, all for the love of you._____ It won't be a sty - lish mar - riage,_____ I can't af - ford a car - riage_____ but you'll look sweet up - on the seat of a bi - cy - cle made for two._____

DS al Fine — DS is short for Dal Segno, which means 'from the sign'. At DS al Fine, go back to 𝄋 and play until Fine (finish).

53 EGGY BREAD (47)

AP

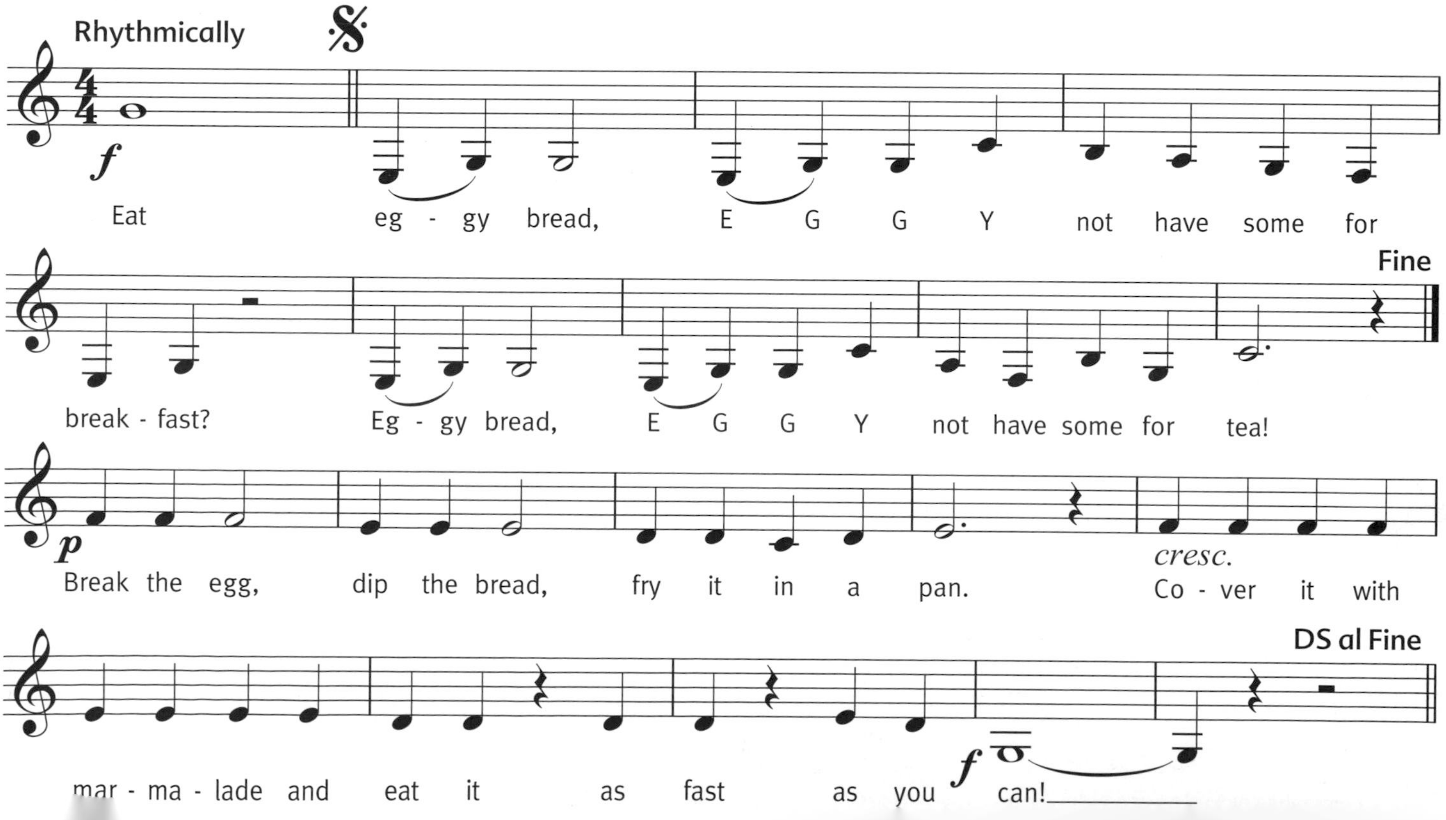

Eat eg - gy bread, E G G Y not have some for break - fast? Eg - gy bread, E G G Y not have some for tea!

Break the egg, dip the bread, fry it in a pan. Co - ver it with mar - ma - lade and eat it as fast as you can!_____

54 OH SOLDIER, SOLDIER (48)

traditional

With a strong beat

'Oh sol - dier, sol - dier, won't you mar - ry me? With your mus - ket, fife and drum.' 'Oh

Fine

no, sweet maid, I can - not mar - ry thee for I have no coat to put on.'

Then off she went to her grand - fa - ther's chest and got him a coat of the ve - ry, ve - ry best, She

DS al Fine

got him a coat of the ve - ry, ve - ry best and the sol - dier put it___ on. 'Oh

$\frac{6}{8}$ (time signature) — six quaver beats to the bar.

Count two beats to the bar, eg.   or count six quavers, eg.

55 STROLLING ALONG (49)

Lorna Rutland

56 ROW, ROW, ROW YOUR BOAT (round) (50)

traditional

* entry point when played as a round

57 THREE BLIND MICE (round) 51

traditional

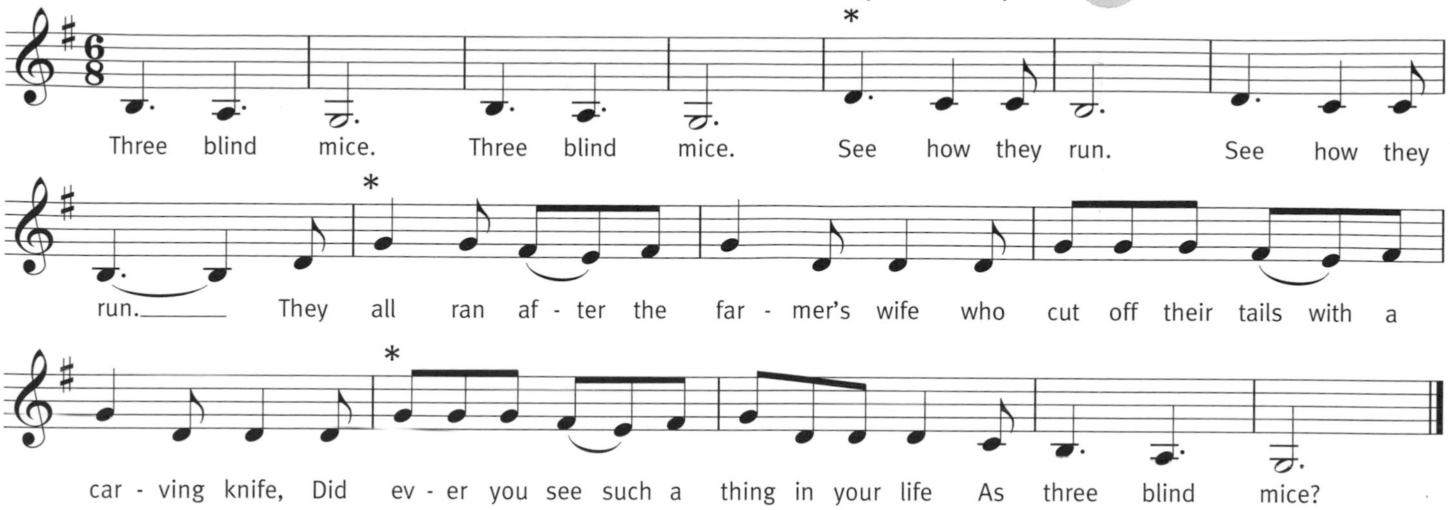

Three blind mice. Three blind mice. See how they run. See how they

run. They all ran af-ter the far-mer's wife who cut off their tails with a

car-ving knife, Did ev-er you see such a thing in your life As three blind mice?

*entry point when played as a round

58 SUSAN AND CATHERINE 52

*words: English version by
Patrick R Chalmers
music: traditional Angevin*

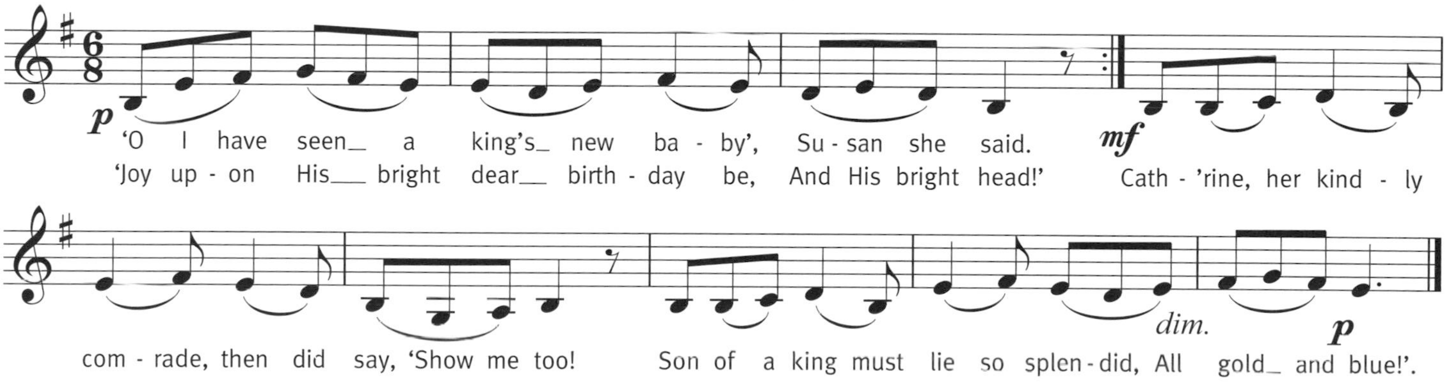

'O I have seen a king's new ba-by', Su-san she said.
'Joy up-on His bright dear birth-day be, And His bright head!' Cath-'rine, her kind-ly

com-rade, then did say, 'Show me too! Son of a king must lie so splen-did, All gold and blue!'.

59 THE BEAR WENT OVER THE MOUNTAIN 53

traditional

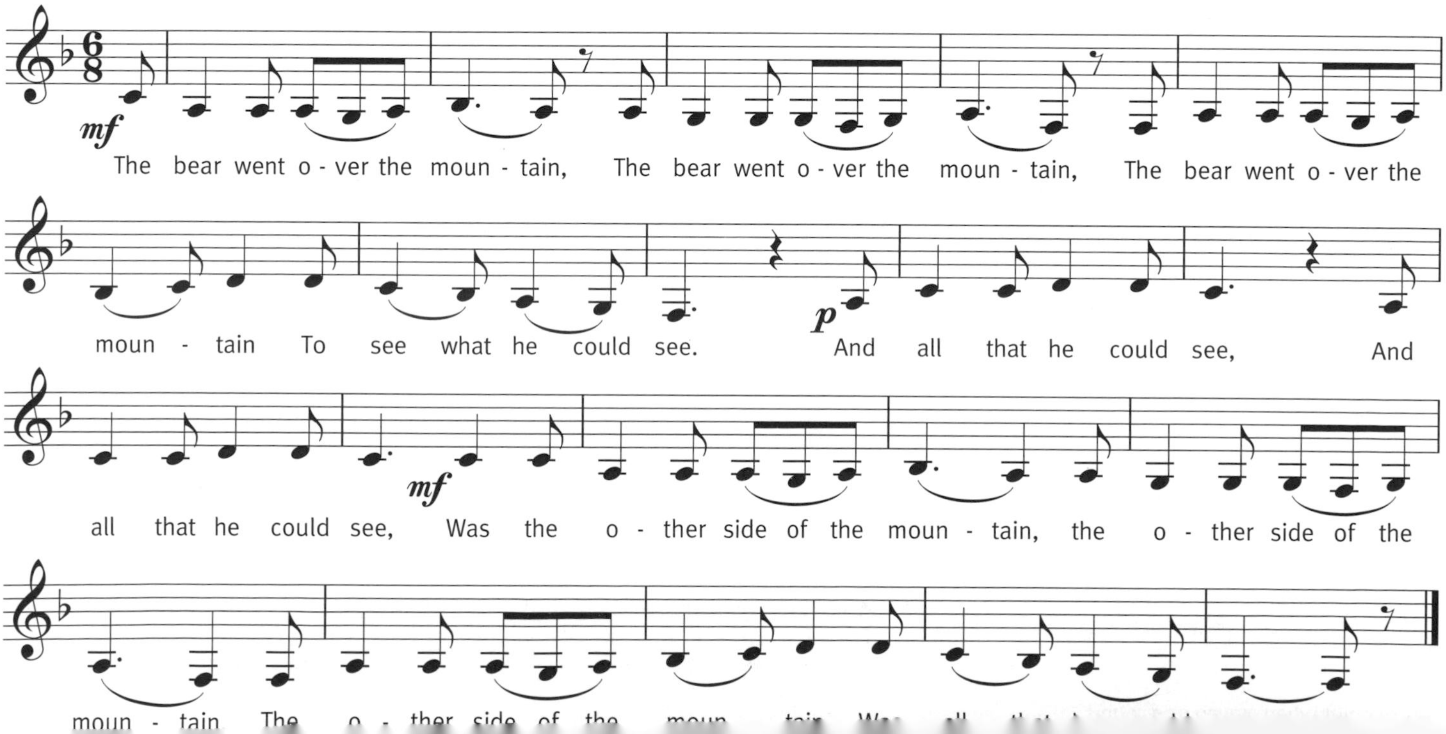

The bear went o-ver the moun-tain, The bear went o-ver the moun-tain, The bear went o-ver the

moun-tain To see what he could see. And all that he could see,	And

all that he could see, Was the o-ther side of the moun-tain, the o-ther side of the

moun-tain The o-ther side of the moun-tain Was all that he could

$\frac{9}{8}$ (time signature) — nine quaver beats to the bar. The quavers are grouped in threes.

60 MORNING HAS BROKEN 54

words: Eleanor Farjeon
music: Gaelic

Morn - ing has bro - ken   Like the first morn - ing,   Black - bird has spo - ken   Like the first bird.____

Praise for the sing - ing!   Praise for the morn - ing!   Praise for them, spring - ing   Fresh from the Word!____

♪ semiquaver — worth a quarter of a crotchet beat.   ♬♬ = ♩

The semibreve rest ▬ is used to show a whole bar's rest in any time signature.

61 BERCEUSE D'AUVERGNE (duet)

French arr. JR

NEW NOTE

B♭

62 OVER THE HILLS AND FAR AWAY 55

English

63 PLAISIR D'AMOUR (56)

G P Martini

mp Plai - sir d'a - mour___ ne du - re qu'un__ mo - ment.___ Cha -

- grin d'a - mour du - re toute__ la vie.___

64 KOL DŌDI (57)

Israeli

♩· ♩· staccato dots — a dot above or below a note indicates that the note
should be played short and detached.

ff (fortissimo) — very loud

65 RAKES OF MALLOW (58)

traditional

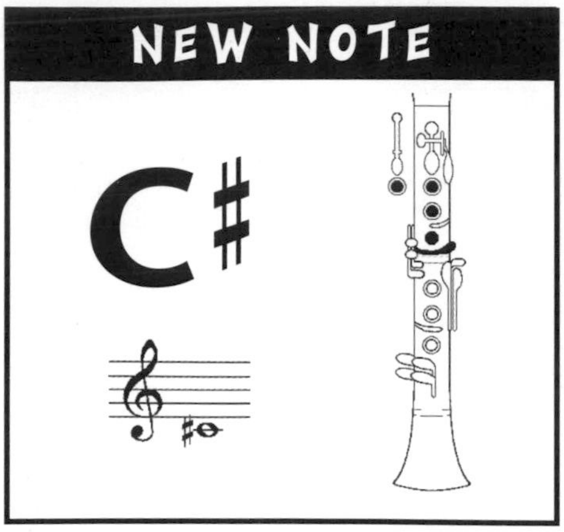

NEW NOTE

C#

6/4 (time signature) — six crotchet beats to the bar

pp (pianissimo) — very quiet

Andante (tempo indication) — at a walking pace
(tempo = speed)

66 O LITTLE ONE SWEET 59

Scheidt

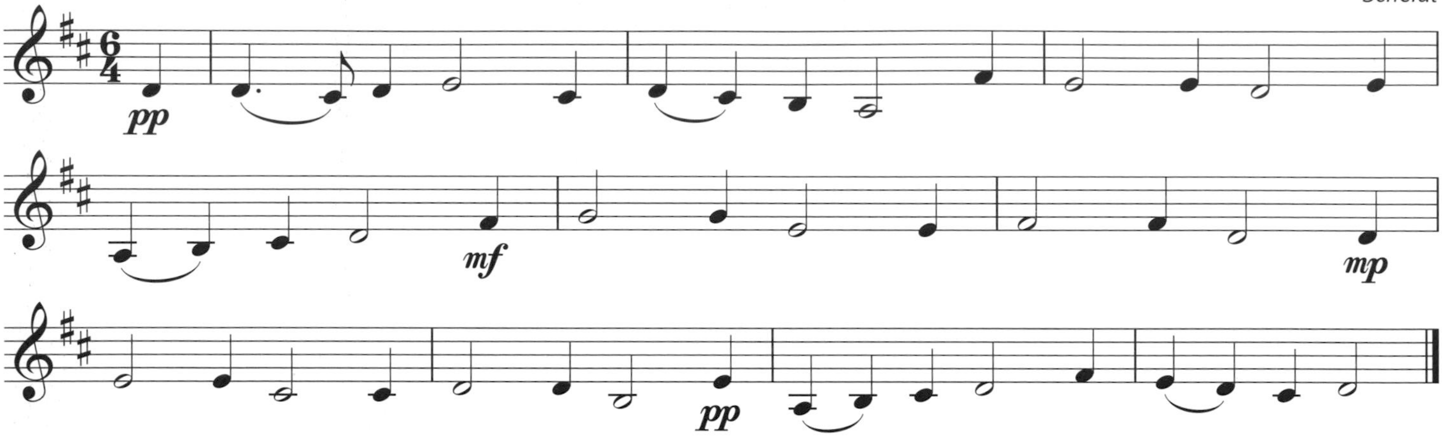

♮ (natural) — it cancels the effect of a sharp or flat. Its influence lasts until the next barline.

67 PATAPAN (duet)

Burgundian arr. L H Page

With a bounce

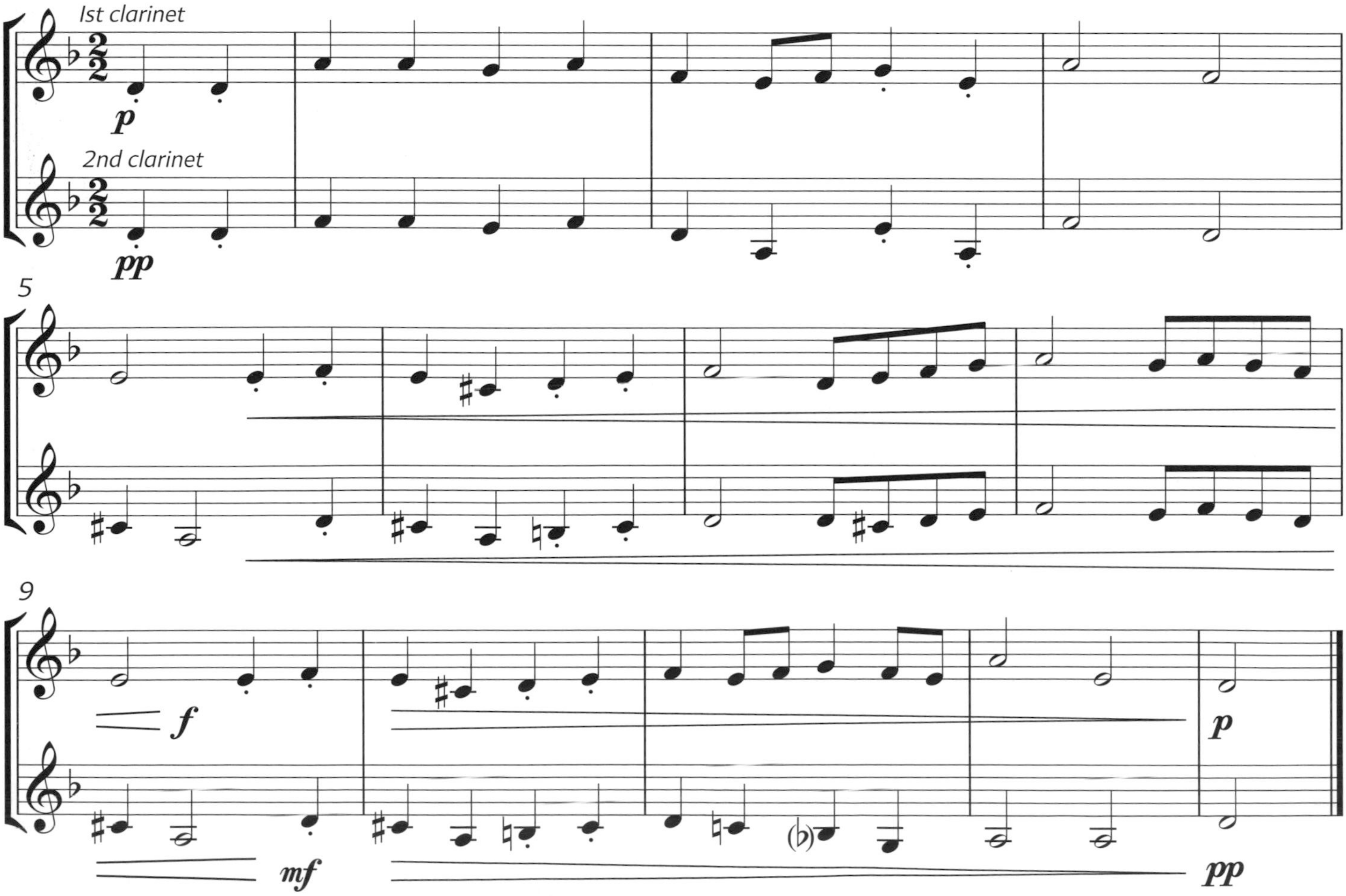

NEW NOTE

E♭

or

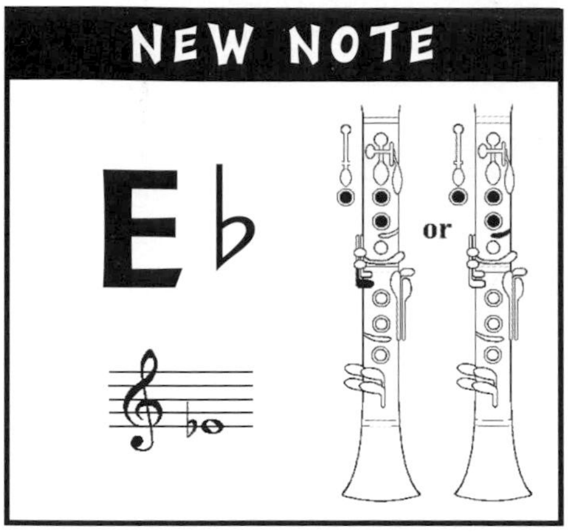

$\frac{3}{2}$ (time signature) — three minim beats to the bar

68 BROTHER JAMES' AIR

J L M Bain

Andante

mf

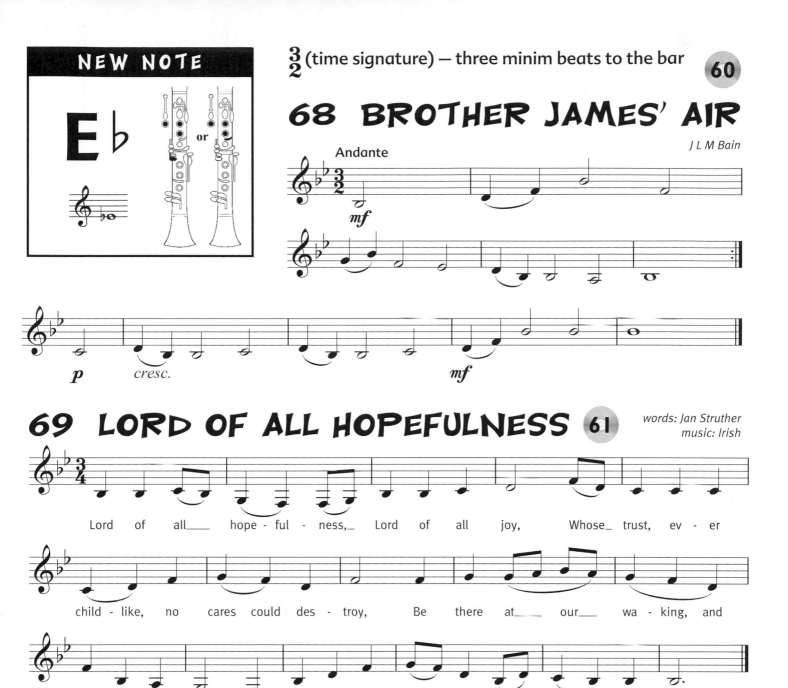

p   *cresc.*   *mf*

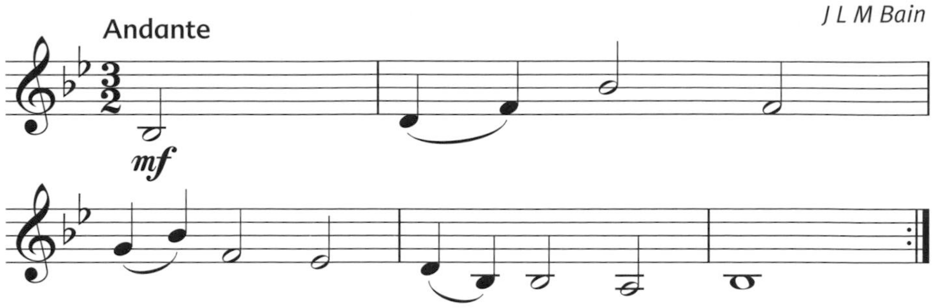

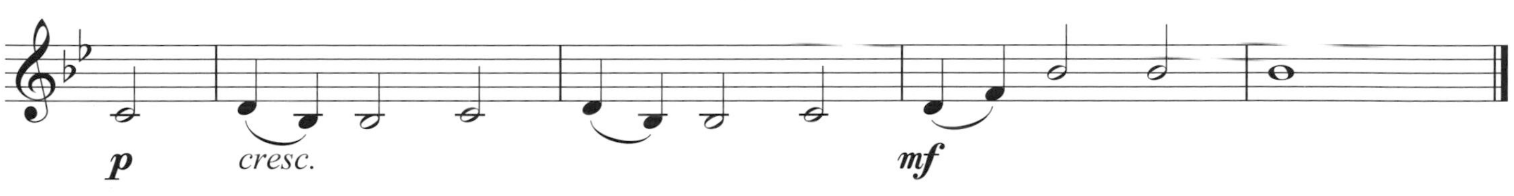

69 LORD OF ALL HOPEFULNESS 61

words: Jan Struther
music: Irish

Lord of all___ hope - ful - ness,___ Lord of all joy, Whose_ trust, ev - er

child - like, no cares could des - troy, Be there at___ our___ wa - king, and

give us, we pray, Your bliss in our hearts,___ Lord, at the break of the day.

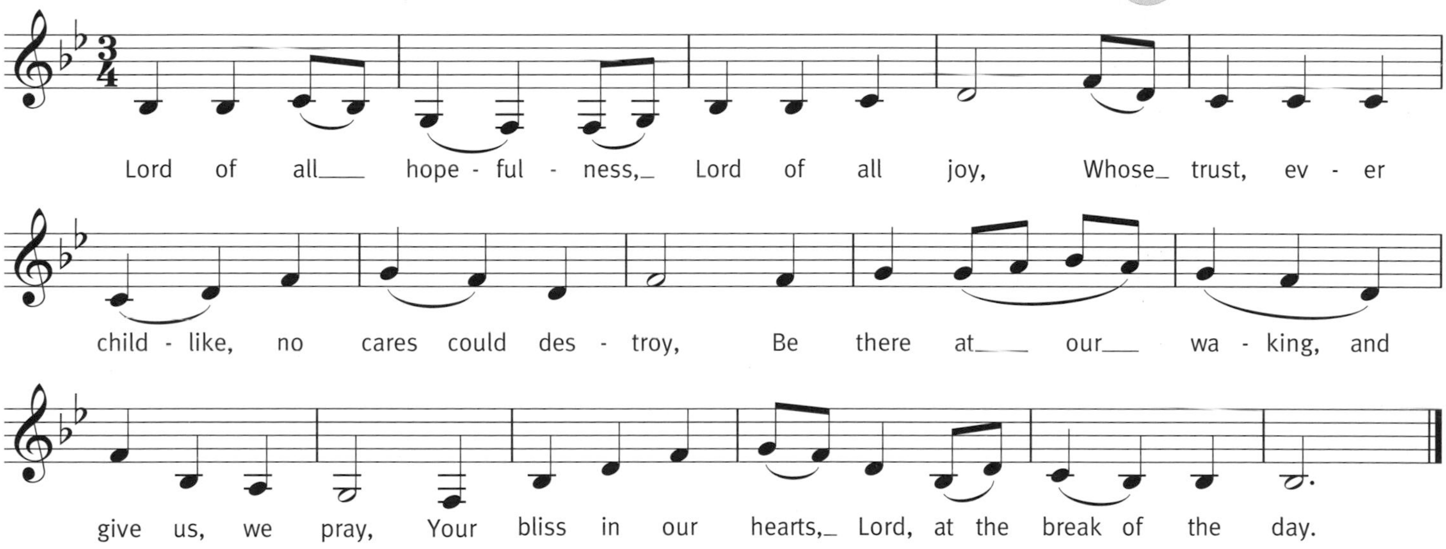

Since a sharp raises a note by a semitone and a flat lowers a note by a semitone, D♯ and E♭ are two different names for the same note, halfway between D and E.
Similarly, F♯ = G♭, C♯ = D♭, etc.

70 YOU ARE MY SUNSHINE 62

Jimmie Davis and Charles Mitchell

Lively

mf

You are my sun - shine,_____ my on - ly sun - shine,_____ You make me

cresc.

hap - py_____ when skies are grey,_____ You'll ne - ver know dear,_____ how much I

f   *dim.*   *mf*

love you,_____ Please don't take my sun - shine a - way._____

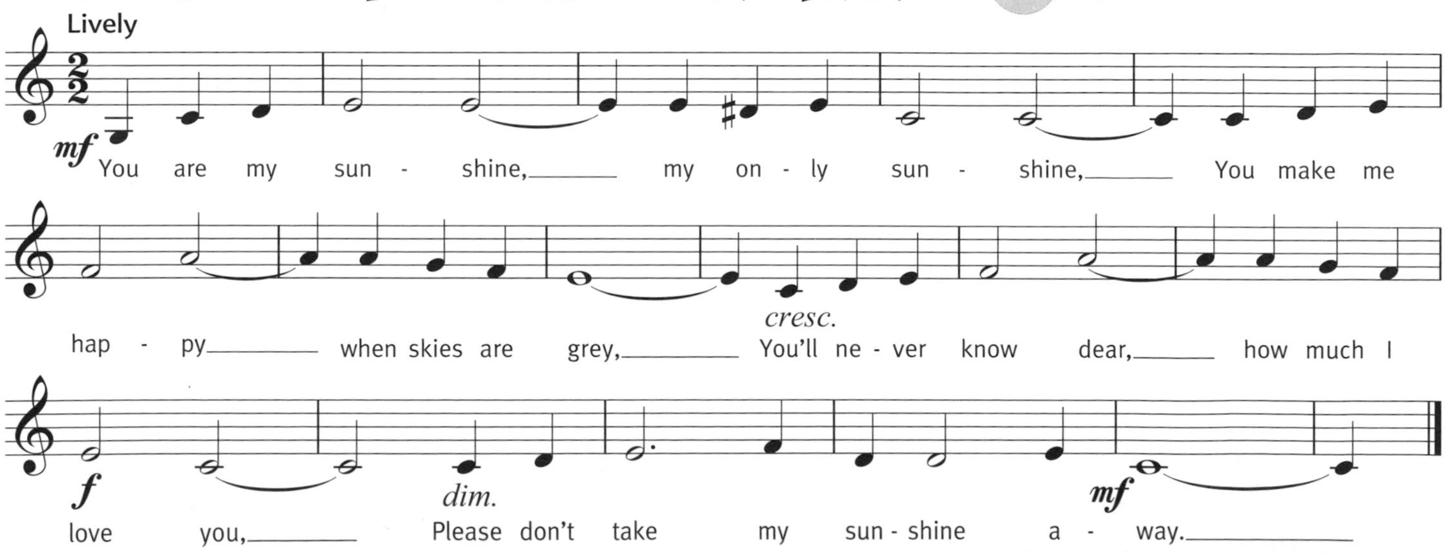

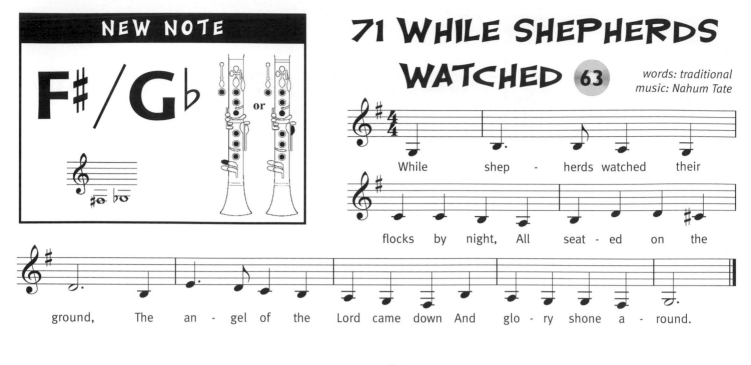

NEW NOTE

F♯/G♭

71 WHILE SHEPHERDS WATCHED 63

words: traditional
music: Nahum Tate

While shep - herds watched their flocks by night, All seat - ed on the ground, The an - gel of the Lord came down And glo - ry shone a - round.

72 DECK THE HALL 64

Welsh

Cheerfully

ff Deck the hall with boughs of hol - ly, *mp* Fa - la - la - la - la, Fa - la - la - la. *ff* 'Tis the sea - son

to be jol - ly, *mp* Fa - la - la - la, Fa - la - la - la. *pp* Fill the mead cup, drain the bar - rel,

cresc. Fa - la - la - la - la, *ff* la - la - la. Troll the an - cient Christ - mas ca - rol, *mp* Fa - la - la - la - la, *ff* Fa - la - la - la.

⌢ pause — hold the note marked with a pause sign for a little longer than its written value.

73 HURON INDIAN CAROL 65a first 36 secs

Canadian

Andante

mp

f   *dim.*

mp   *pp*

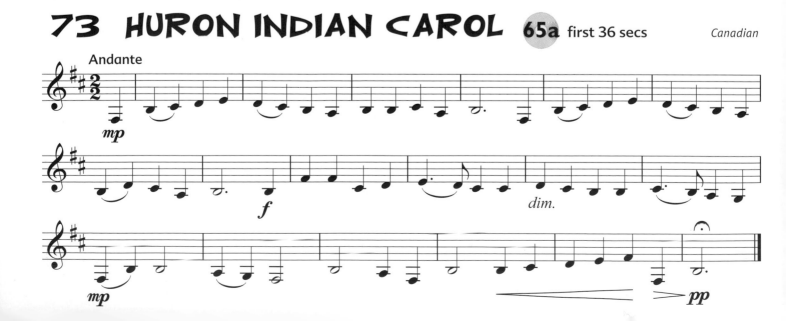

74 HEY, LITTLE BULL   65b after 36 secs

words: A H Green
music: Brazilian carol

mf Hey,__ lit-tle bull be-hind the gate, What are you do-ing up so late?

And,__ lit-tle bull, what have you seen On this__ star-ry__ Christ-mas Eve?

mp If you raise your eyes to hea-ven You will see the Vir-gin's Son,

He is clothed in white ap-pa-rel And is bless-ing ev-'ry-one.

mf La-la la-la la la la la la La la-la la-la la-la-la-la-la.

cresc. La-la la-la la la la la la *f* La la-la la la-la la la la.

NEW NOTE

G♯/A♭

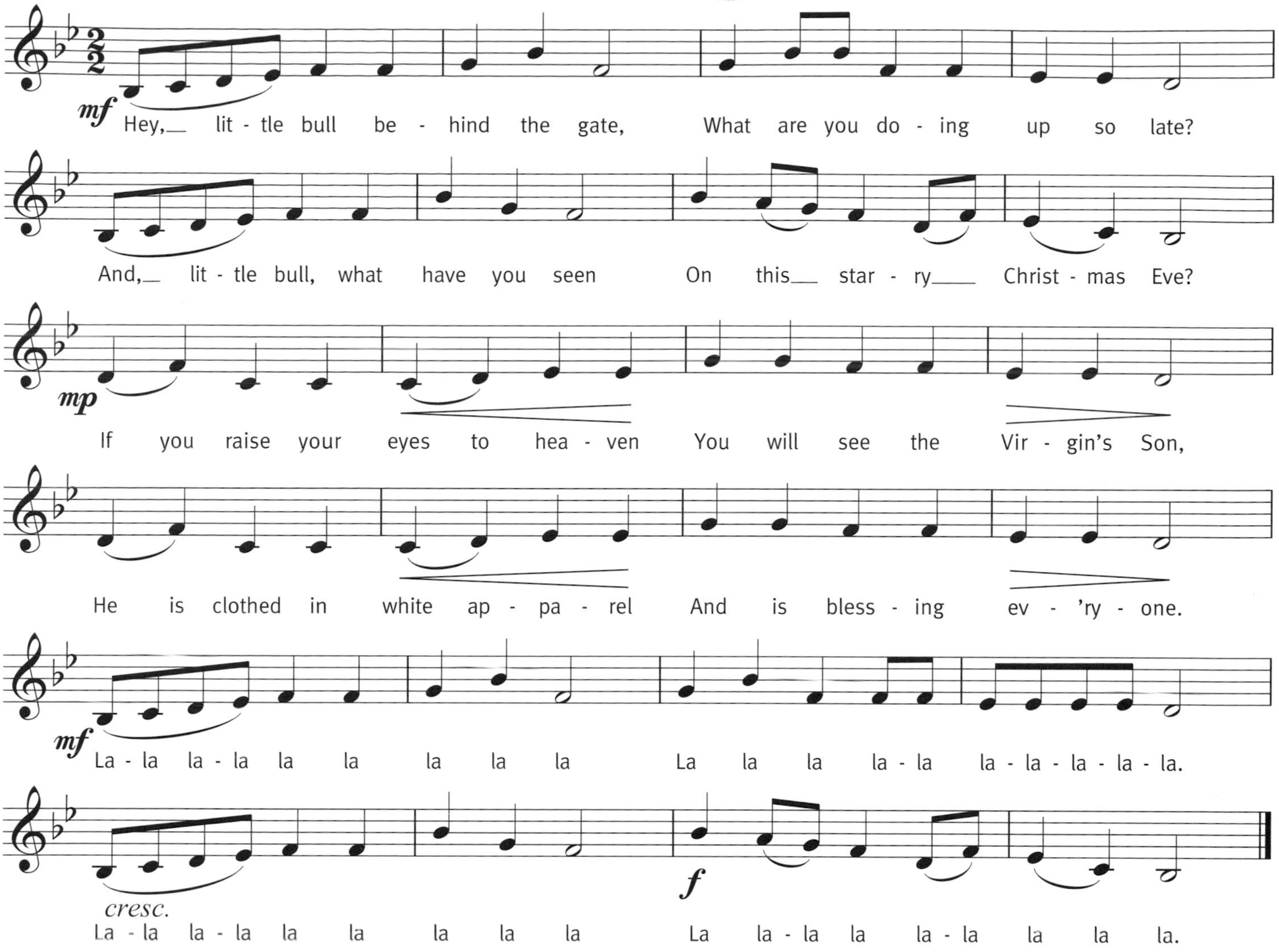

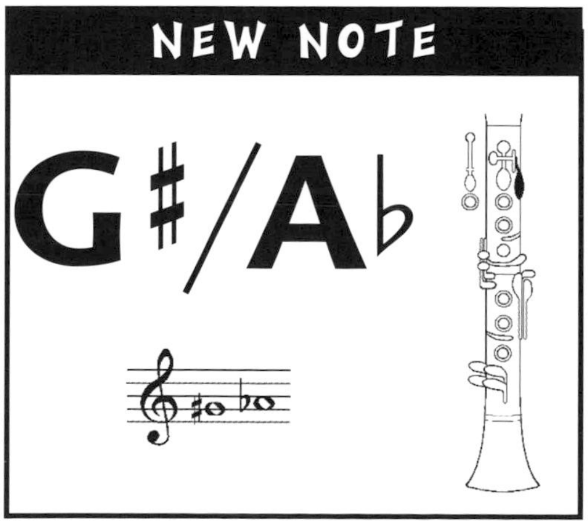

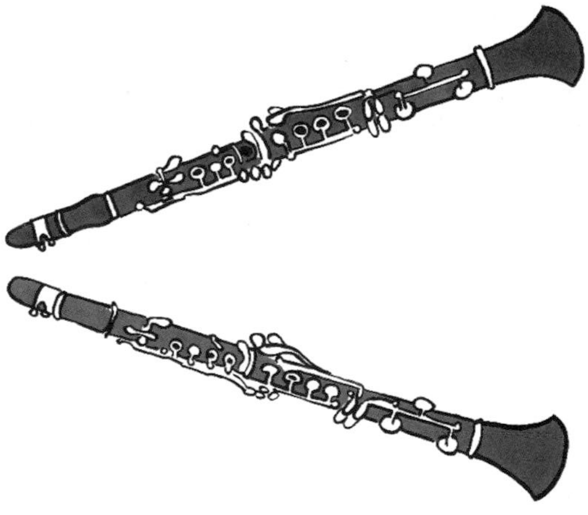

75 SING THIS SONG (round)   66a first 25 secs

words: Michael Jesset,
adapted John Bannister
music: traditional

Sing this song whilst you play,

Sing it in the eve-ning and at break of day.

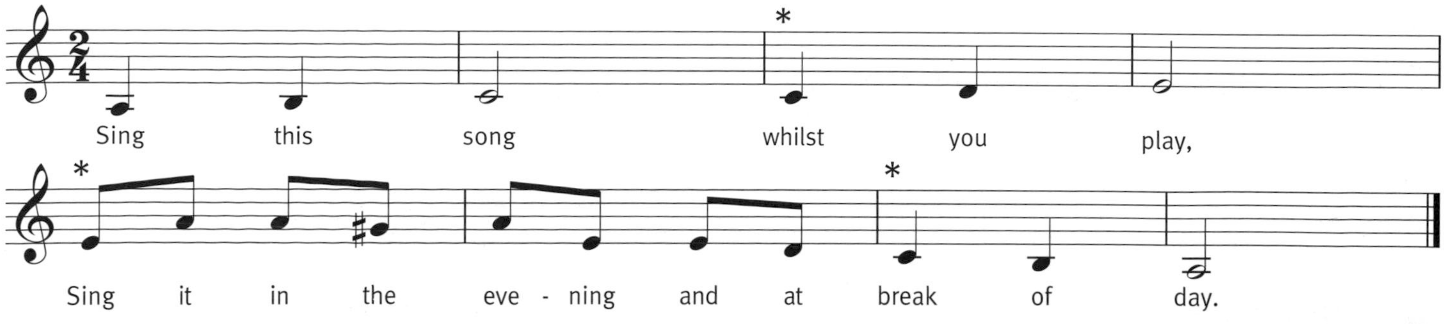

76 LILLIBURLERO

66b after 25 secs

traditional

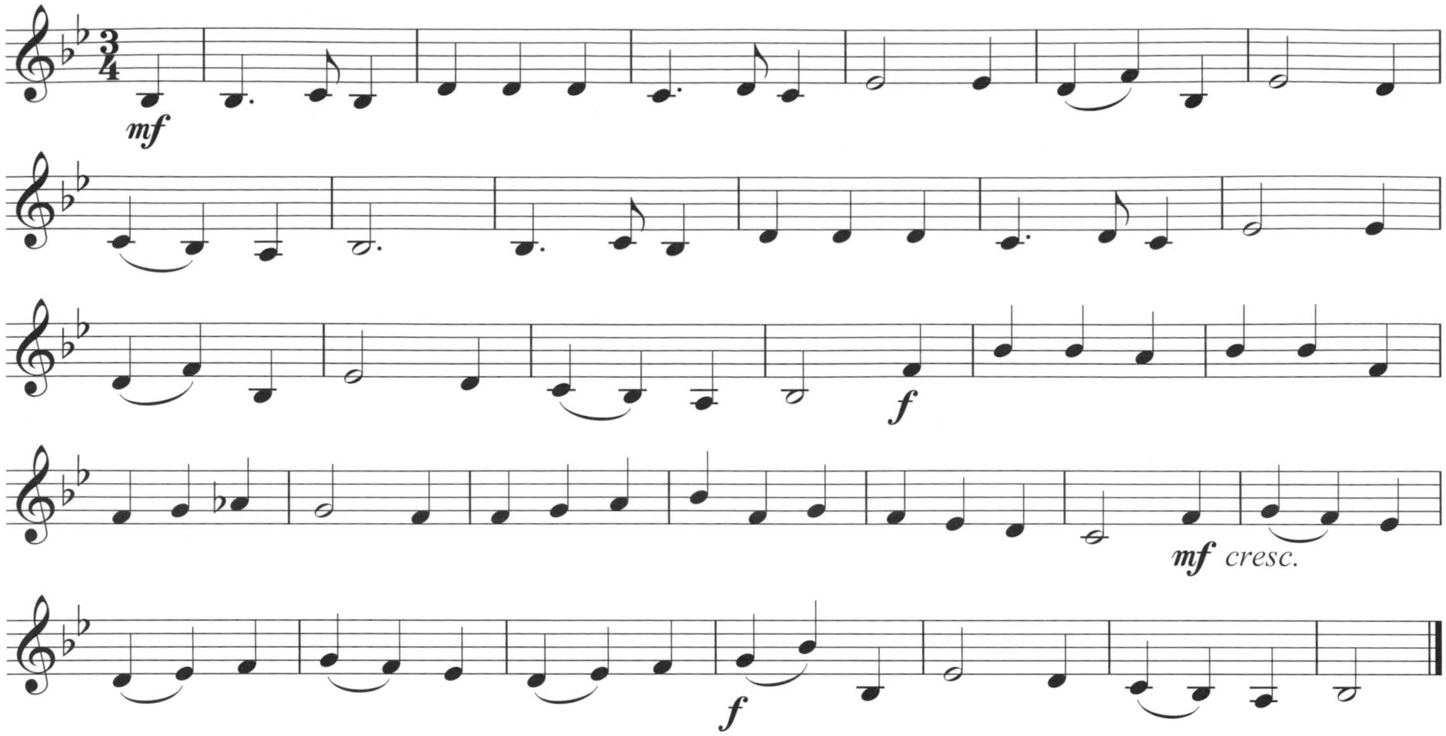

77 NOËL NOUVELET

67a first 26 secs

French carol

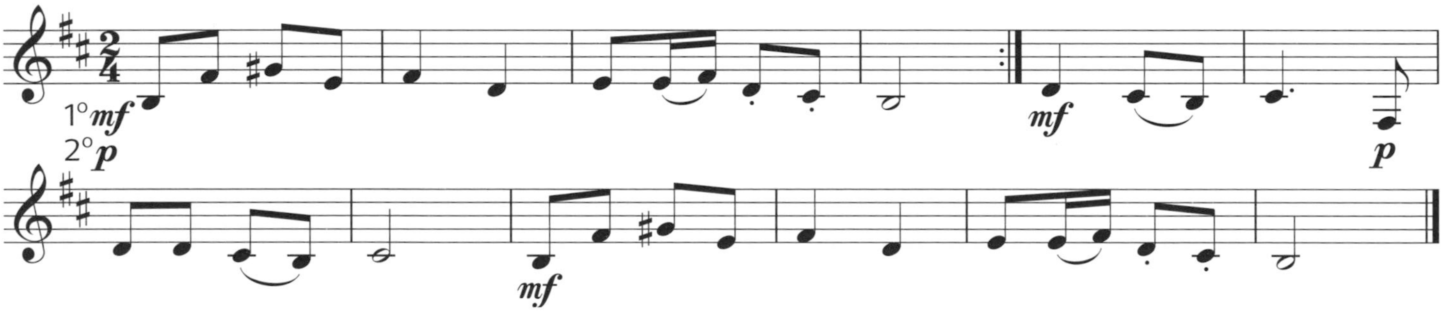

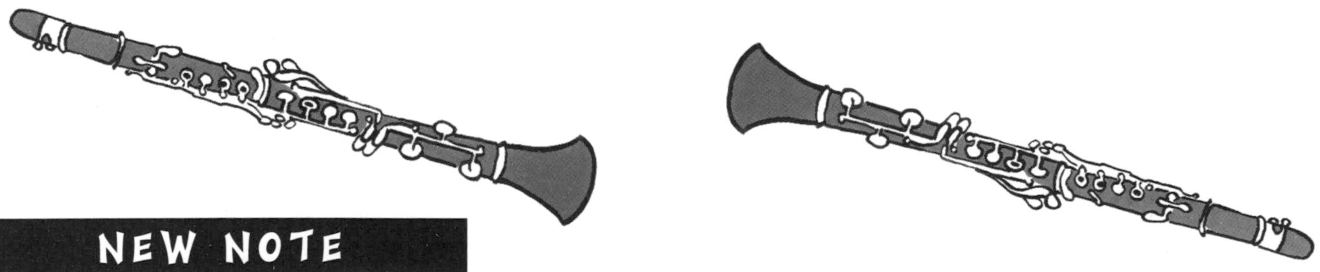

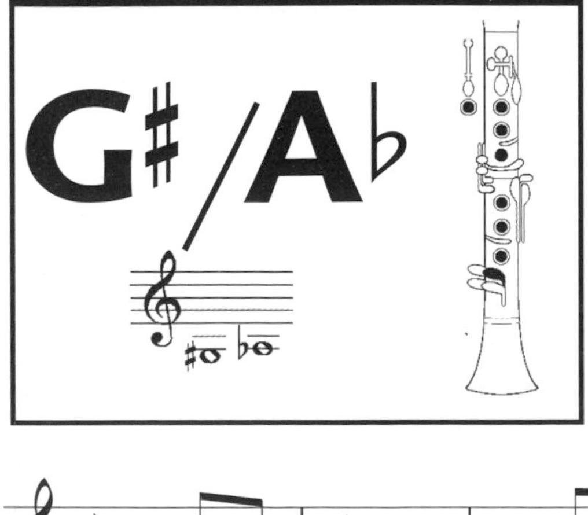

78 EL CONDOR PASA

67b after 26 secs

South American

With a singing tone

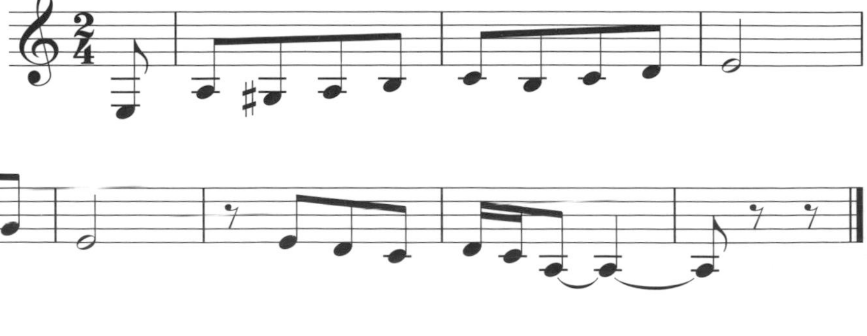

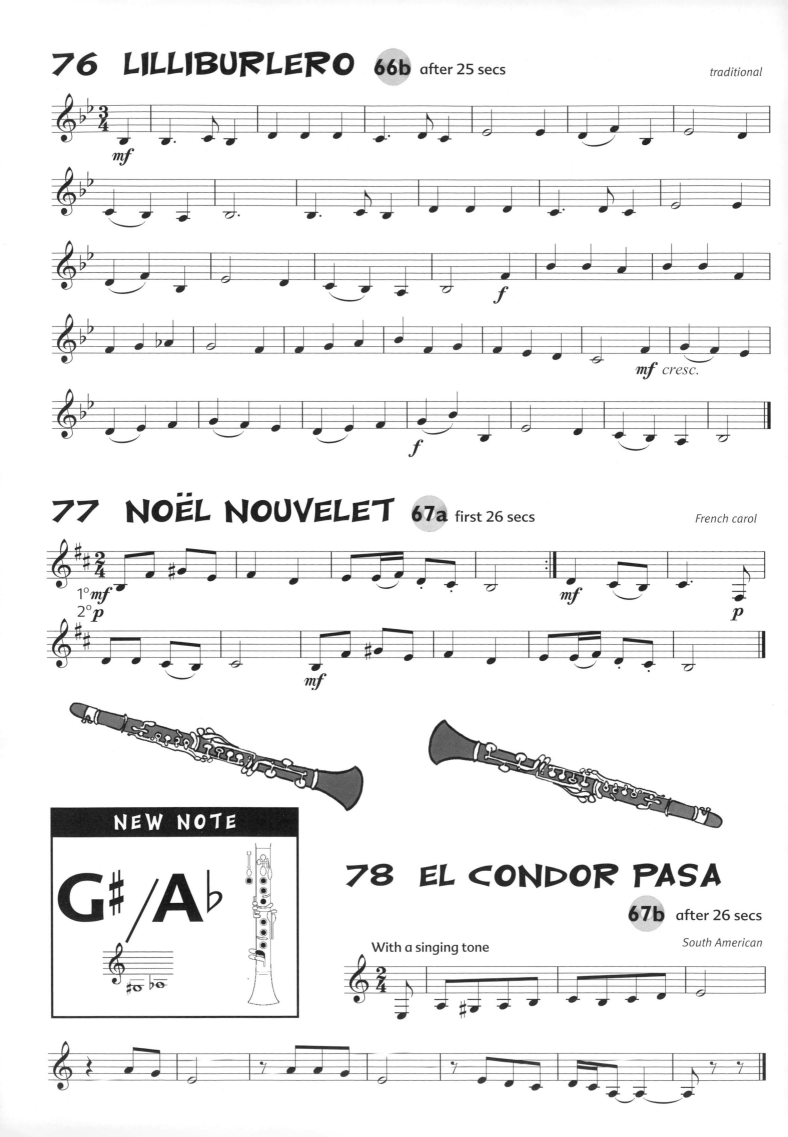

79 SANTA LUCIA 68a first 1 min 7 secs

Neopolitan

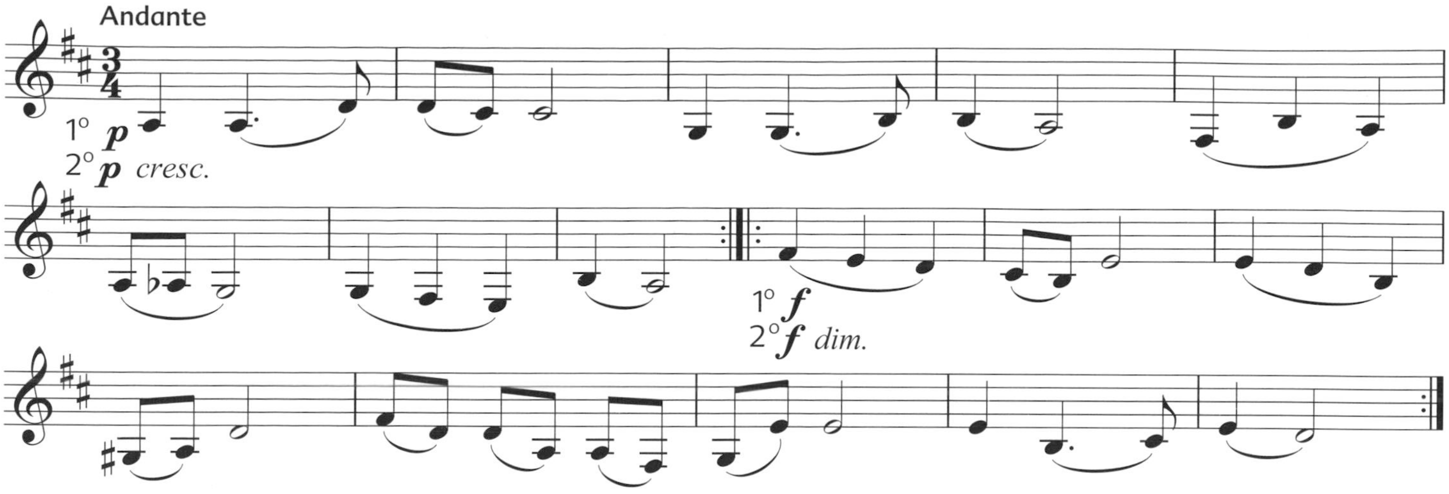

80 OH SUSANNA (duet)

North American arr. JR

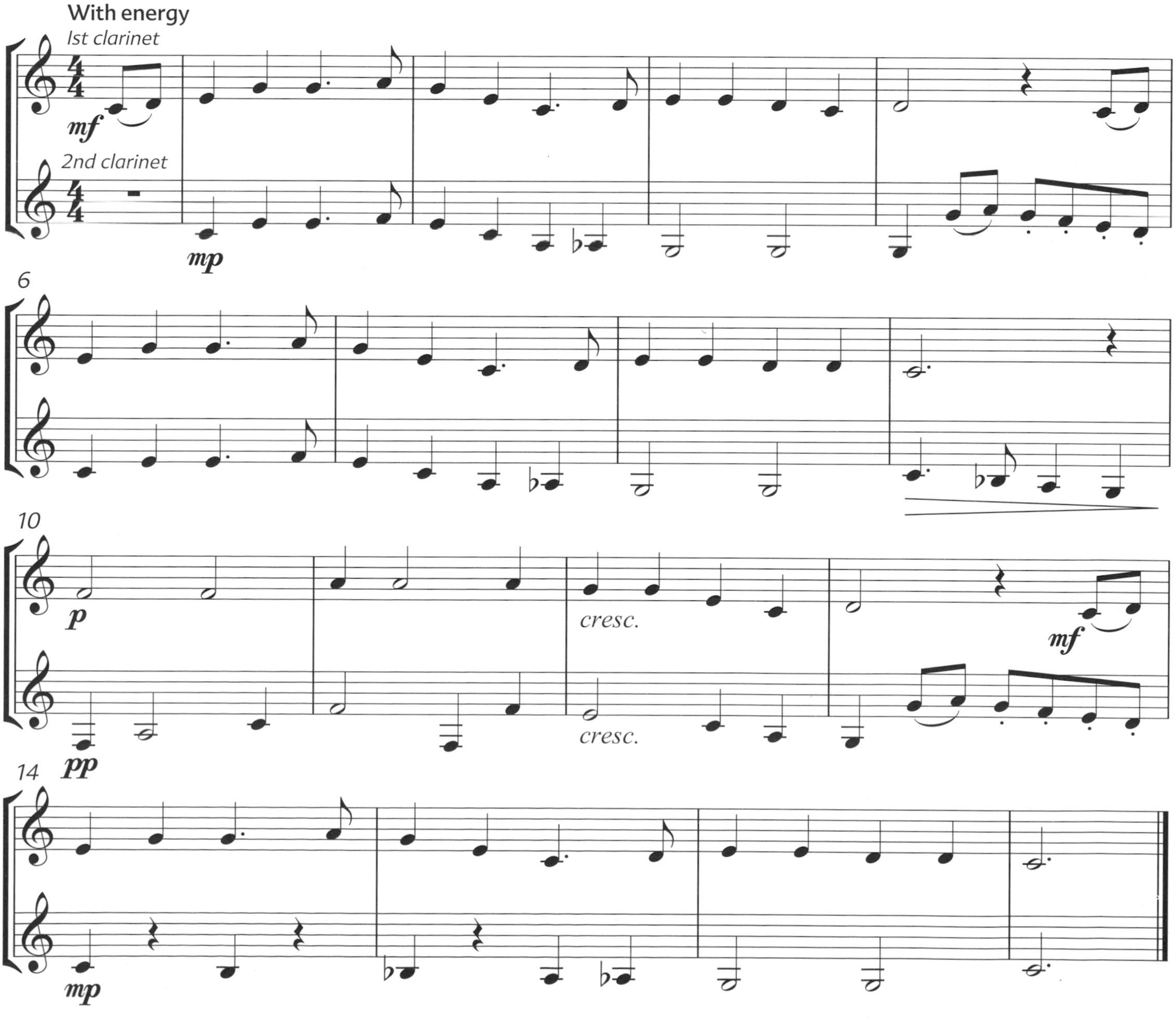

This is a useful fingering when moving between B and B♭ (A♯).

NEW FINGERING

B

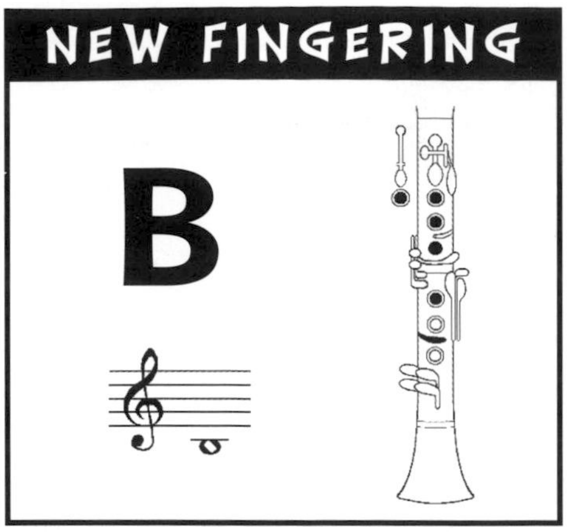

81 OOM PAH PAH 68b after 1 min 7 secs

Lionel Bart

mf

There's a lit - tle dit - ty they're sing - ing in the ci - ty Es - pec - ially when they've been on the gin or the beer; If you've got the pat - ience your own i - ma - gi - na - tions will tell you just ex - act - ly what you want to hear. Oom pah pah, oom pah pah, that's how it goes, Oom pah pah, oom pah pah, ev - 'ry - one knows. They all sup - -pose what they want to sup - pose When they hear 'oom pah pah'.____

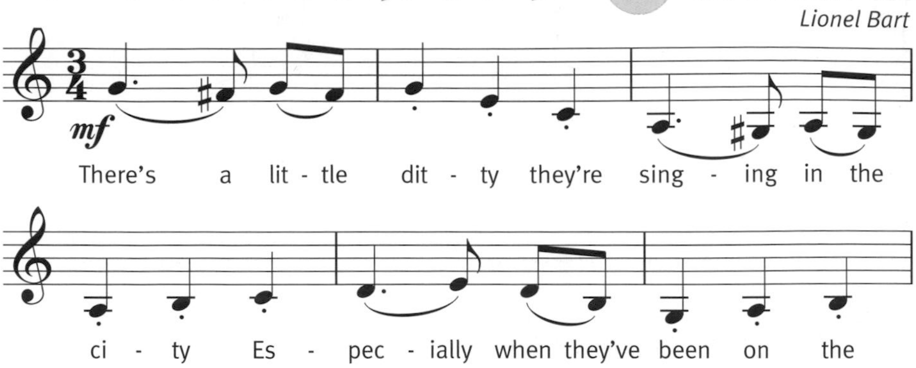

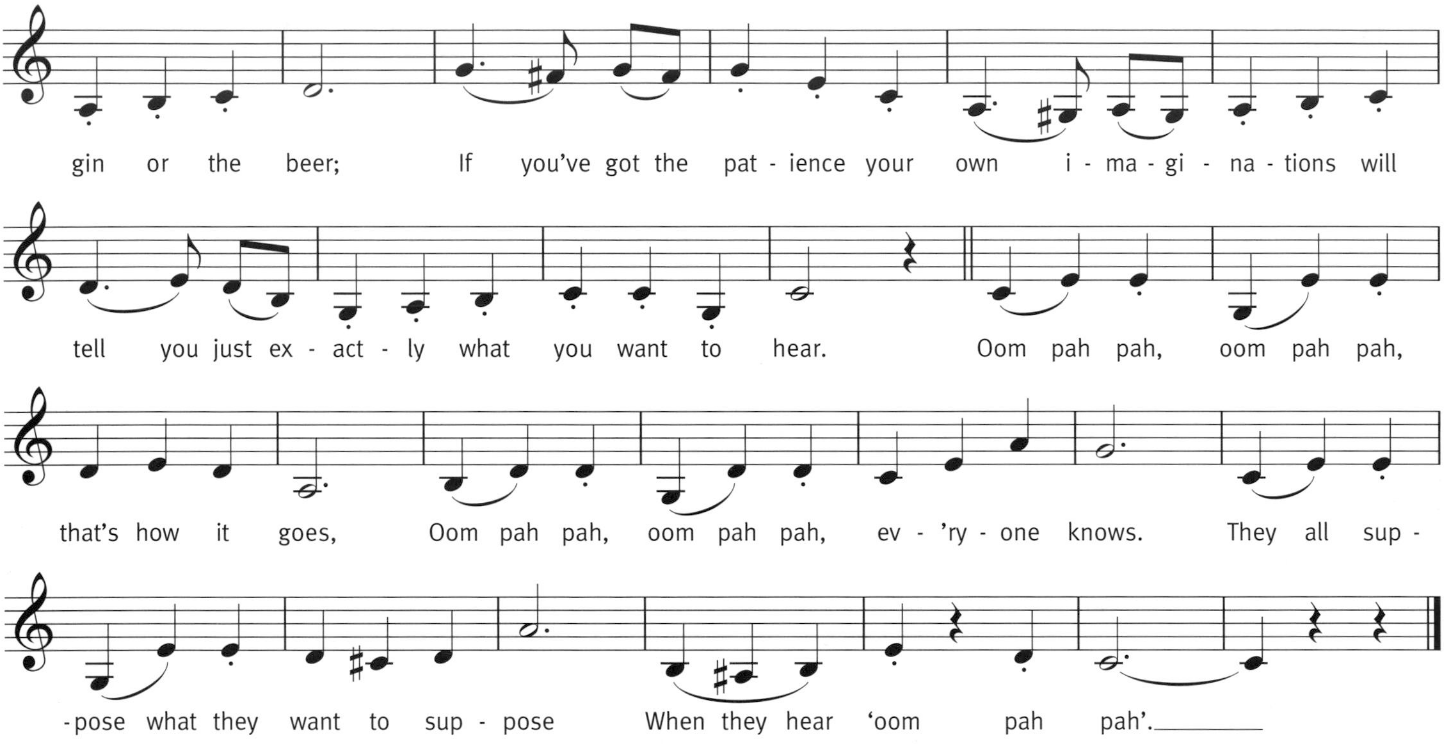

> accent — an accent above or below a note tells you to give extra attack at the start of the note

moderato — at a moderate speed

82 THE CAT FROM 'PETER AND THE WOLF' 69a first 27 secs

Prokofieff

Moderato - elegantly

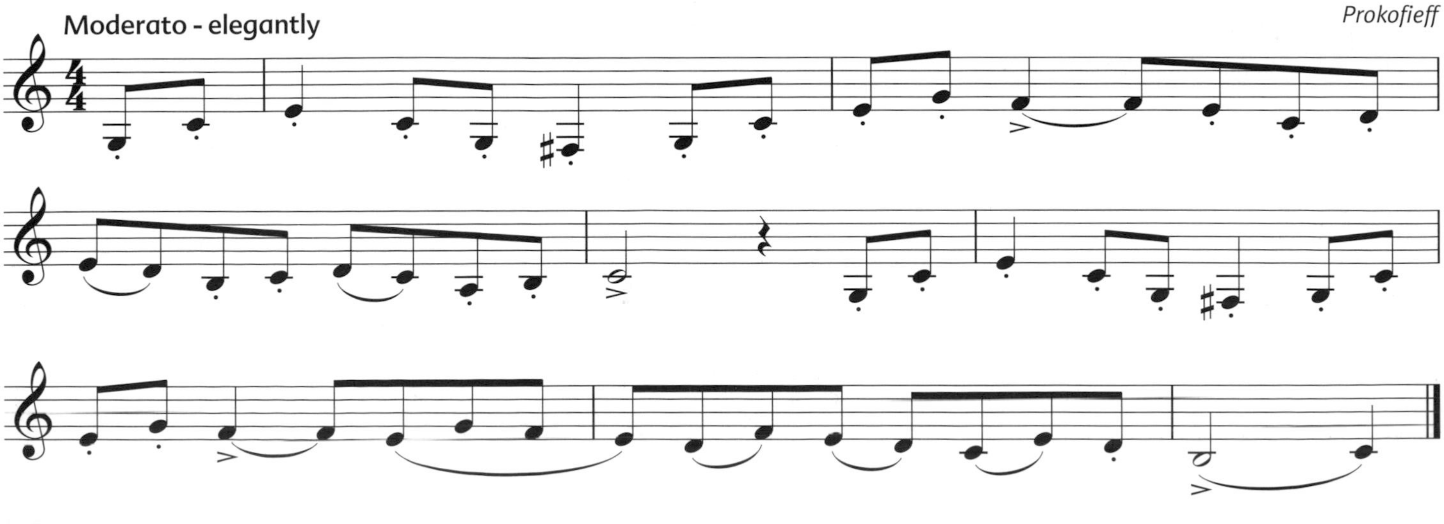

83 FEED ME 69b after 27 secs

AP

84 OLD JOE CLARK (duet)

North American

Jauntily

85 BLUE MIST 70a first 17 secs

JS

Smoothly

ritardando (rit.) — gradually get slower

♩ ♩ tenuto marks — a tenuto mark above or below a note tells you to hold the note for its full value and lean on it slightly.

86 SADNESS (70b) after 17 secs

Lorna Rutland

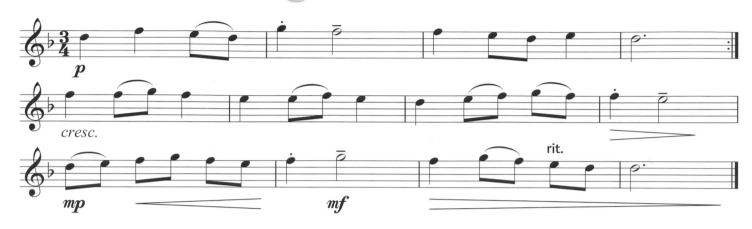

NEW NOTE

87 NOW THE DAY IS OVER

(71a) first 20 secs *S. Baring-Gould*

Gently

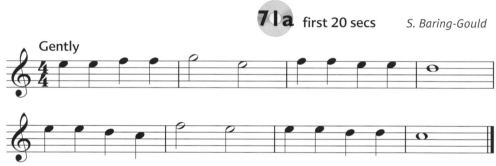

88 HUMMING SONG (71b) after 20 secs

Schumann

In a singing style

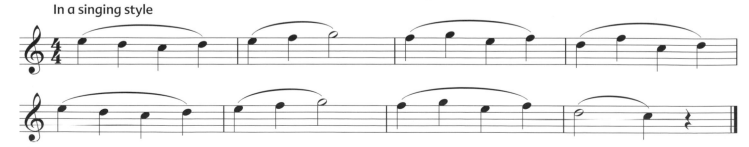

WINTER GOODBYE 72a first 24 secs *German*

Moderato
mf

90 ANDREW MINE, JASPER MINE

72b after 24 secs

words: C K Offer
music: Moravian carol

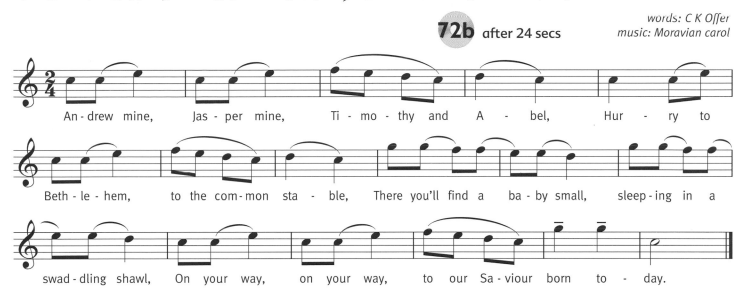

An - drew mine, Jas - per mine, Ti - mo - thy and A - bel, Hur - ry to

Beth - le - hem, to the com - mon sta - ble, There you'll find a ba - by small, sleep - ing in a

swad - dling shawl, On your way, on your way, to our Sa - viour born to - day.

91 UPIDEE 73a first 12 secs *French*

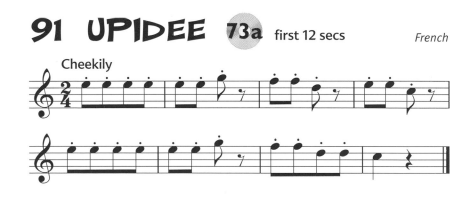

Cheekily

NEW NOTE

F#

92 A CUCKOO 73b after 12 secs *French*

NEW FINGERING

F♯

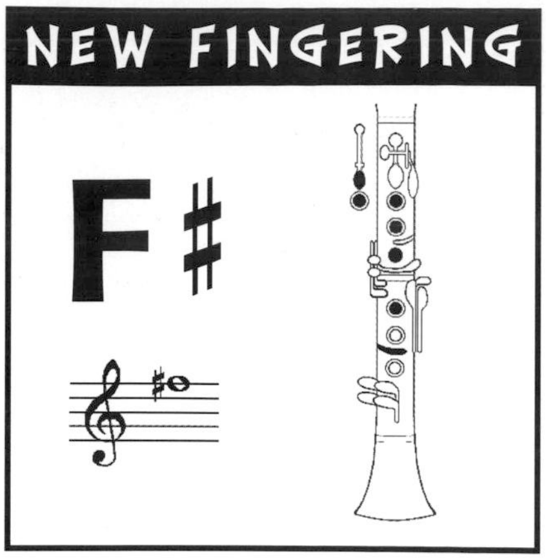

allegro — fast and lively

93 JIGSAW **74a** first 33 secs

L H and R H Page

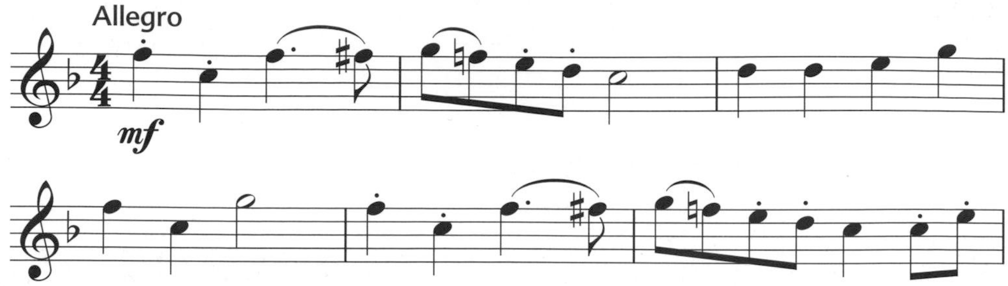

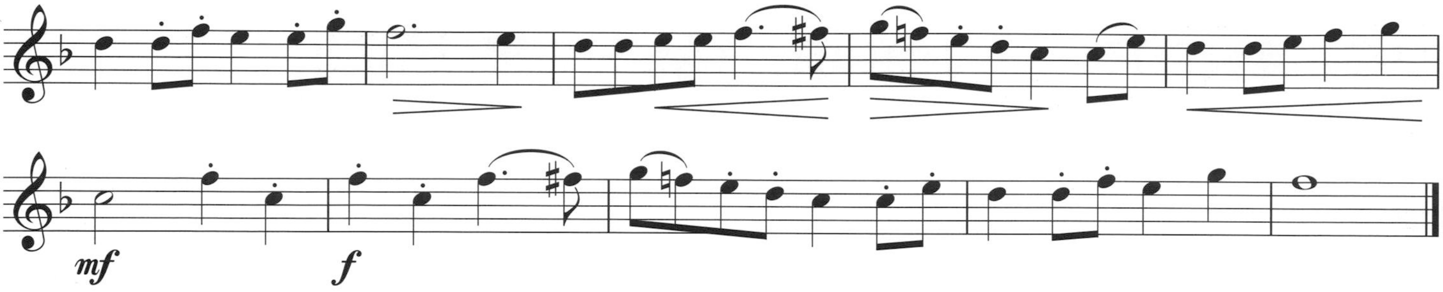

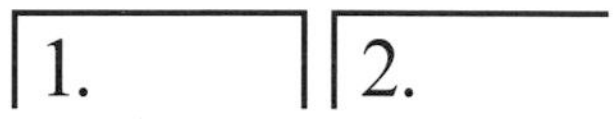

1. | 2. | first and second time bars — when you repeat the music, miss out the first time bar and go straight to the second time bar.

allegretto — fairly fast, but less so than allegro

94 GAVOTTE (duet)

Hook arr. Nick Munns

Allegretto
Lightly tongued throughout
1st clarinet

2nd clarinet

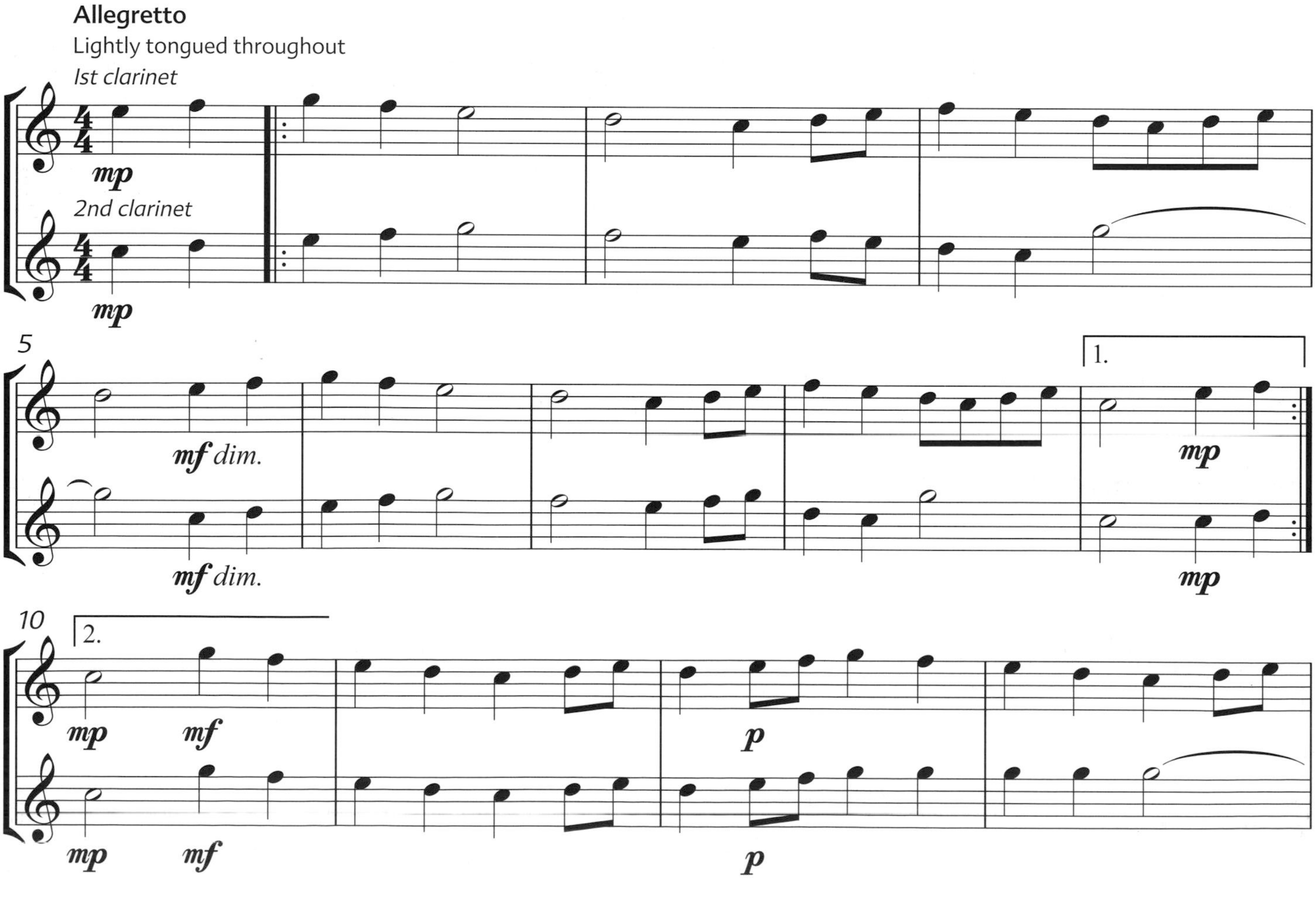

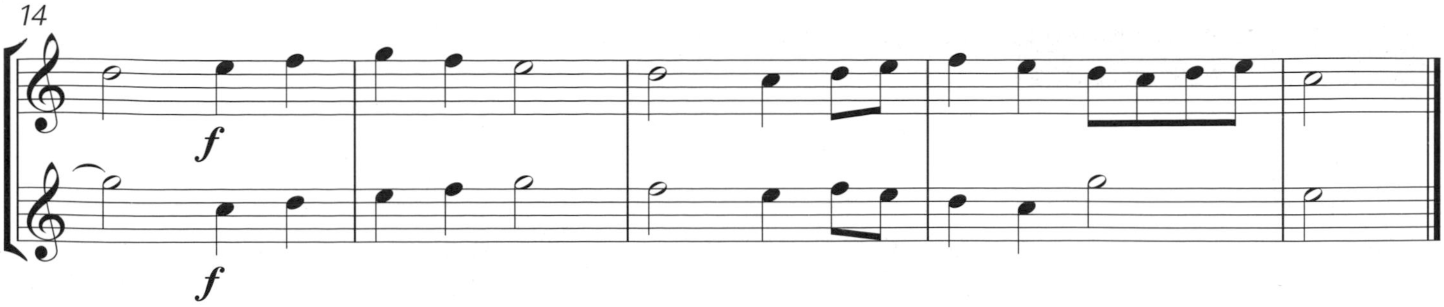

allegro moderato — moderately fast

95 CANON FROM 'MIKROKOSMOS' (duet)

Bartok arr. Suchoff

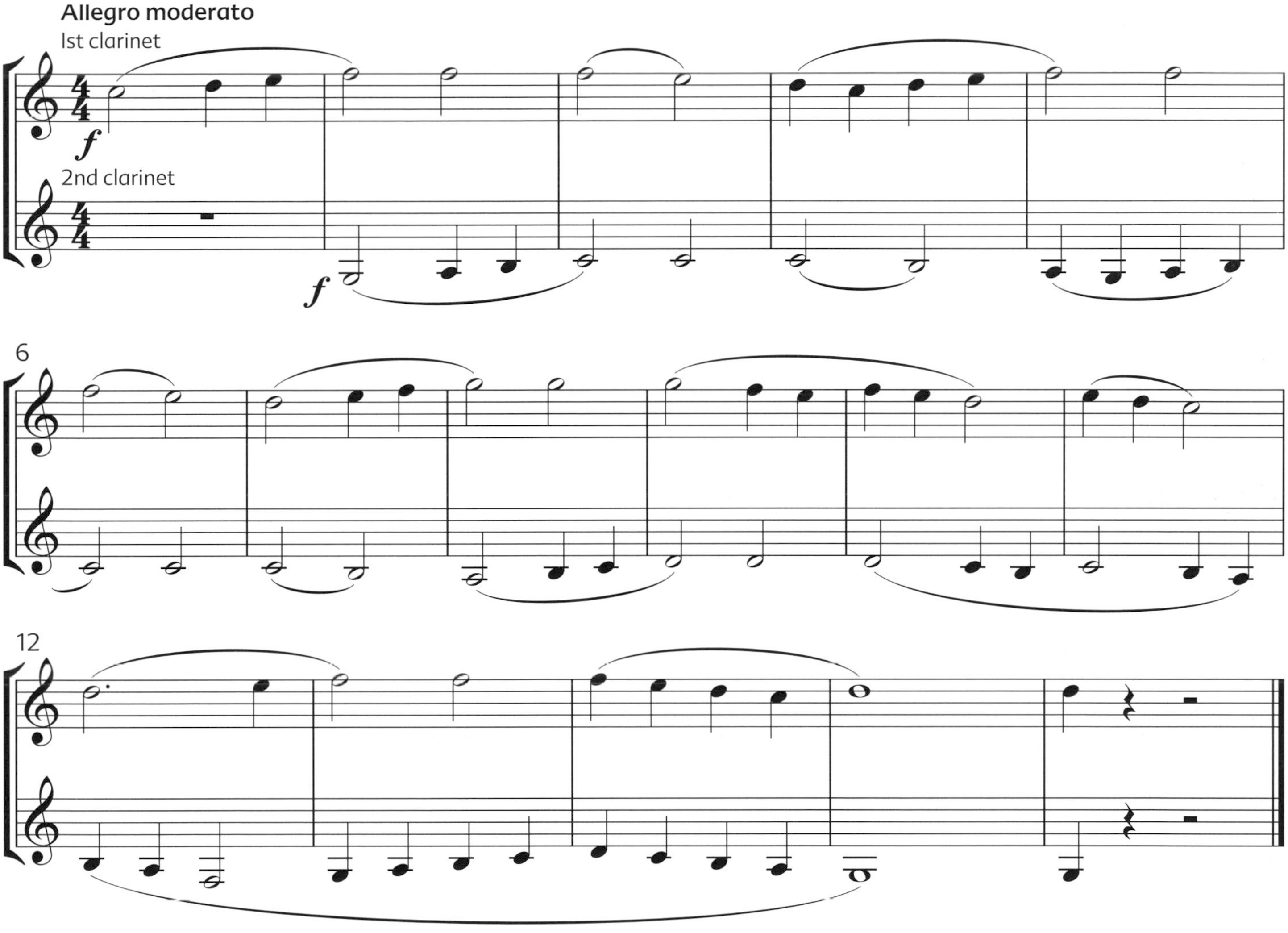

96 COUNTRY GARDENS 74b after 33 secs *traditional Morris tune*

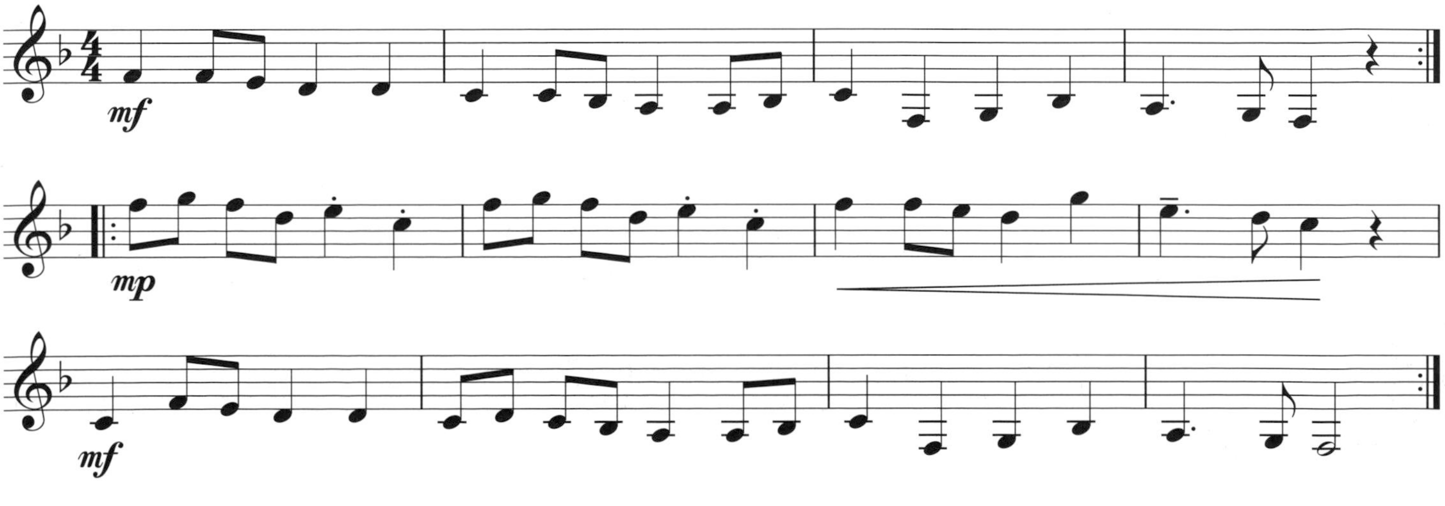

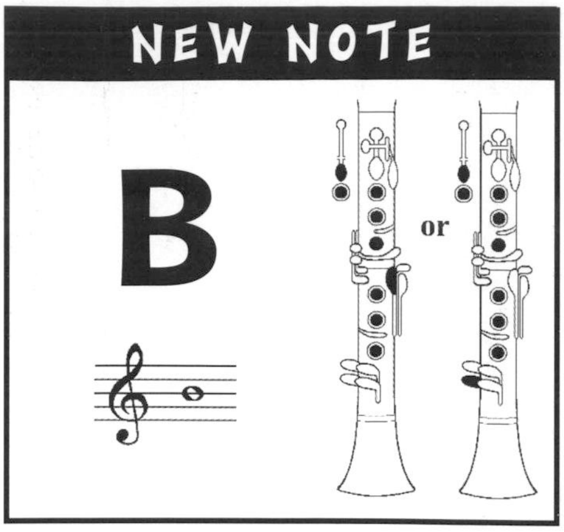

NEW NOTE

B

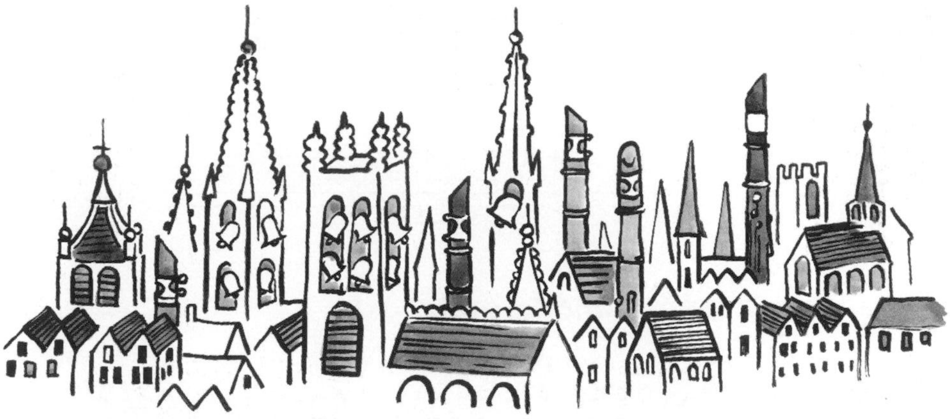

97 ORANGES AND LEMONS · 75a · first 40 secs · *traditional*

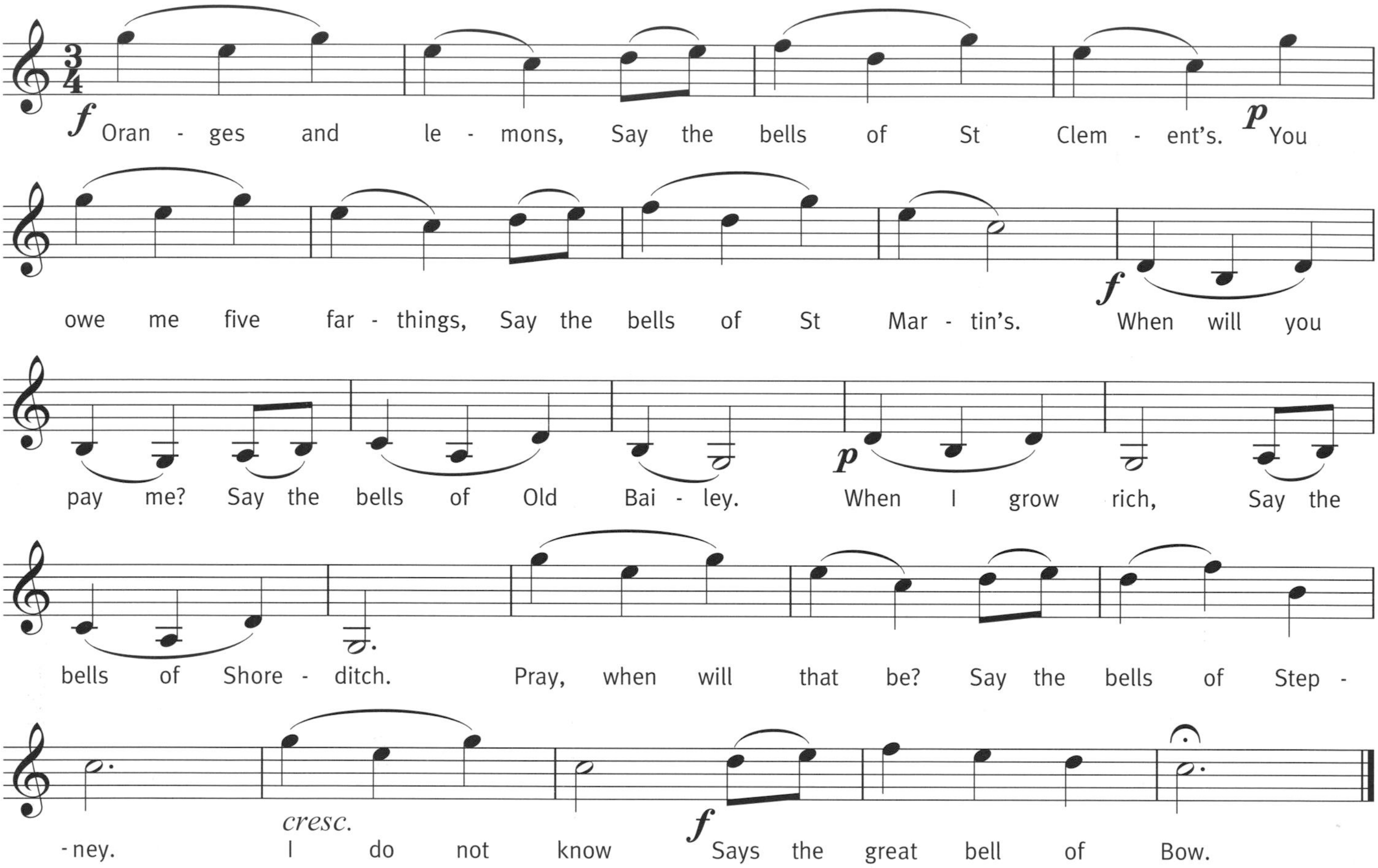

f Oran - ges and le - mons, Say the bells of St Clem - ent's. *p* You owe me five far - things, Say the bells of St Mar - tin's. *f* When will you pay me? Say the bells of Old Bai - ley. *p* When I grow rich, Say the bells of Shore - ditch. Pray, when will that be? Say the bells of Step - ney. *cresc.* I do not know *f* Says the great bell of Bow.

98 ST ANTHONY CHORALE · 75b · after 40 secs · *Haydn (attributed)*

Andante

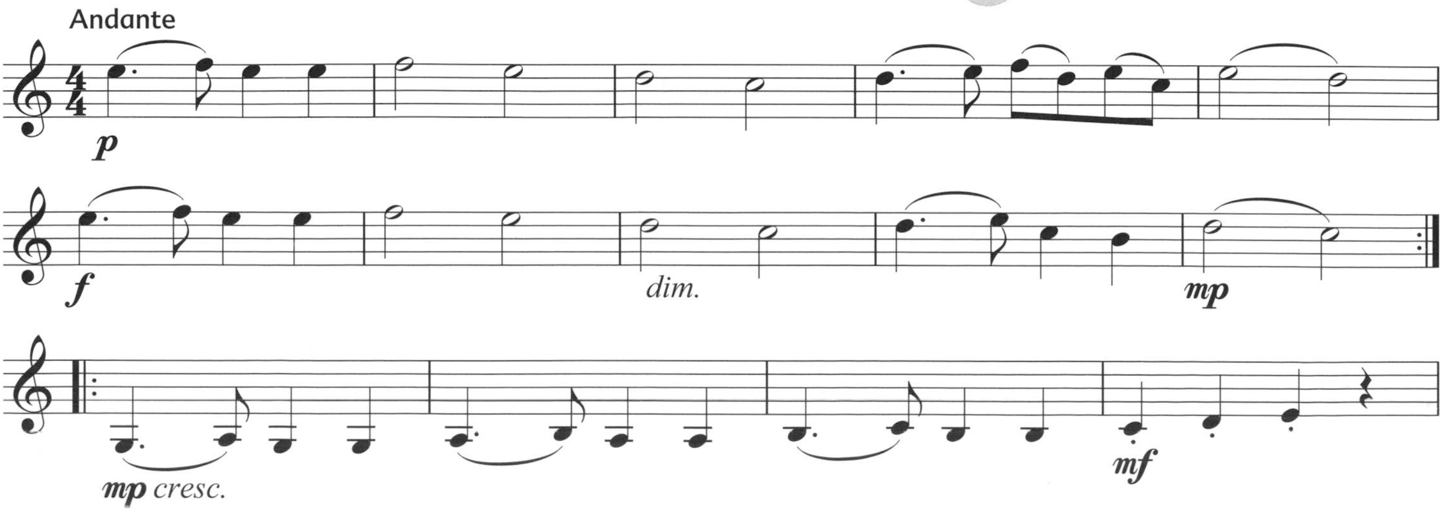

p   *f*   *dim.*   *mp*

mp cresc.   *mf*

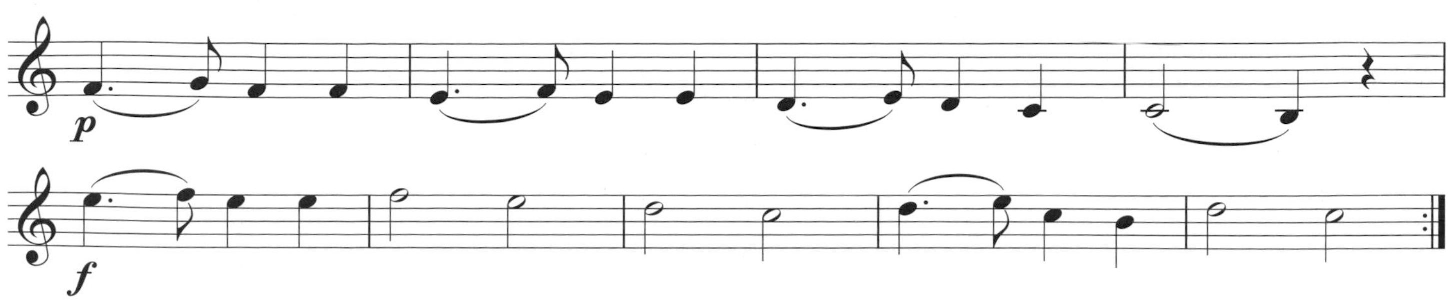

99 DONKEY IN THE RAIN 76a first 22 secs AP

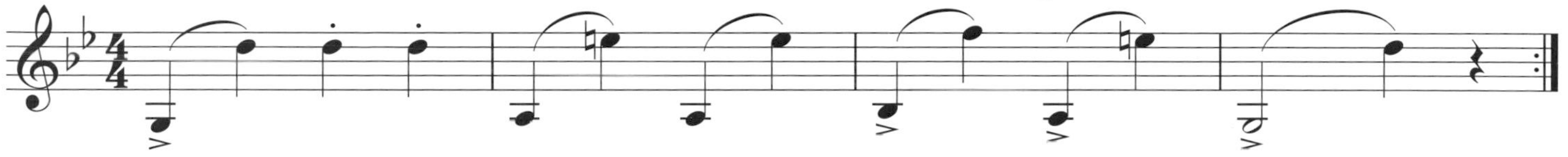

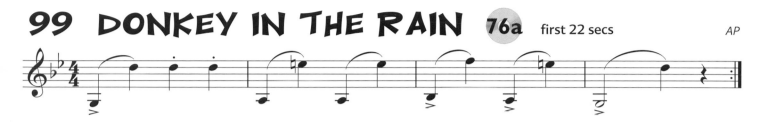

100 FROG IN MY THROAT 76b after 22 secs DF

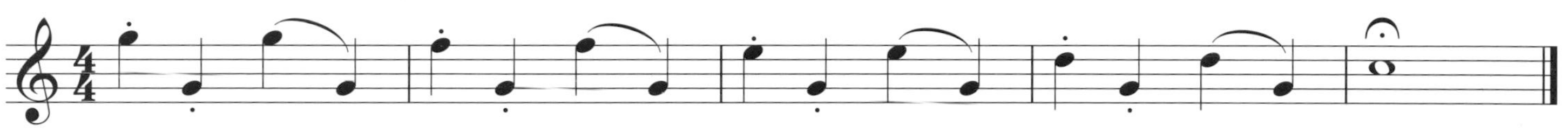

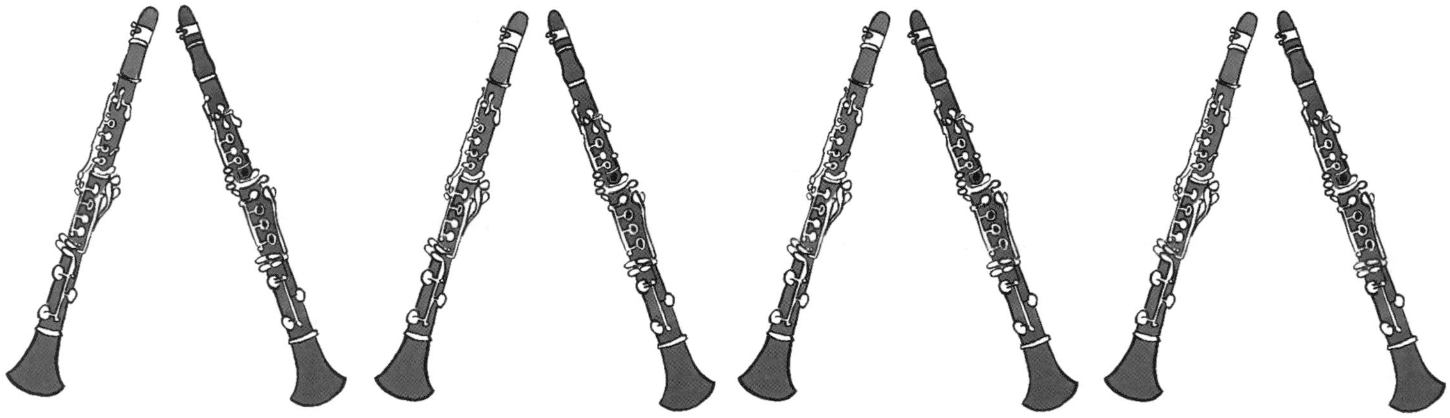

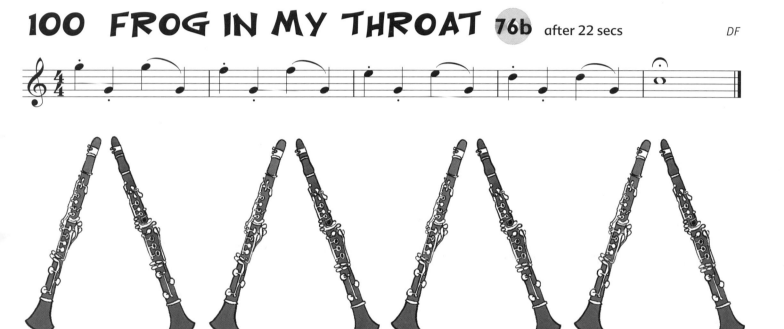

101 OFF TO FRANCE IN THE MORNING

77a first 29 secs *Peter Davey*

With energy

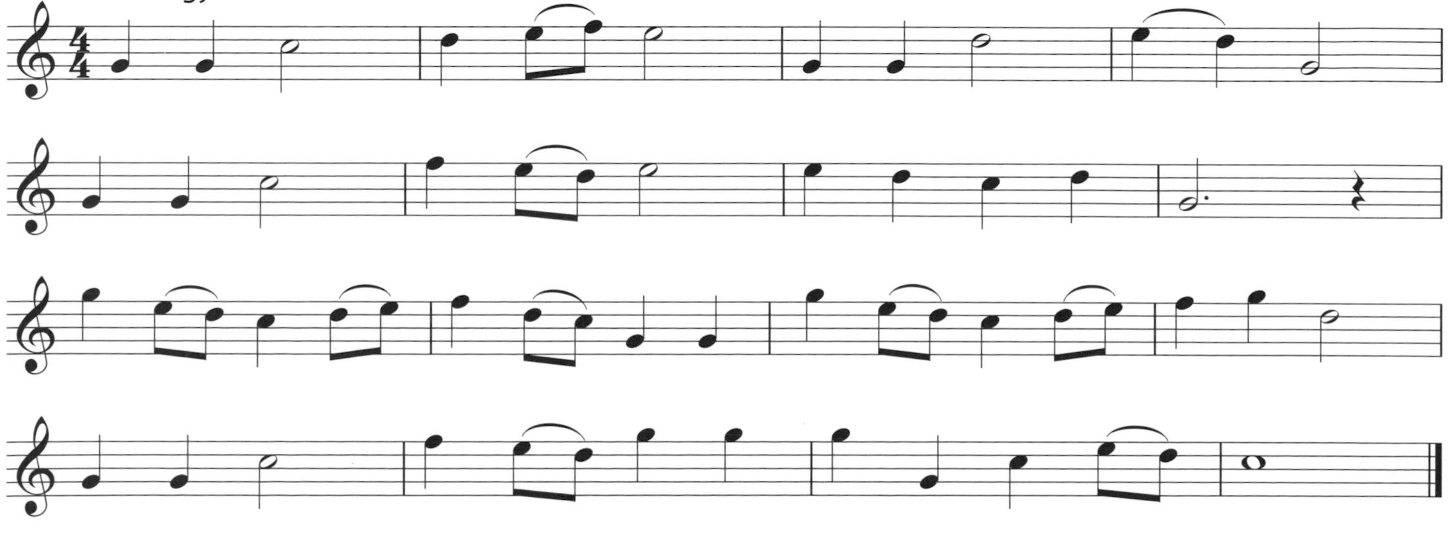

102 COAL-HOLE CAVALRY 77b after 29 secs

Ted Edwards

Ear - ly mor - ning, dream - ing is shat - tered, One clit - ter clat - ter ont' flags out - side,

Old knock - er up - per rat - tat - ting ont' win - dows, Ma - king sure_ no - bo - dy's o'er - lied.

Clit - ter - ing, clat - ter - ing, coal - hole cav - al - ry, gal - lop - ing rain or fine,___

Clit - ter - ing, clat - ter - ing, coal - hole cav - al - ry, gal - lop - ing down to t'mine.___

103 SHEPHERDS' HEY 78a first 30 secs

traditional Morris tune

Dancing

mf

f

104 THE GRAND OLD DUKE OF YORK

78b after 30 secs *traditional*

March tempo

mf
Oh, the grand old Duke of York, He had ten thou-sand men, He

f *f*
marched them up to the top of the hill And he marched them down a - gain. And

pp *mf*
when they were up they were up. And when they were down they were down. And

when they were on - ly half - way up They were nei - ther up nor down.

NEW NOTE

A

105 THE MILLER OF DEE

79a first 24 secs *traditional*

mp
There was a jol - ly mil - ler once lived on the Ri - ver Dee; He

p
worked and sang from morn till night, No lark so blithe as he. And__

this the bur - den of his song For ev - er used to be:_____ 'I

mf
care for no - bo - dy, no not I, If no - bo - dy cares for me'._____

106 LONDON'S BURNING (round) 79b after 24 secs

traditional

Lon-don's burn-ing, Lon-don's burn-ing, Fetch the en-gines, Fetch the

en-gines, Fire! Fire! Fire! Fire! Pour on wa-ter, pour on wa-ter.

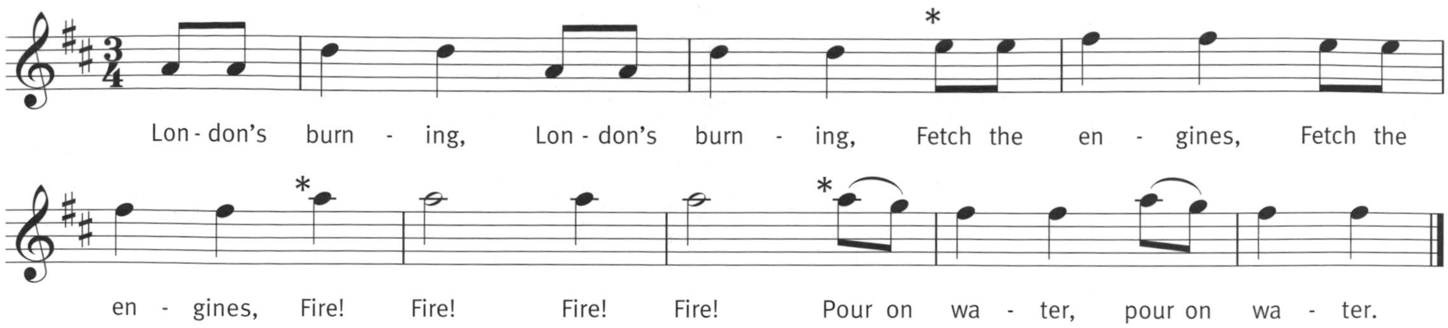

* entry point when played as a round

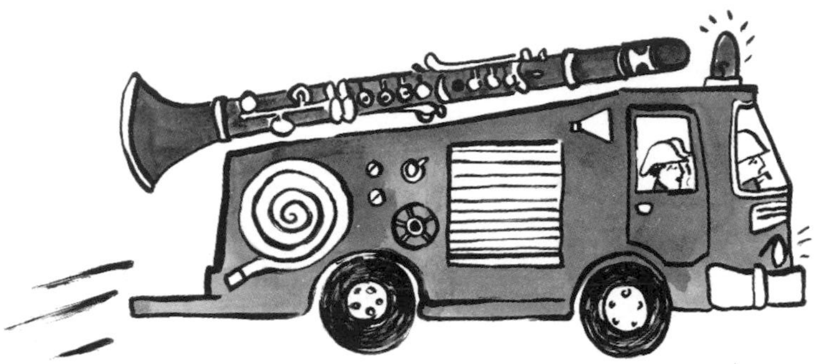

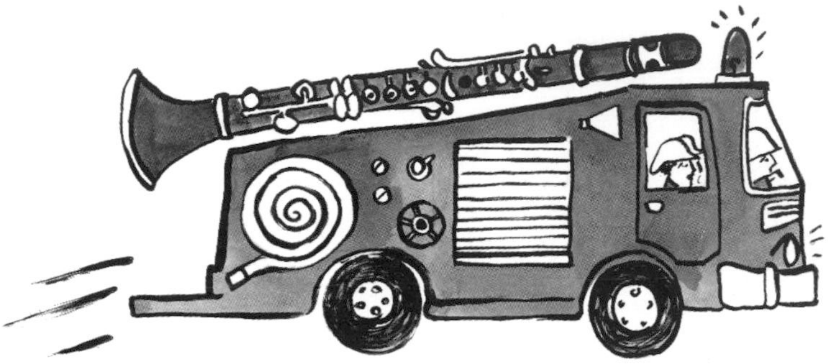

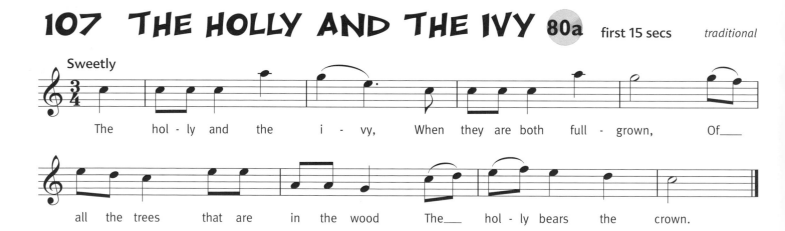

107 THE HOLLY AND THE IVY 80a first 15 secs

traditional

Sweetly

The hol-ly and the i-vy, When they are both full-grown, Of___

all the trees that are in the wood The___ hol-ly bears the crown.

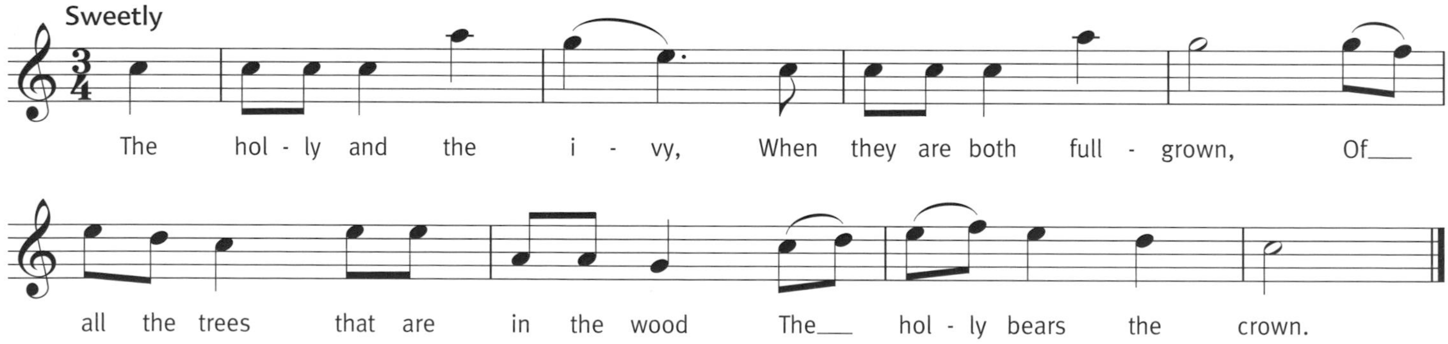

cantabile — in a singing style

$\frac{3}{8}$ (time signature) — three quaver beats to the bar

108 I WONDER AS I WANDER 80b after 15 secs

traditional

Cantabile

p

I won-der as I wan-der, out un-der the sky, How Je-sus the

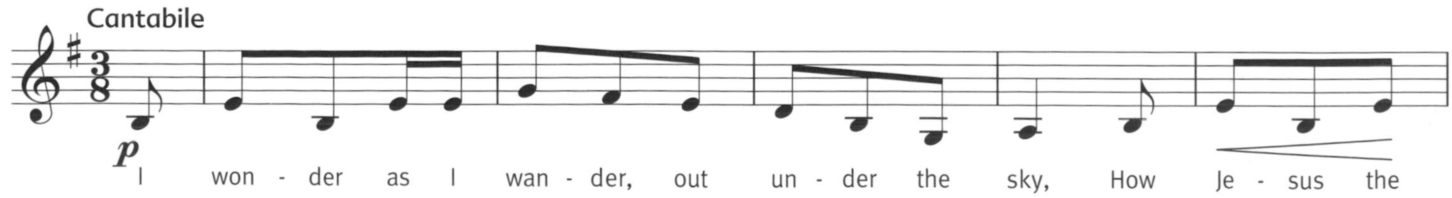

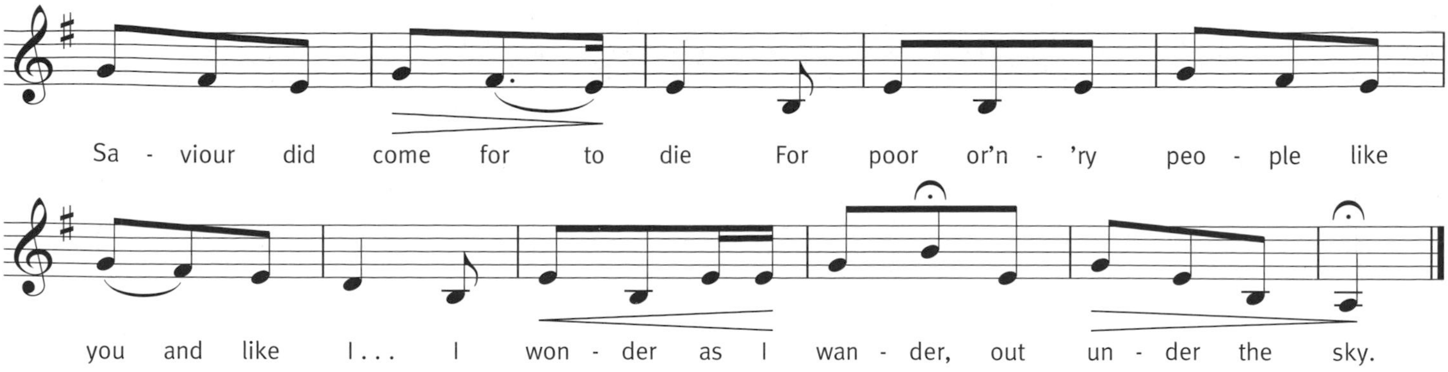

Sa - viour did come for to die For poor or'n - 'ry peo - ple like

you and like I . . . I won - der as I wan - der, out un - der the sky.

109 MACPHERSON'S FAREWELL 81a first 37 secs

words: Robert Burns
music: traditional

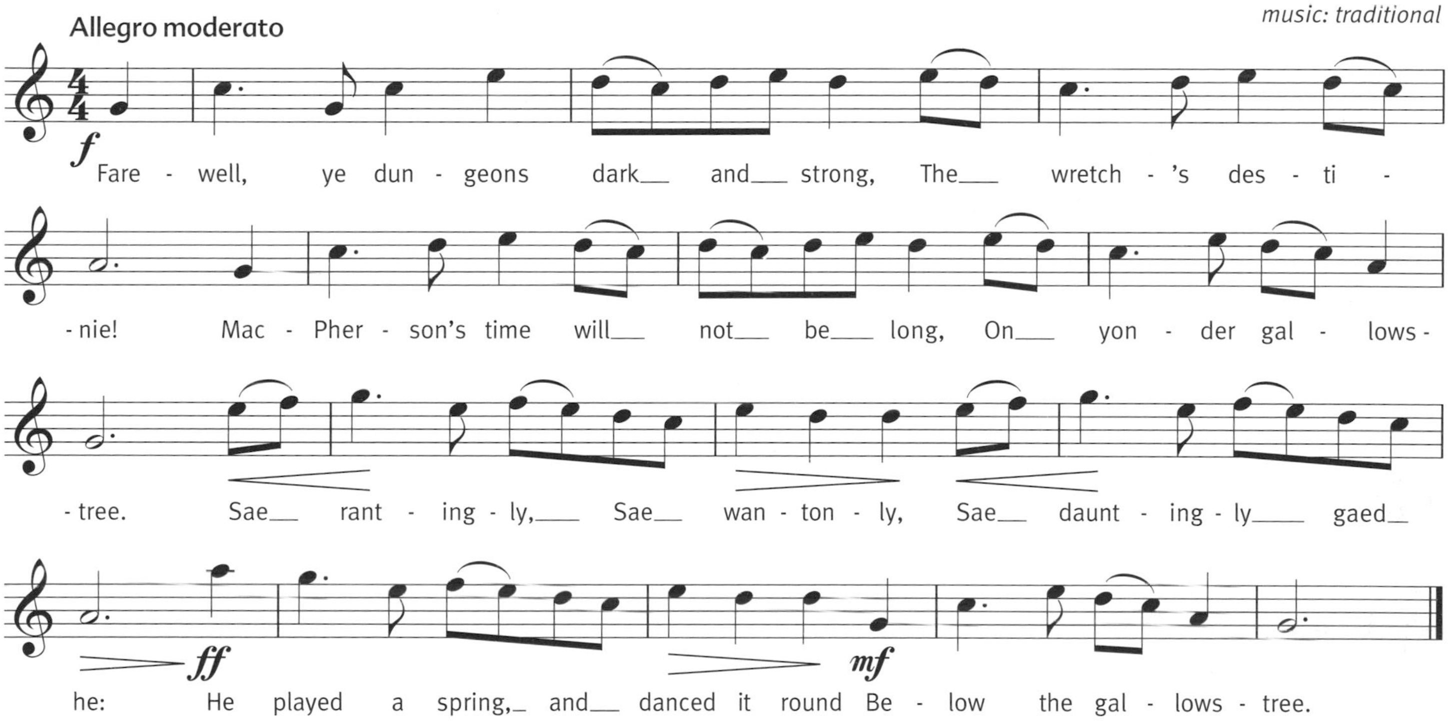

Allegro moderato

Fare - well, ye dun - geons dark__ and__ strong, The__ wretch - 's des - ti -

- nie! Mac - Pher - son's time will__ not__ be__ long, On__ yon - der gal - lows -

- tree. Sae__ rant - ing - ly,__ Sae__ wan - ton - ly, Sae__ daunt - ing - ly__ gaed__

he: He played a spring,__ and__ danced it round Be - low the gal - lows - tree.

110 LITTLE BOXES 81b after 37 secs

Malvina Reynolds

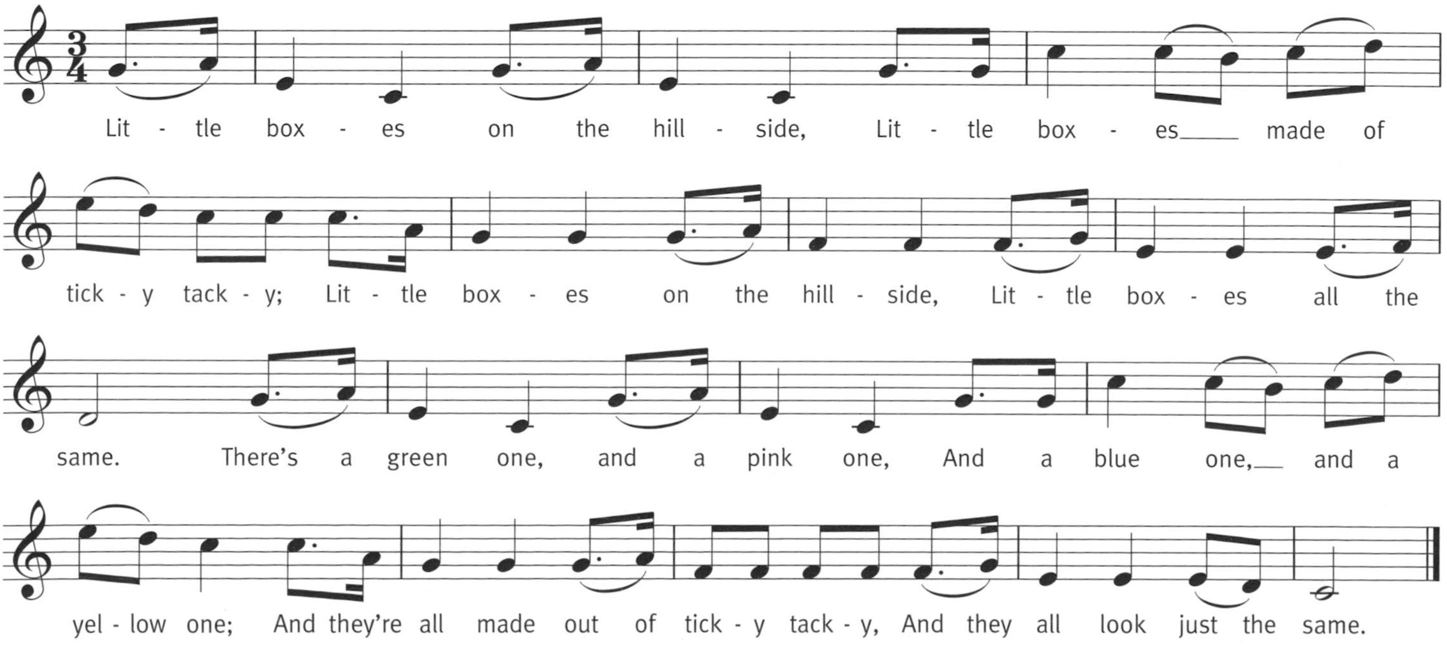

Lit - tle box - es on the hill - side, Lit - tle box - es__ made of

tick - y tack - y; Lit - tle box - es on the hill - side, Lit - tle box - es all the

same. There's a green one, and a pink one, And a blue one,__ and a

yel - low one; And they're all made out of tick - y tack - y, And they all look just the same.

tr (trill) — quickly alternate the written note with the note above.

111 HORNPIPE FROM 'THE WATER MUSIC' (duet)

Handel arr. JR

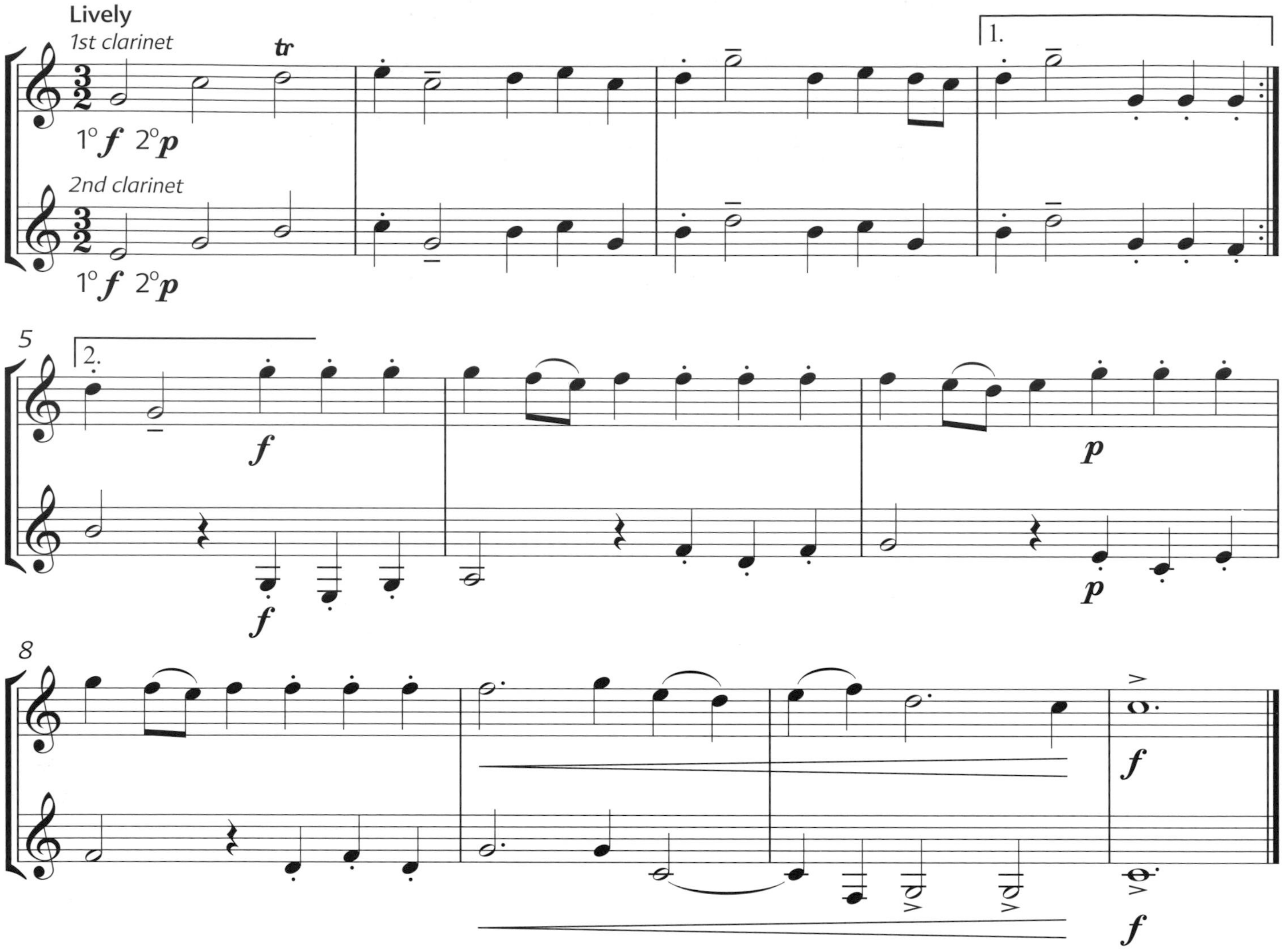

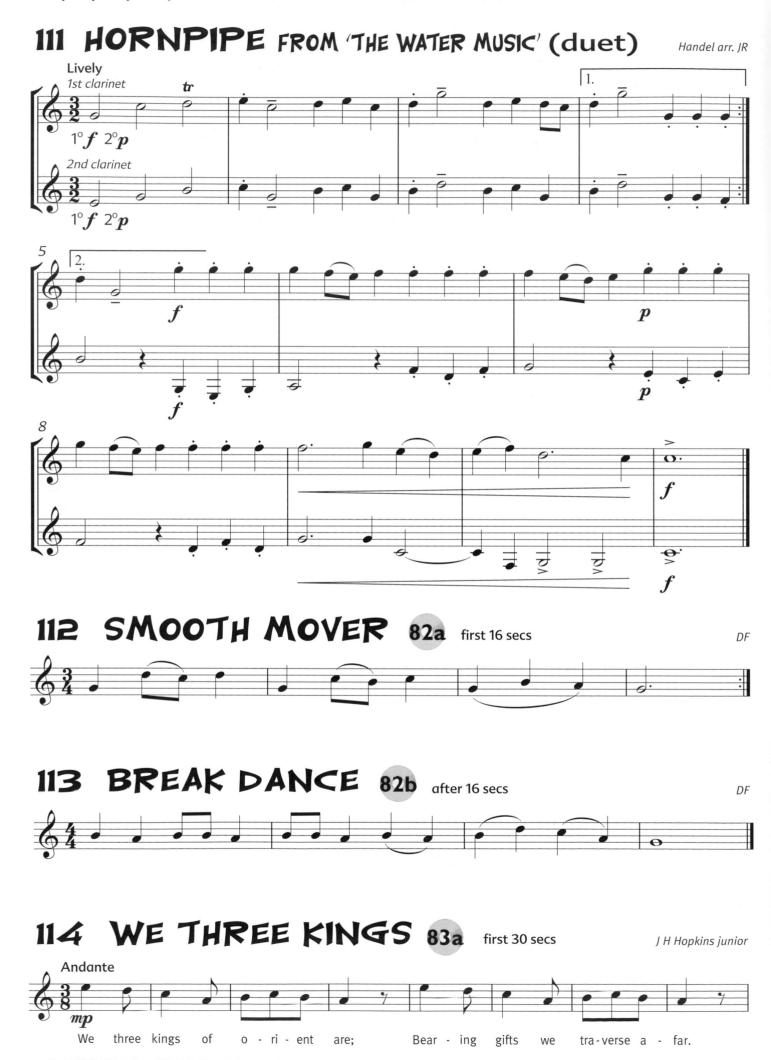

112 SMOOTH MOVER 82a first 16 secs

DF

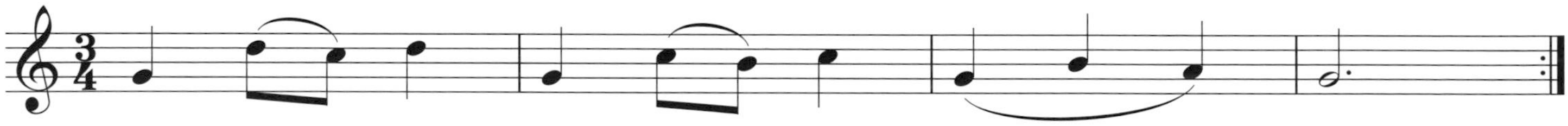

113 BREAK DANCE 82b after 16 secs

DF

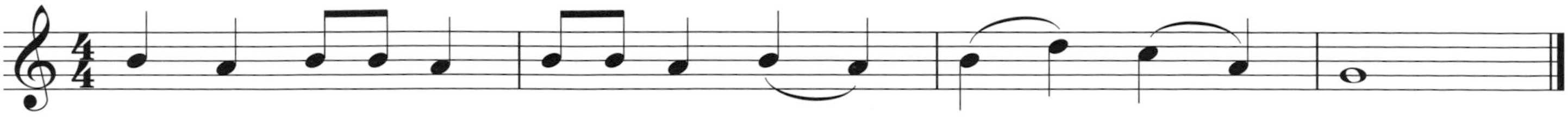

114 WE THREE KINGS 83a first 30 secs

J H Hopkins junior

Andante

We three kings of o - ri - ent are; Bear - ing gifts we tra - verse a - far.

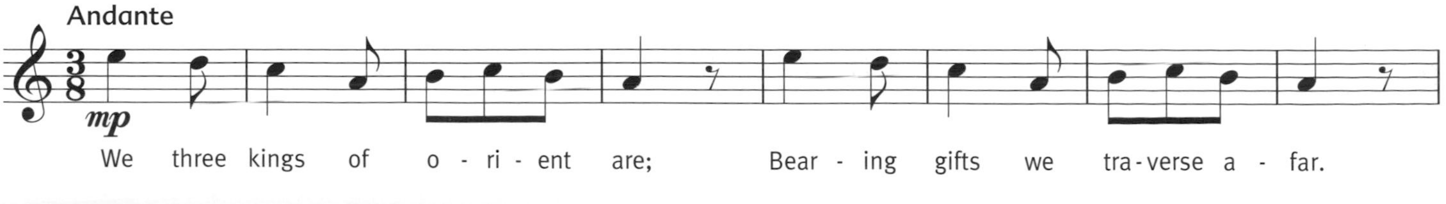

cresc. _mf_ _mp_

Field and foun - tain, moor and moun - tain, Fol - low - ing yon - der star:

_mf_ O_____ star of won - der, star of night, Star with roy - al beau - ty bright,

West - ward lead - ing, still pro - ceed - ing, Guide us to thy per - fect light.

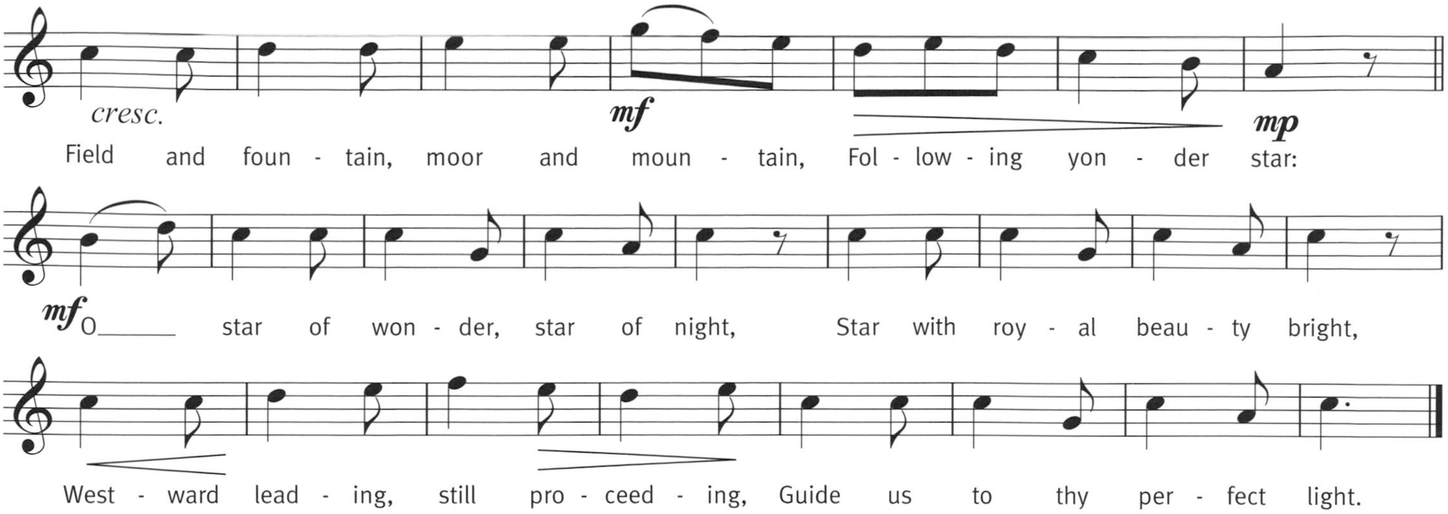

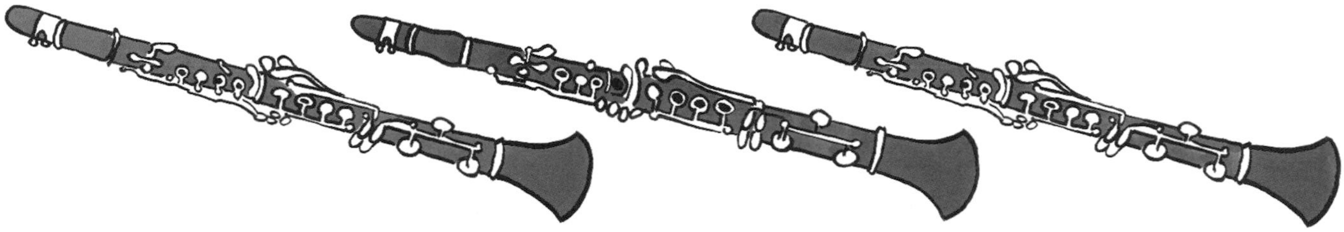

115 HOME! SWEET HOME 83b after 30 secs

Sir Henry Bishop

Andante

p cantabile

_pp_

116 TURA-LAI-AY 84a first 24 secs

traditional

_mf_

_f_ _mf_

_mp_

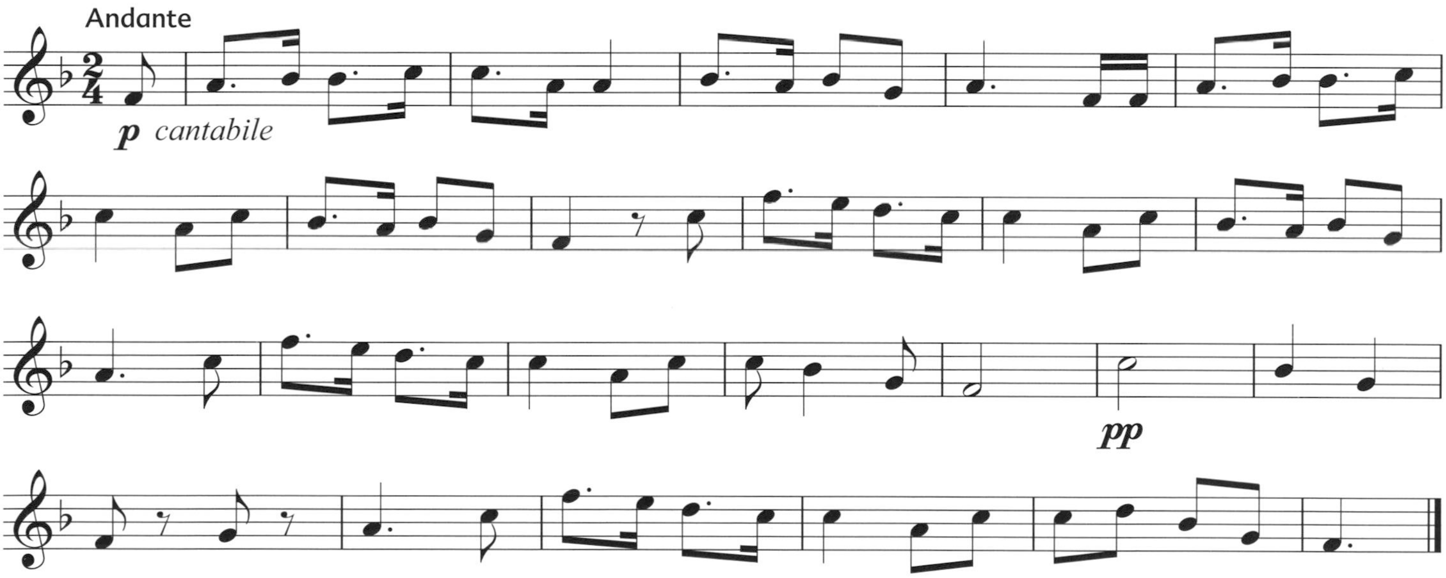

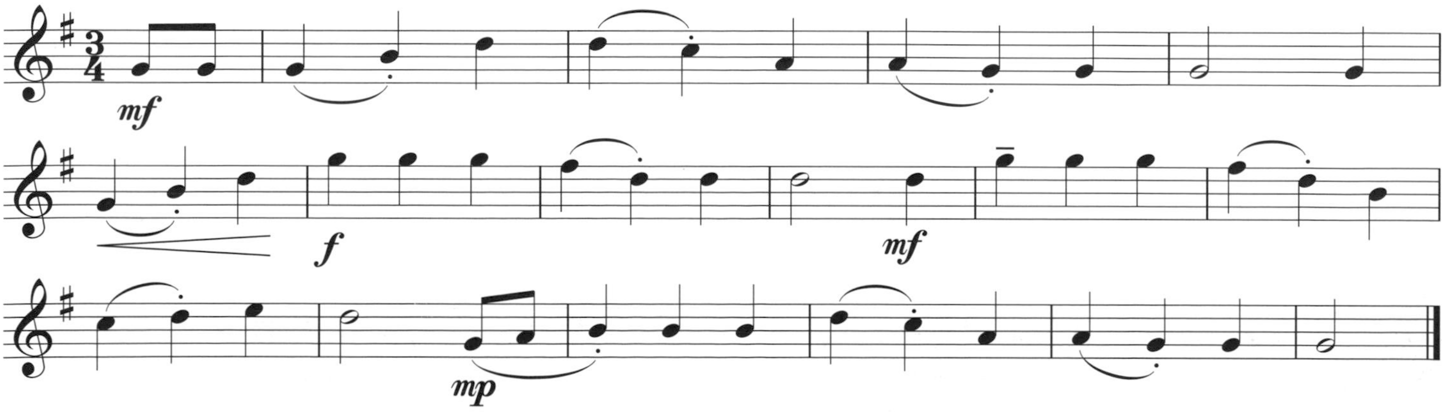

117 OVER THE EARTH IS A MAT OF GREEN

84b after 24 secs

words: Ruth Brown
music: Scottish, arr. Herbert Wiseman

O - ver the earth is a mat_ of_ green,_ O - ver the green_ is_

dew,_ O - ver the dew are the arch - ing_ trees,_

O - ver the trees_ the_ blue._ *f* A - cross the blue are scud - ding_ clouds,

O - ver the clouds the sun,_ *mf* O - ver it all is the love_ of_ God,_

Bless - ing us ev - 'ry - one,_ *p morendo* Bless - ing us ev - 'ry - one._

NEW NOTE

E♭

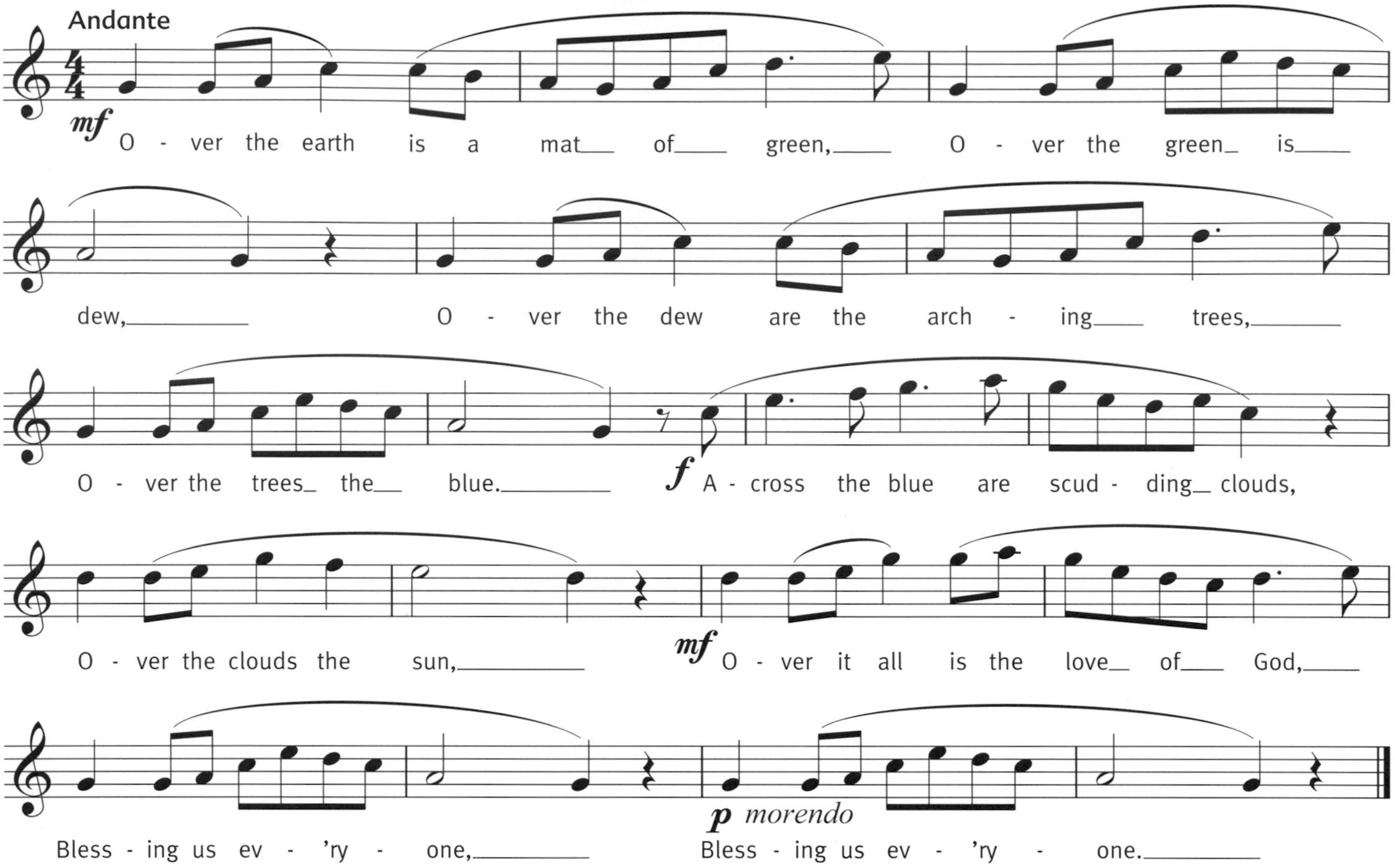

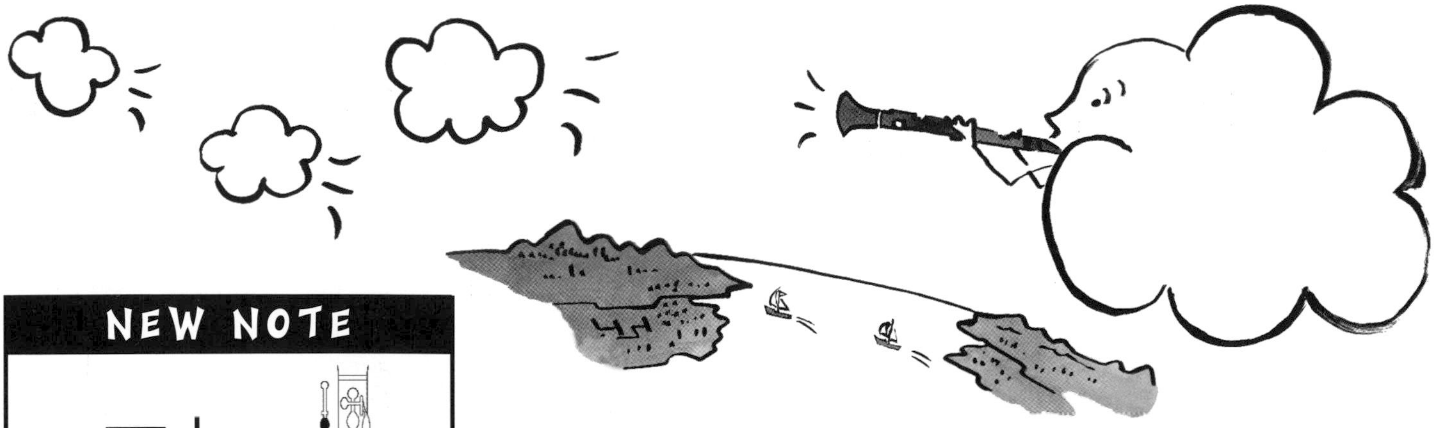

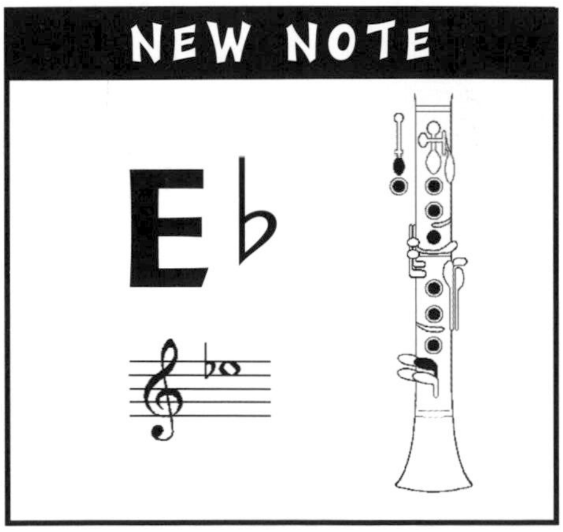

118 CLEMENTINE **85a** first 17 secs

North American

With a bounce

mf

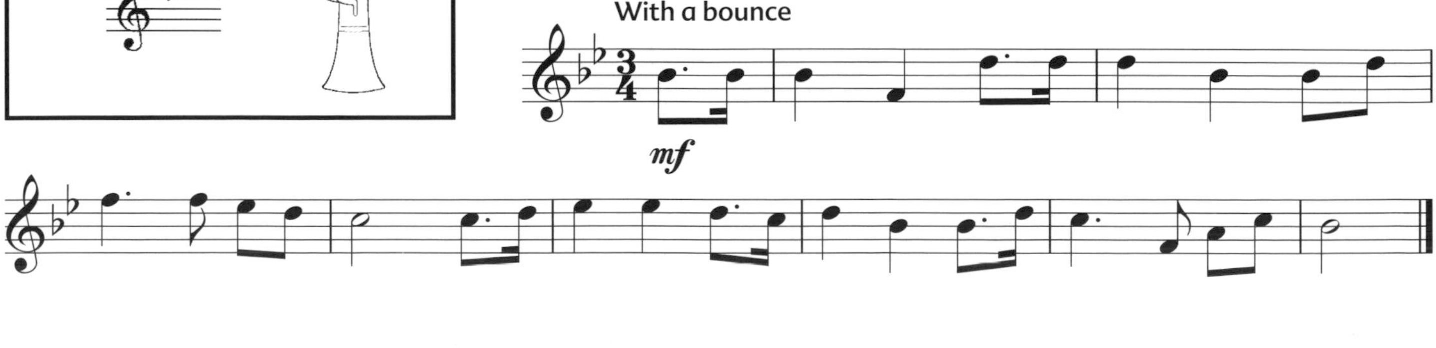

119 HAIL THE CONQUERING HERO

FROM 'JUDAS MACCABAEUS' (duet)

Handel arr. R H Page

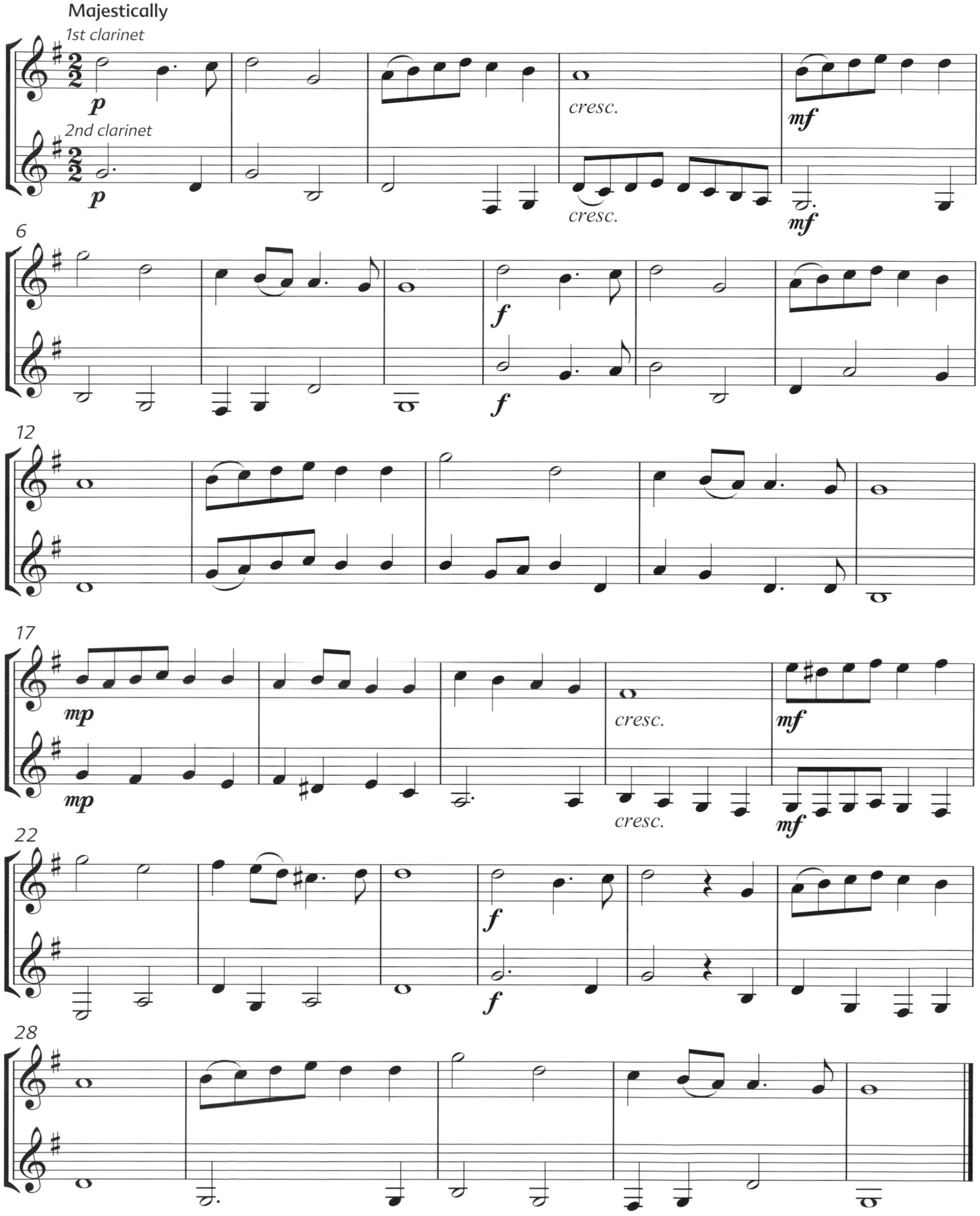

dolce — sweetly

120 SILENT NIGHT 85b after 17 secs

words: Joseph Mohr
music: Franz Grüber

Si - lent night, ho - ly night. All is calm, all is bright,

Round yon Vir - gin Mo - ther and child. Ho - ly In - fant so ten - der and mild,

Sleep in hea - ven - ly peace,___ Sleep___ in hea - ven - ly peace.___

DC al Fine — DC is short for Da Capo, which means 'from the beginning'. At DC al Fine, repeat from the beginning up to the bar marked Fine.

121 SKYE BOAT SONG 86a first 1 min 4 secs

Scottish

122 LULLABY OF THE SPINNING WHEEL

86b after 1 min 4 secs

words: trans S Taylor Coleridge
music: F T Durrant

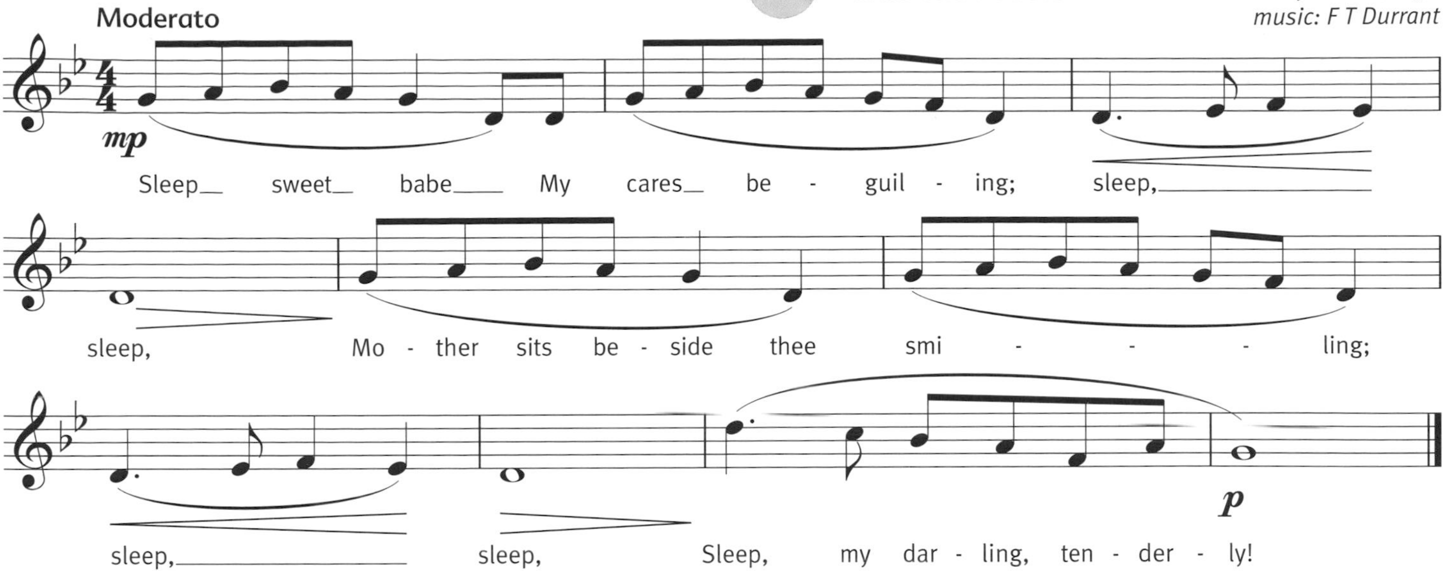

Moderato

mp

Sleep__ sweet__ babe__ My cares__ be - guil - ing; sleep,__

sleep, Mo - ther sits be - side thee smi - - - ling;

sleep,__ sleep, Sleep, my dar - ling, ten - der - ly!

p

♩.. **double dotted crotchet** — the first dot after a note adds half the value of the note; the second dot adds half the value of the first dot. ♩.. = ♩ ♪ ♪

When two or more notes of the same pitch follow each other under a slur, they should be gently tongued — just enough to separate them.

molto moderato — at a very moderate pace (molto = very, moderato = moderate)

123 OLD FRENCH SONG **87a** first 53 secs

Tchaikovsky

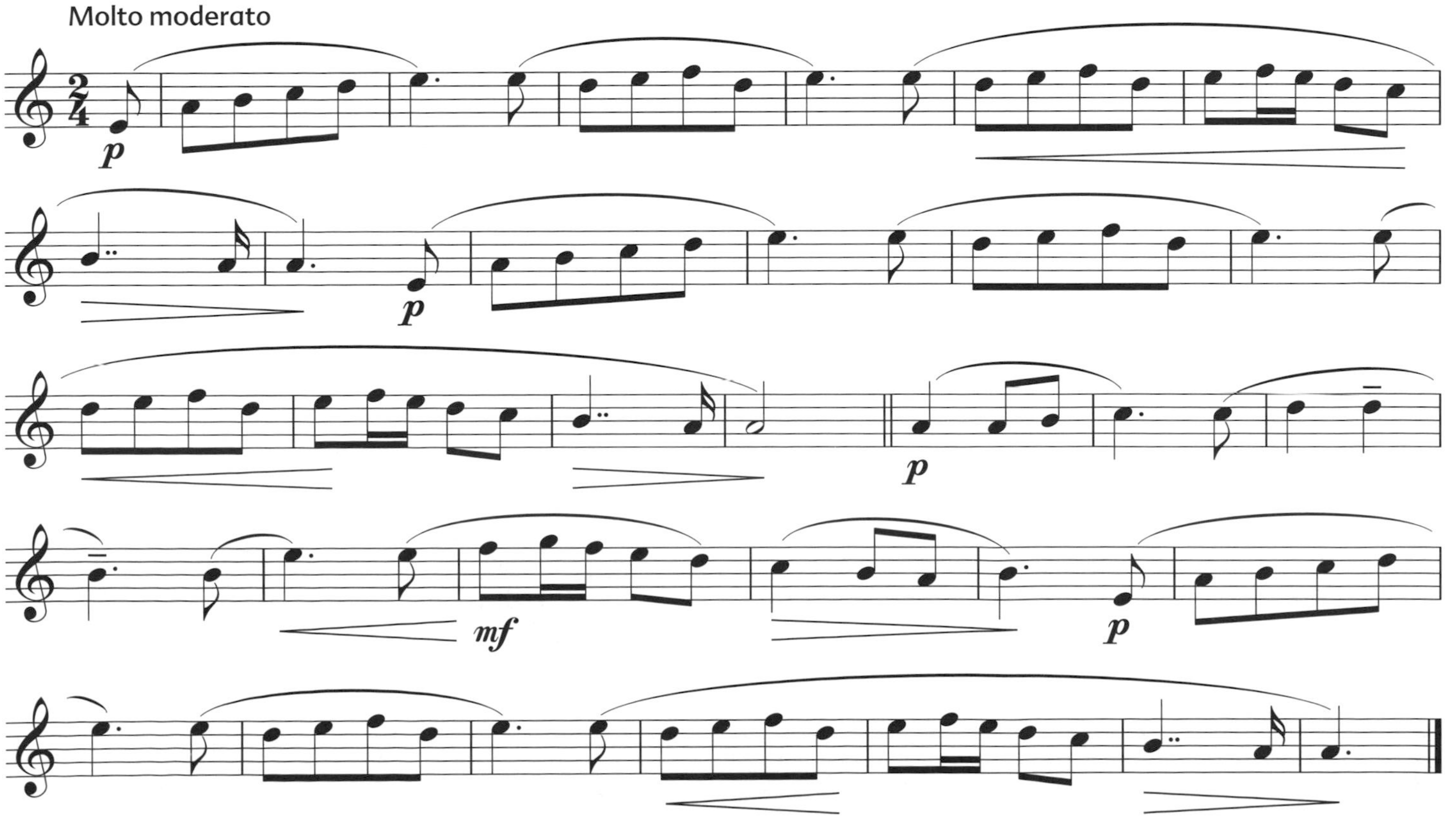

Molto moderato

p

p

p

mf

p

124 PORTSMOUTH (duet)

traditional, arr. Catherine Johnson

adagio — slow

triplet — play three quavers instead of two in a crotchet beat.

125 THE GOLDEN PEACOCK 87b after 53 secs

Jewish folk song

126 THE WATER IS WIDE

88a first 32 secs

traditional

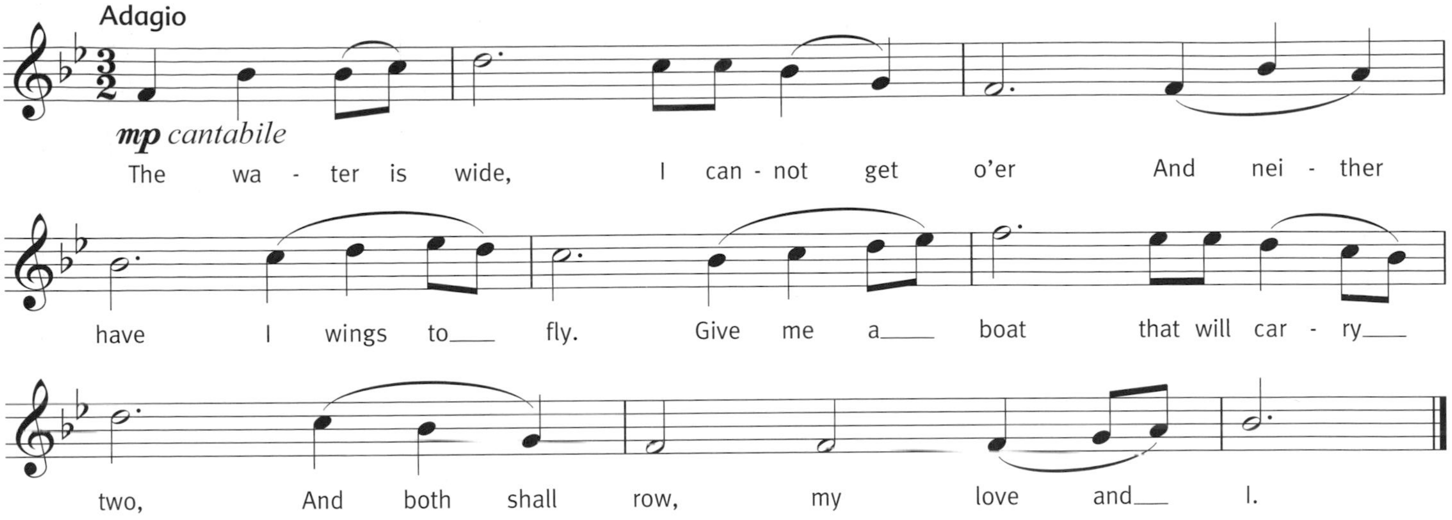

The wa-ter is wide, I can-not get o'er And nei-ther have I wings to fly. Give me a boat that will car-ry two, And both shall row, my love and I.

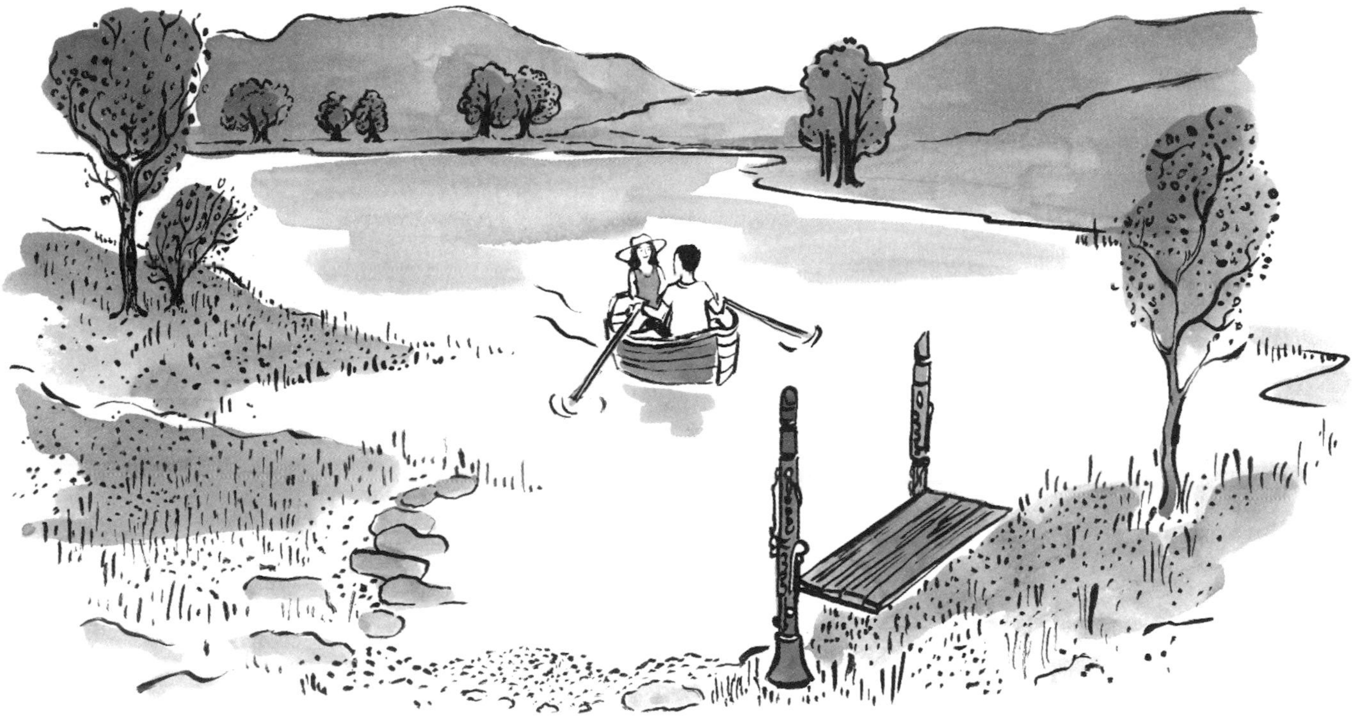

127 HILLS OF THE NORTH, REJOICE

88b after 32 secs

words: Charles Oakley
music: Martin Shaw

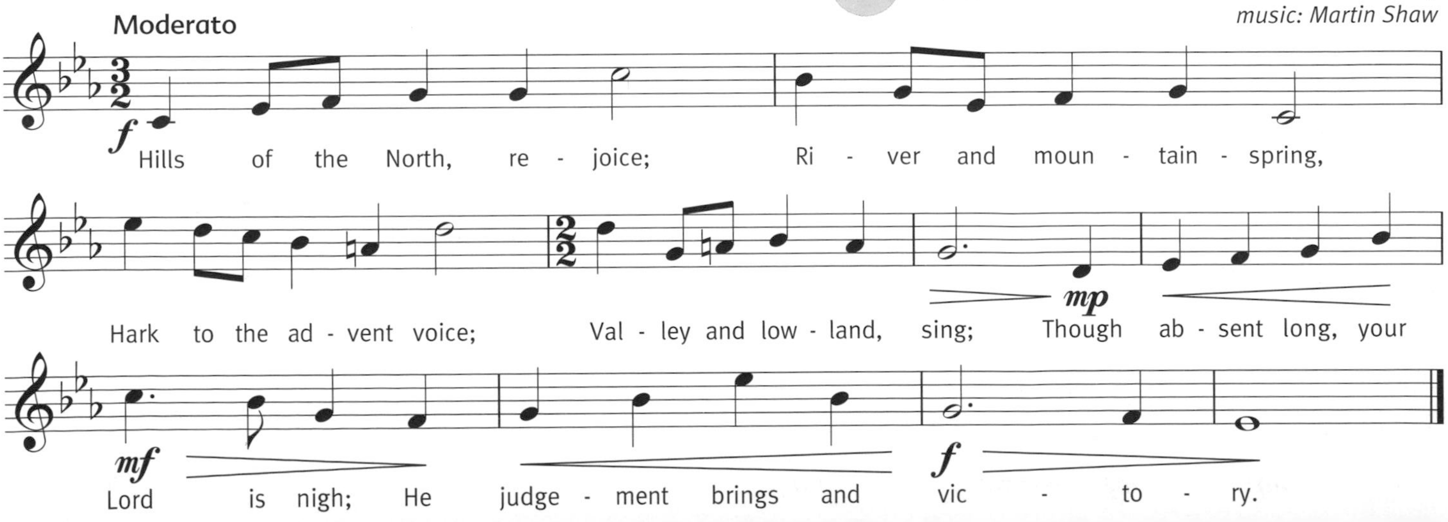

Hills of the North, re-joice; Ri-ver and moun-tain-spring, Hark to the ad-vent voice; Val-ley and low-land, sing; Though ab-sent long, your Lord is nigh; He judge-ment brings and vic-to-ry.

marcato — marked (each note stressed)

128 MARCH OF THE KINGS 89a first 32 secs

French

Allegro moderato

f marcato

mf

f

LEFT HAND C

C

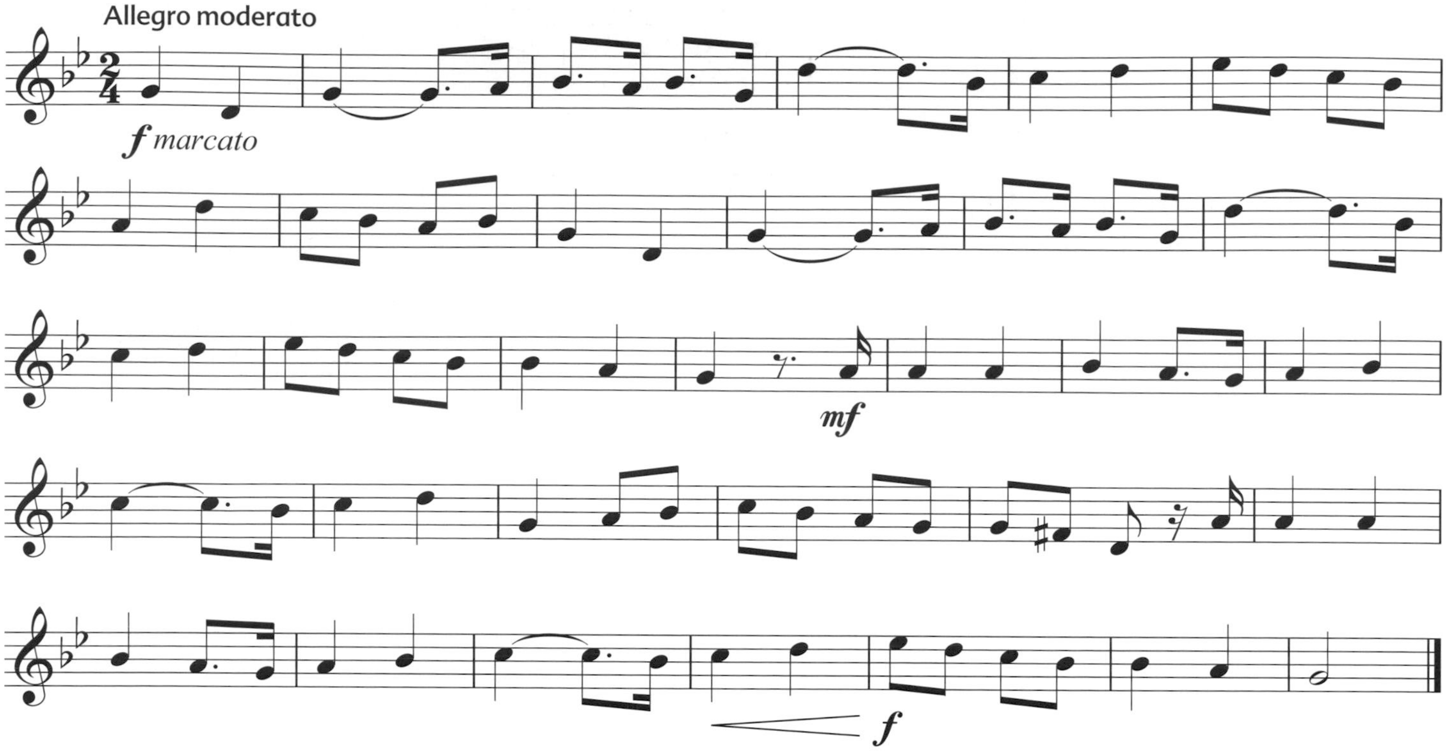

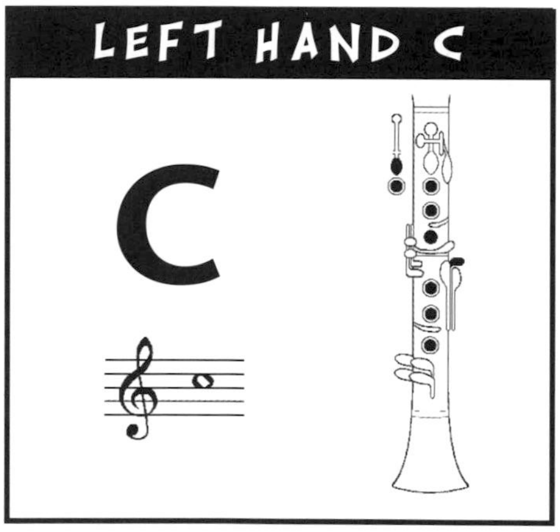

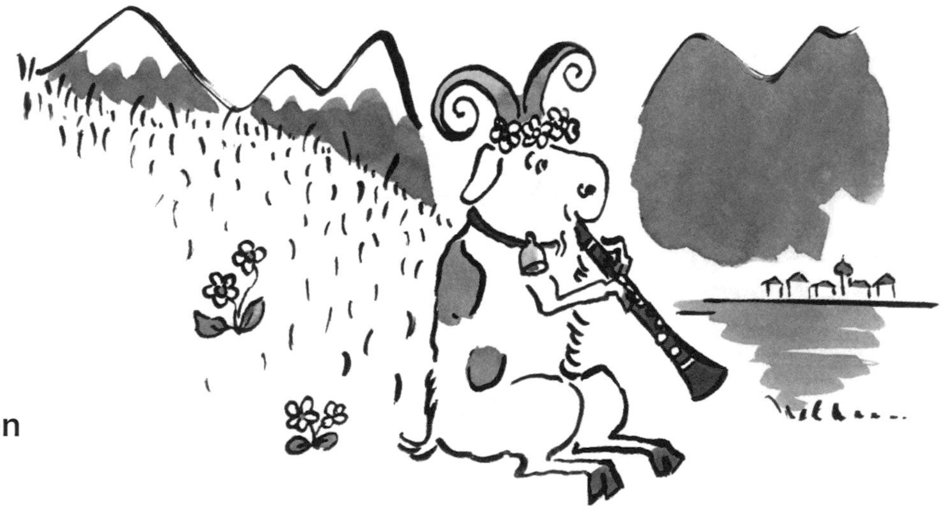

Use the left little finger C when
moving between C and E♭.

129 TYROLEAN WEDDING 89b after 32 secs

Helga Vernau

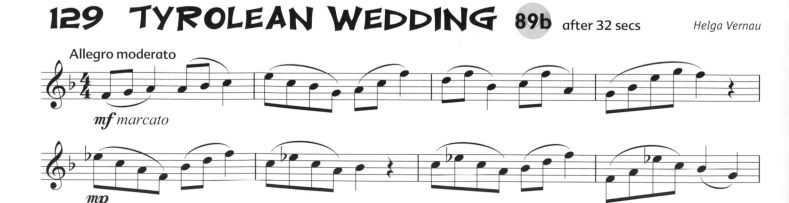

Allegro moderato

mf marcato

mp

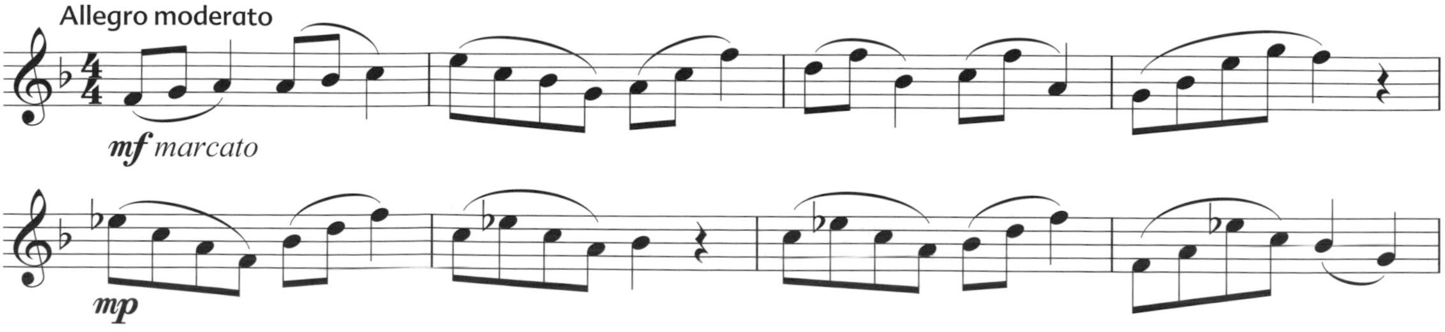

130 LAST OF THE SUMMER WINE

90a first 33 secs

Ronnie Hazlehurst

NEW NOTE

C#

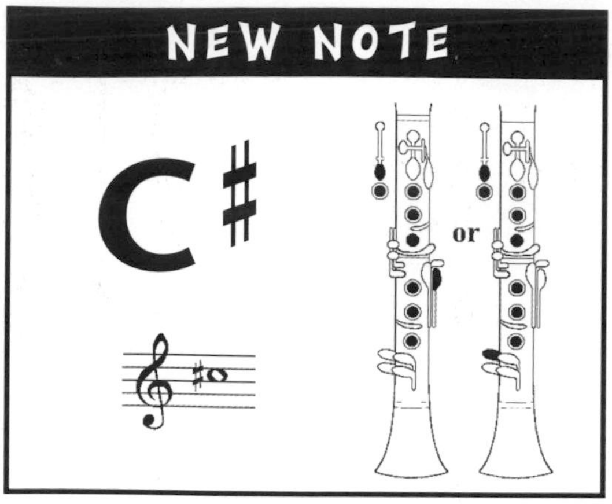

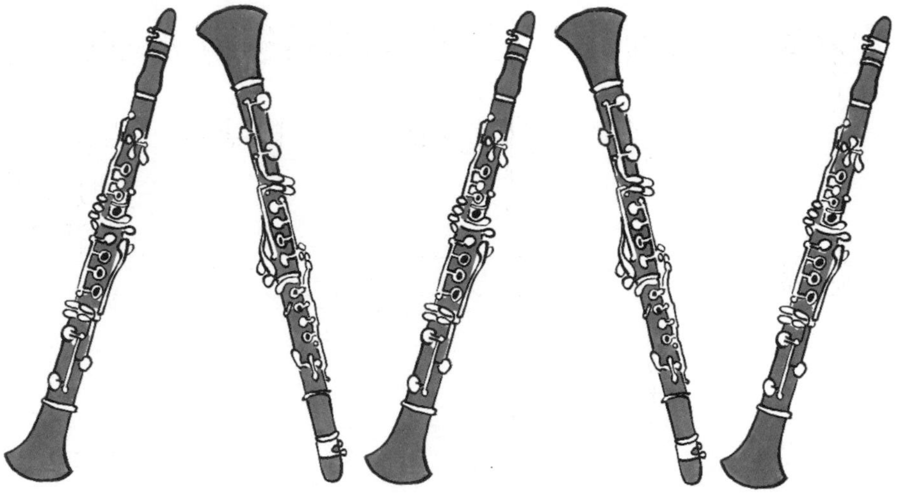

lento — slow

131 SOLOTHURN 90b after 33 secs

Swiss

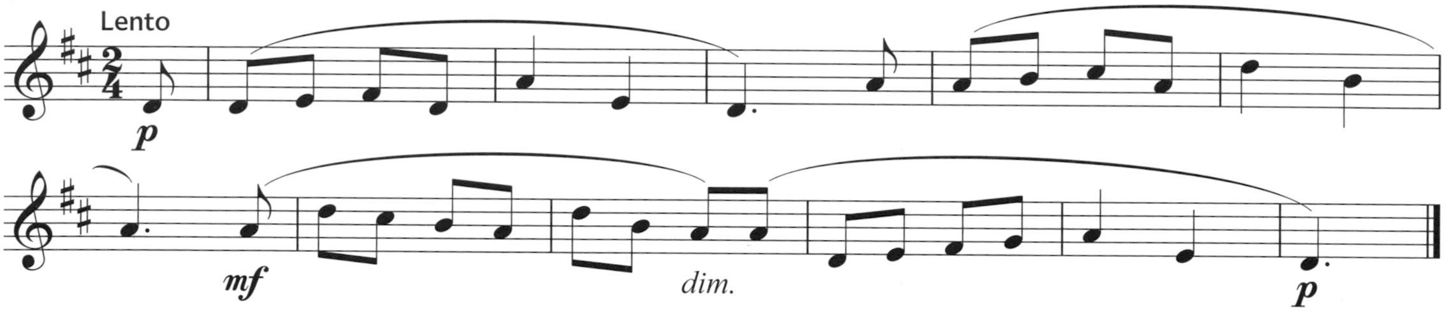

132 I DO LIKE TO BE BESIDE THE SEASIDE

91a first 41 secs

John A Glover-Kind

Oh, I do like to be be-side the sea - side,_____ Oh, I do like to

be be-side the sea._____ I do like to stroll up on the prom, prom,

prom, where the brass bands play, Tid - de - ly - om - pom - pom! So_____

just let me be be-side the sea - side,_____ I'll be be -

side my-self with glee;_____ And there's lots of girls be - sides, I should

like to be be-side, Be-side the sea - side, Be-side the sea._____

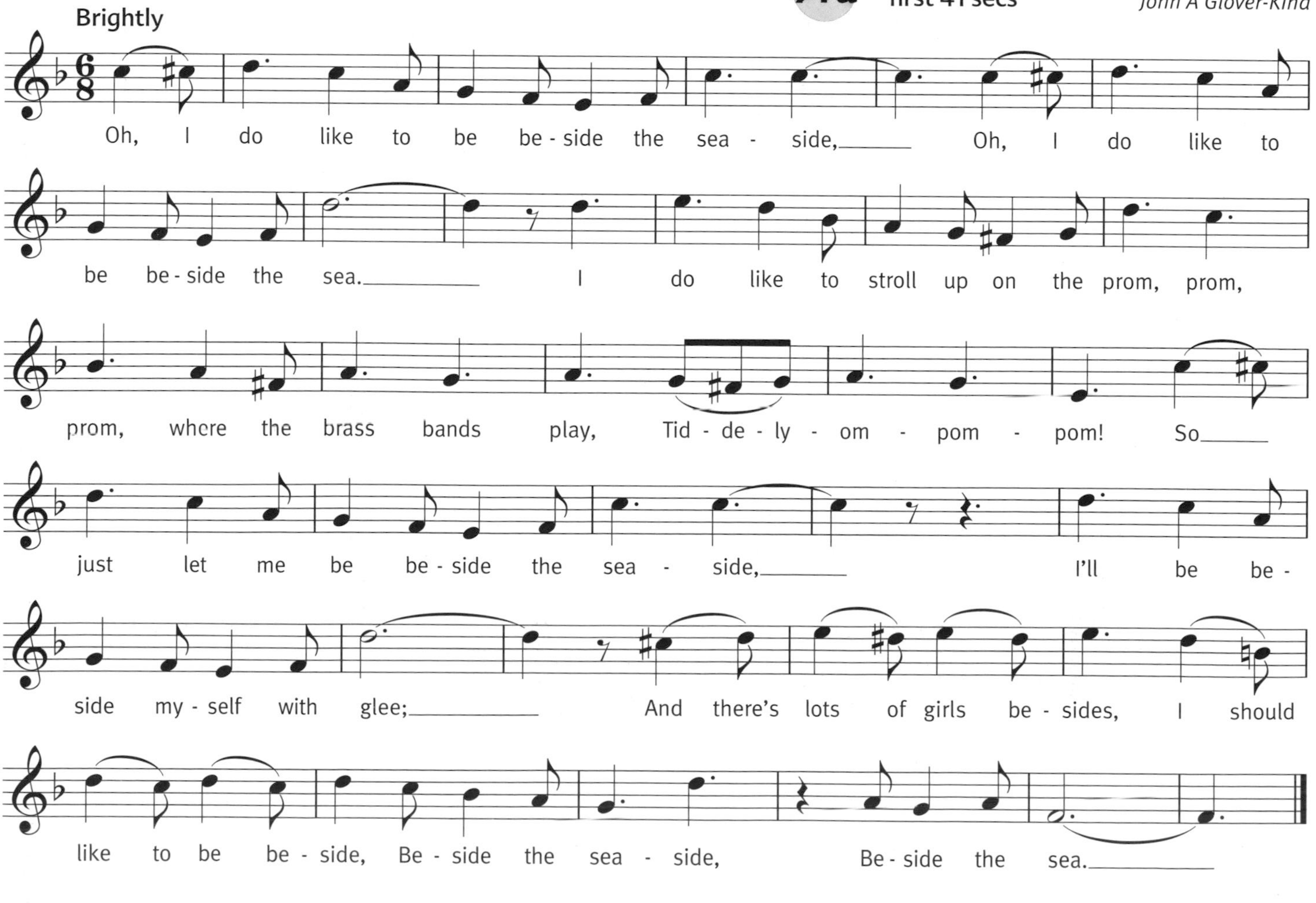

133 LITTLE AUGUSTINE AND COME DANCING (partner pieces)

91b after 41 secs

German/Swedish

leggiero — lightly

134 BOURRÉE FROM 'MUSIC FOR THE ROYAL FIREWORKS' (duet)

Handel arr. JR

Allegro leggiero

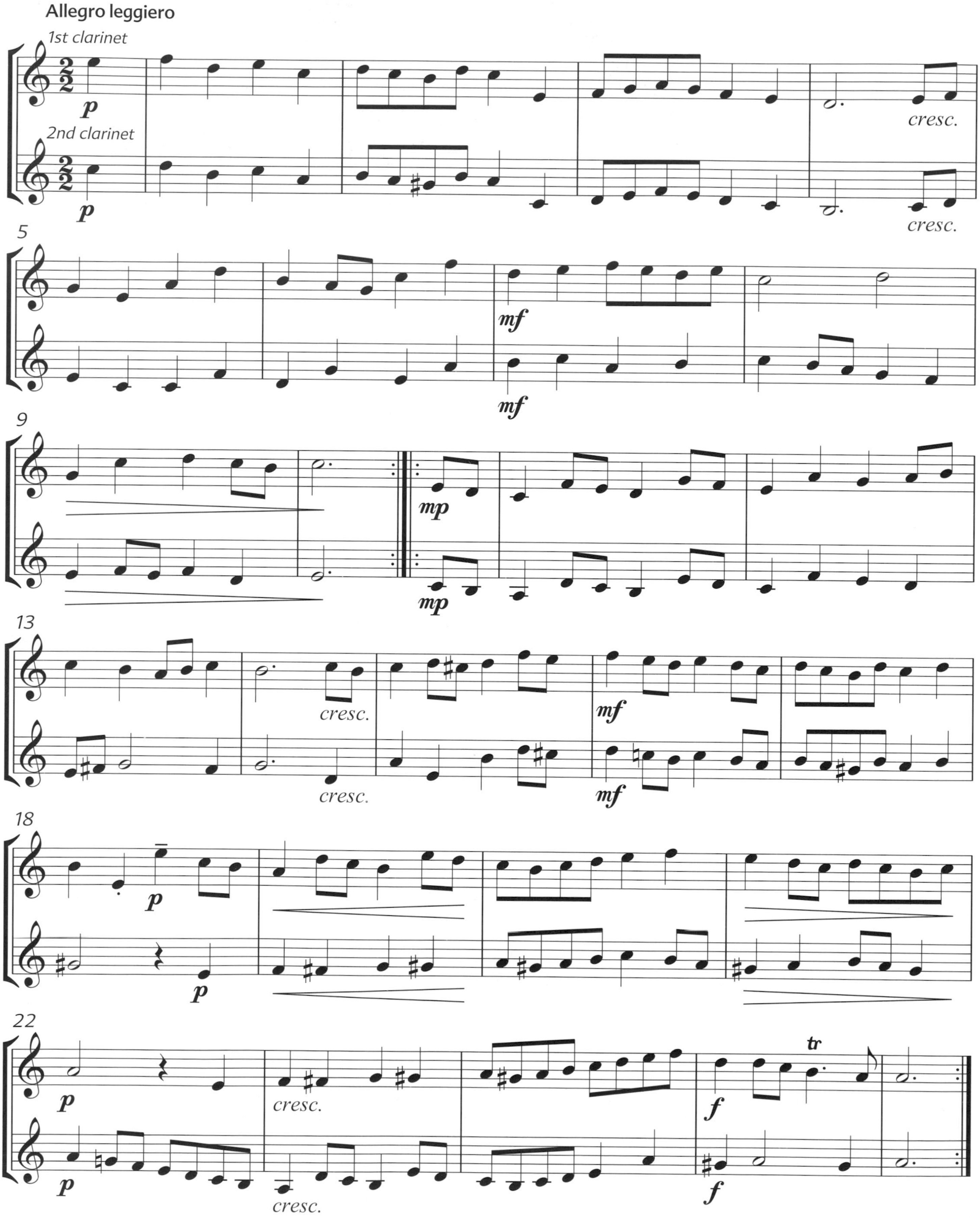

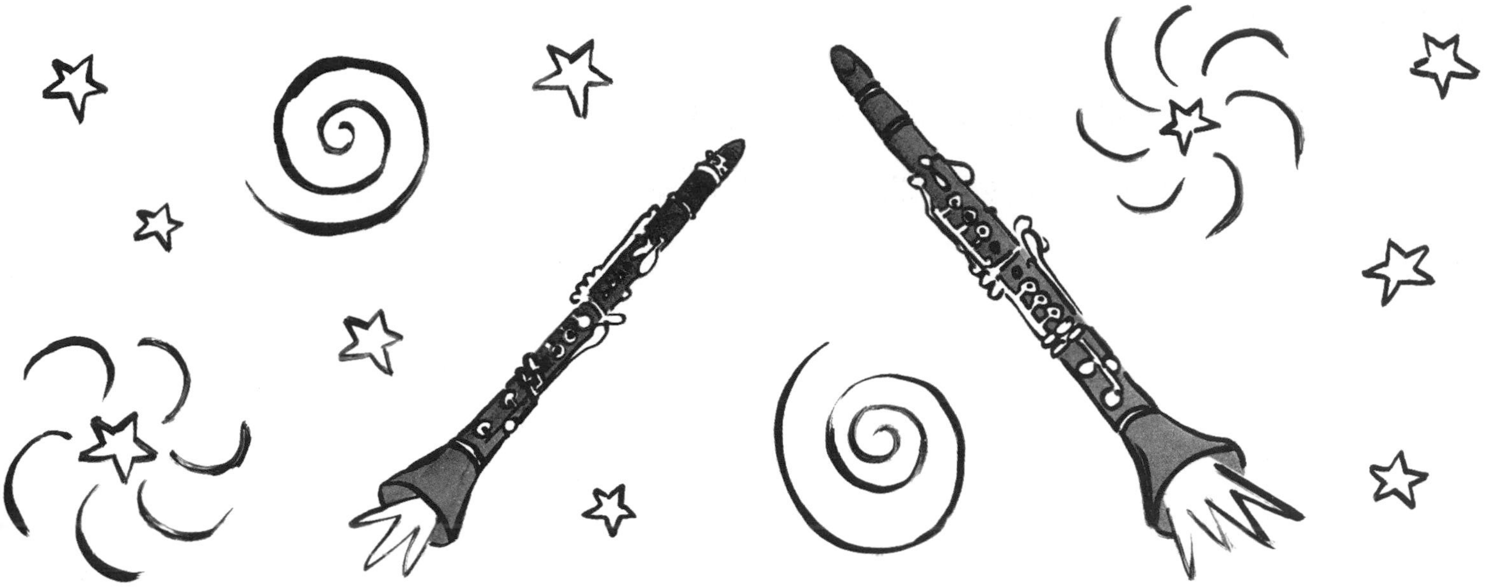

135 DUO (duet)

Berr arr. JR

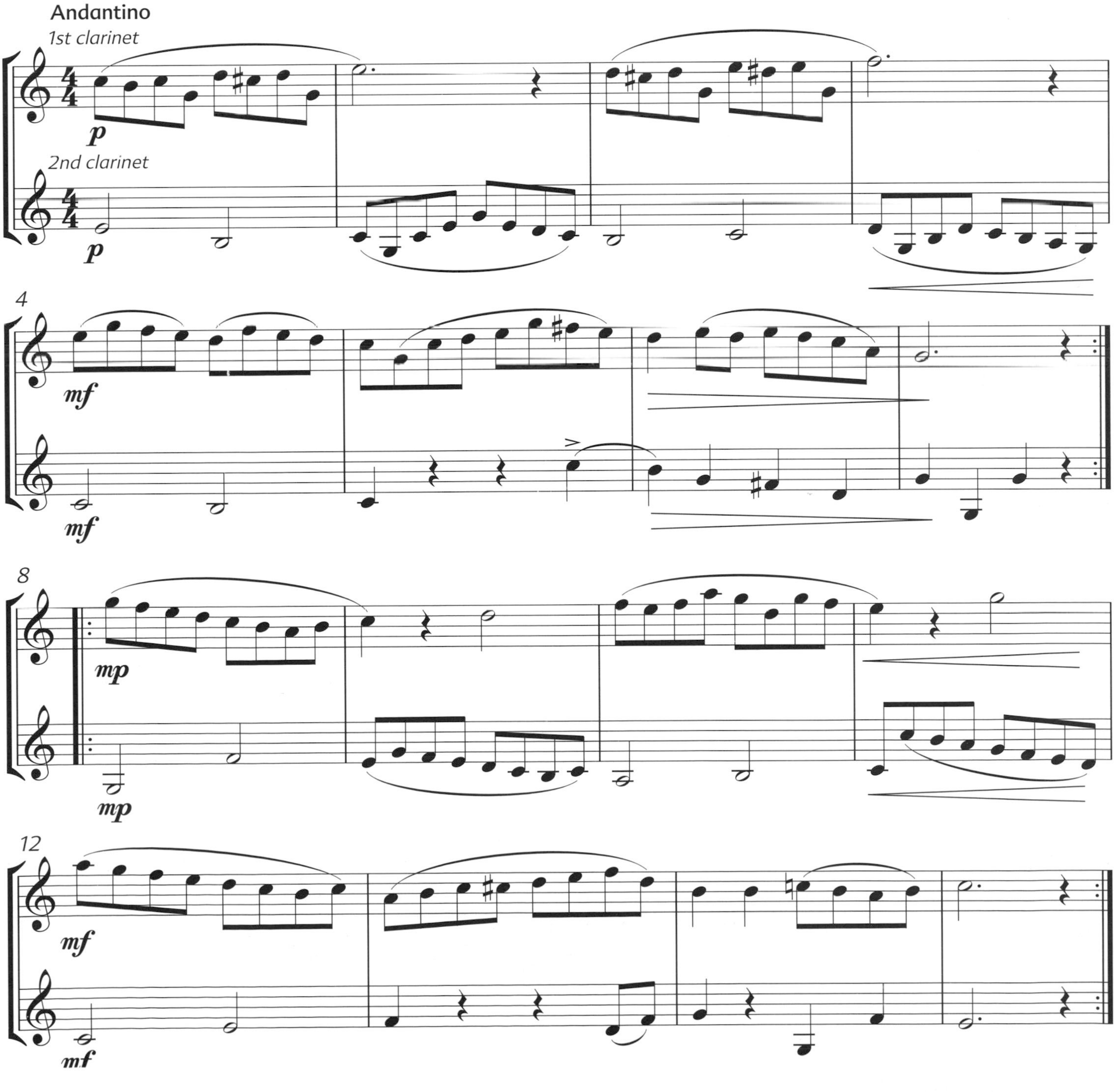

RIGHT HAND E

LEFT HAND F#

Take special care over these next two tunes. To play them fluently it is essential to use the correct sequence of LH and RH little fingers. Alternate left and right little fingers. Do not hop from one key to another with the same little finger.

♪ acciaccatura (crushed note)
Play it as quickly as you can and slur it to the following note.

sempre — always

136 THE SORCERER'S APPRENTICE

92a first 21 secs   *Dukas*

LH/RH — change fingering while playing one note

137 LYKE WAKE DIRGE **92b** after 21 secs   *traditional*

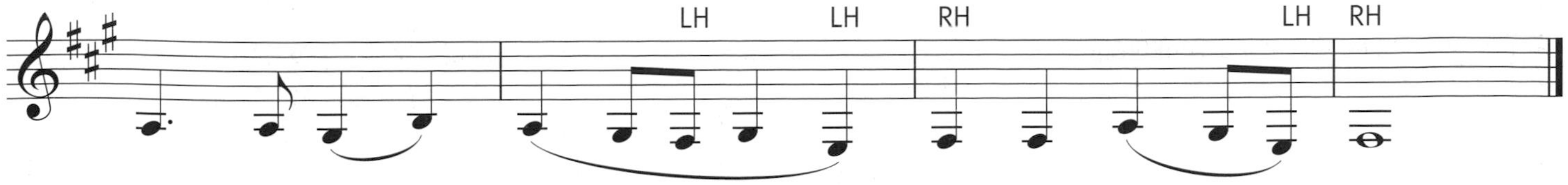

138 ZION, ME WAN GO HOME · 93a · first 19 secs

Rastafarian chant

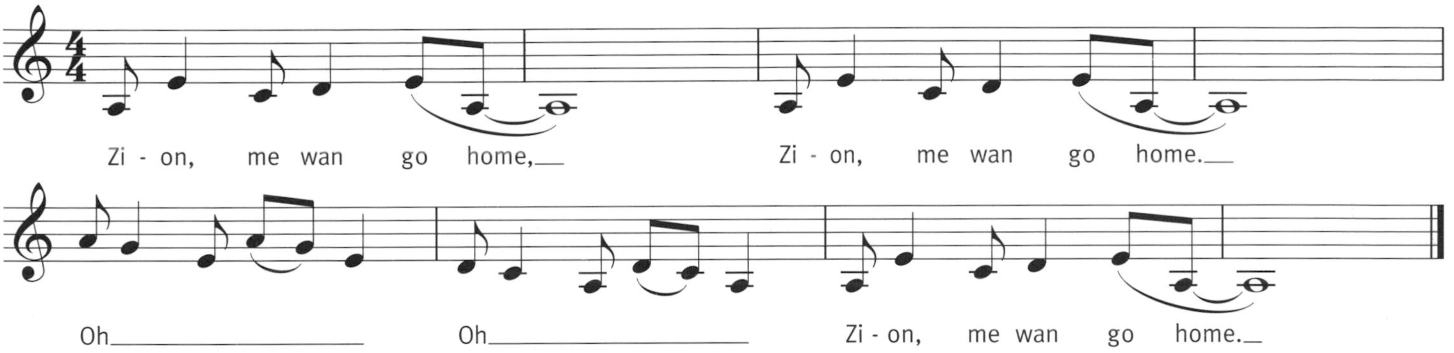

Zi - on, me wan go home,__ Zi - on, me wan go home.__

Oh__ Oh__ Zi - on, me wan go home.__

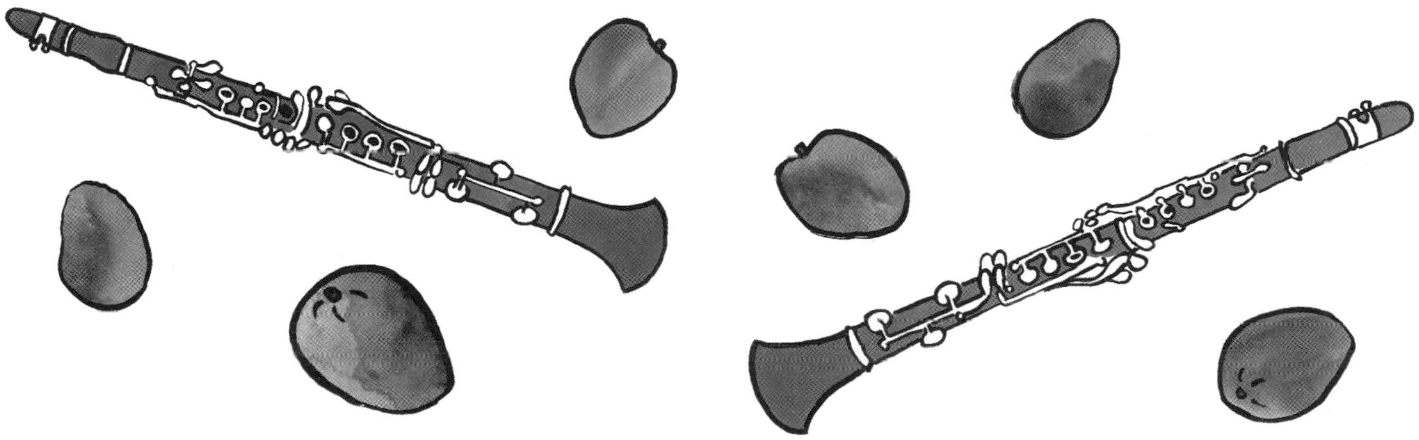

139 MANGO WALK · 93b · after 19 secs

traditional

Lightly

My bro-ther did-a tell me that you go man-go walk, You go man-go walk, you go man-go walk, My

Fine

bro-ther did-a tell me that you go man-go walk And steal all the num-ber 'le-ven.

Now tell me Joe do tell me for true, Do tell me for true, do tell me That

DC al Fine

you don't go to no man-go walk And steal all the num-ber 'le-ven.

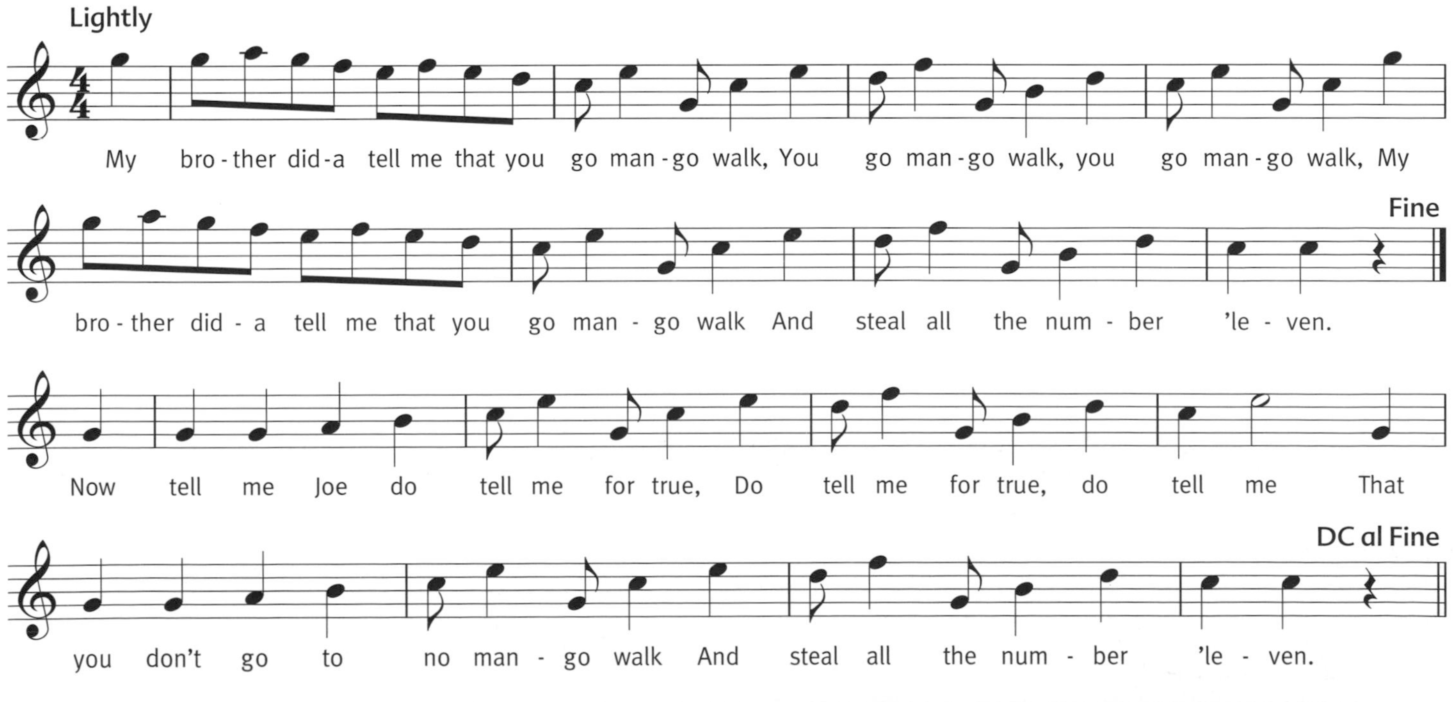

140 SWING LOW, SWEET CHARIOT

94a first 1 min 16 secs *spiritual*

Andante *mp*

Swing low, sweet cha - ri - ot,___ Com - ing for to car - ry me home,

Swing_ low, sweet cha - ri - ot,___ Com - ing for to car - ry me home. *mf* I

looked o - ver Jor - dan and what did I see,___ Com - ing for to car - ry me home? A

band_ of an - gels com - ing af - ter me,___ Com - ing for to car - ry me home.

pp

Swing low, sweet cha - ri - ot,___ Com - ing for to car - ry me home,

Swing_ low, sweet cha - ri - ot,___ Com - ing for to car - ry me home.

morendo

Com - ing for to car - ry me home.___

NEW NOTE

B

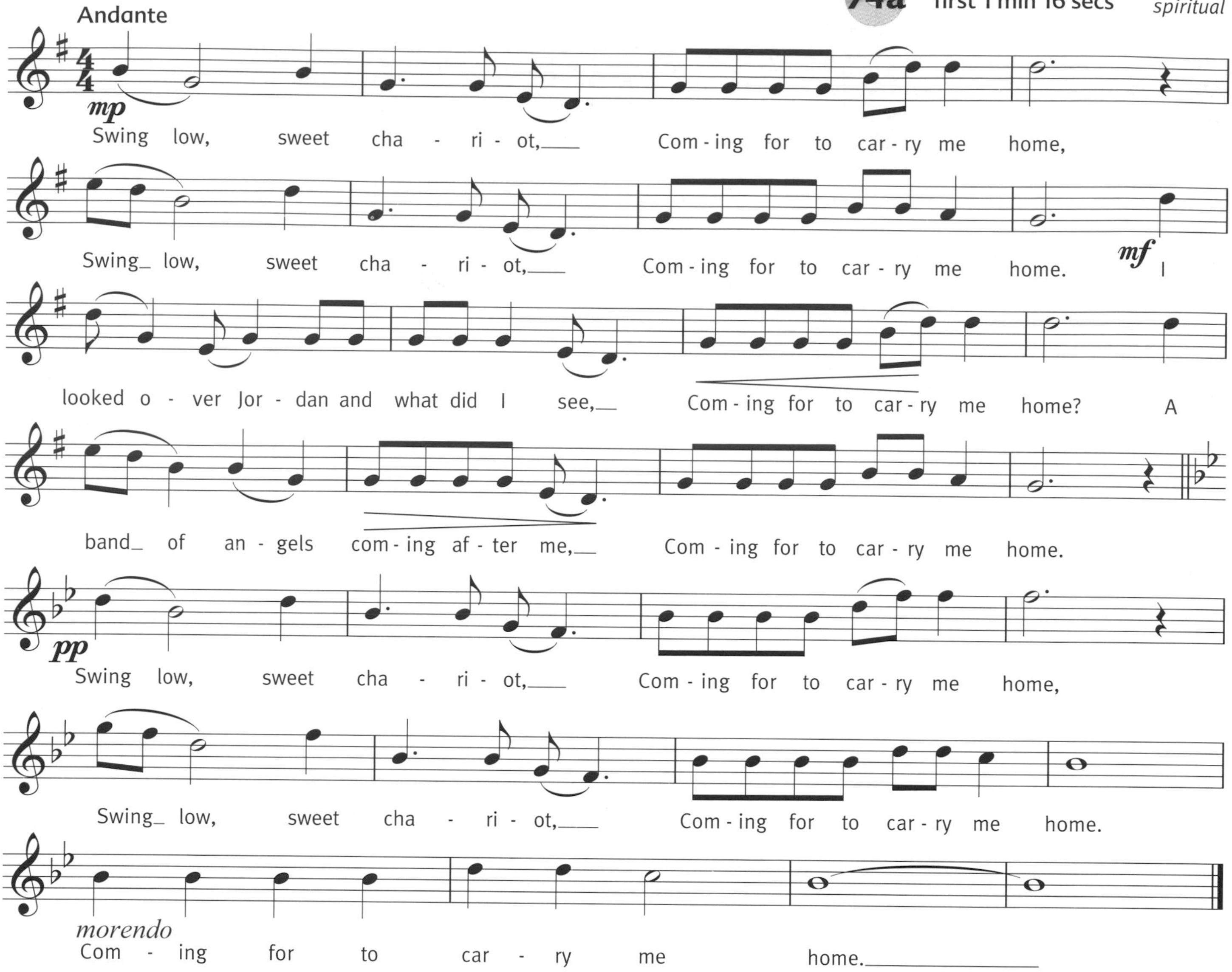

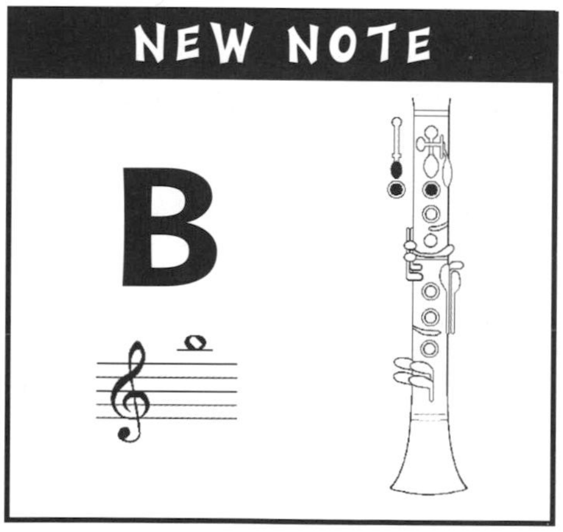

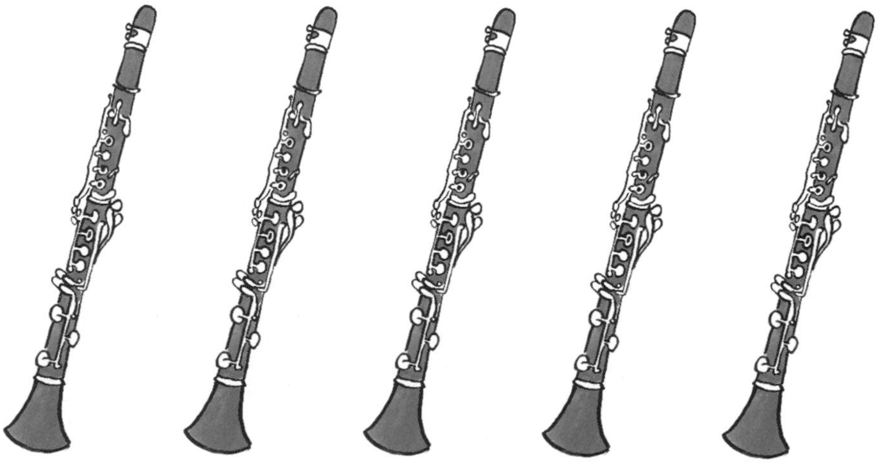

141 GO, TELL IT ON THE MOUNTAIN

94b after 1 min 16 secs *spiritual*

Strong

Go, tell it on the moun - tain, O - ver the hills and ev - 'ry - where,_ Go, tell it on the

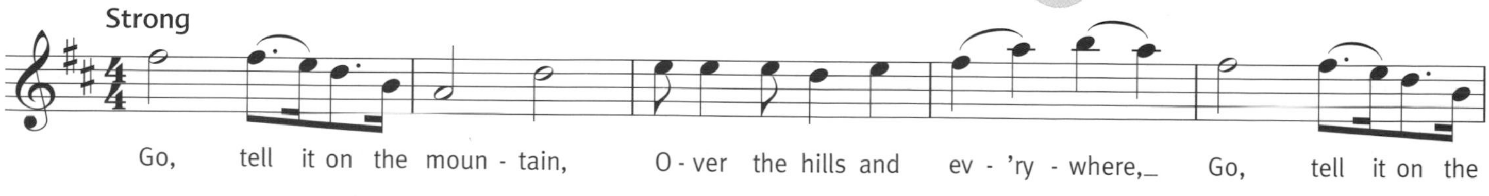

moun-tain That Je-sus Christ_ is born. While shep-herds kept their watch-ing O-ver

wan-d'ring flocks by night,_ Be-hold from out of hea-ven There shone a ho-ly light.

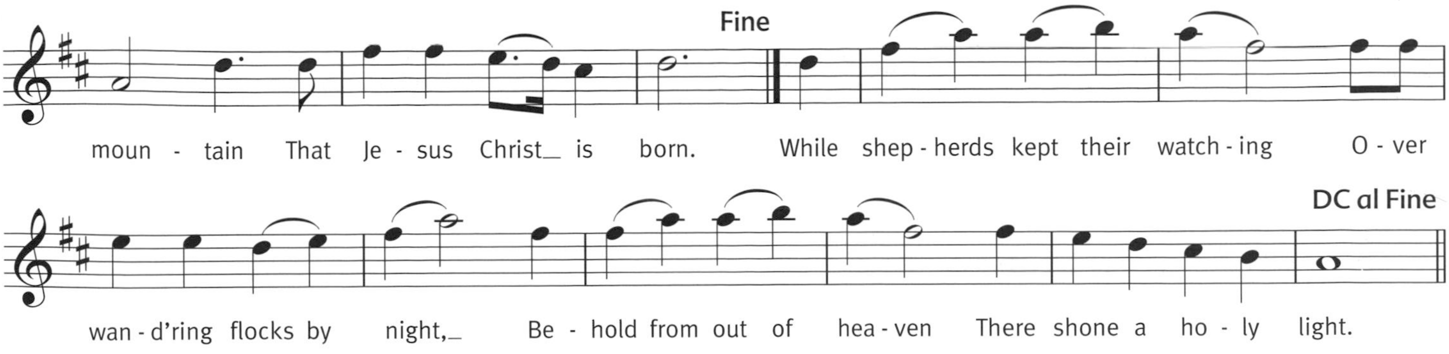

142 MUST I BE BOUND? 95a first 21 secs *traditional*

mp *cresc.* *mf* *mp*

Must_ I be bound_ and_ you go free? Must_ I love one who ne'er loved me Why_

cresc. *mf dim.* *mp*

should I act such a_ child-ish part To_ love a lad_ who will break my heart?

NEW NOTE

G#

143 THE MOCKING BIRD 95b after 21 secs *Haitian*

Allegretto

p Have you heard the song of the mock-ing bird?

When you sad and blue, Then he mock at you, He sing high a-bove, And he laugh at love.

Oh I heard his tune By the Hai-tian moon, When I lost my Chou-coune.

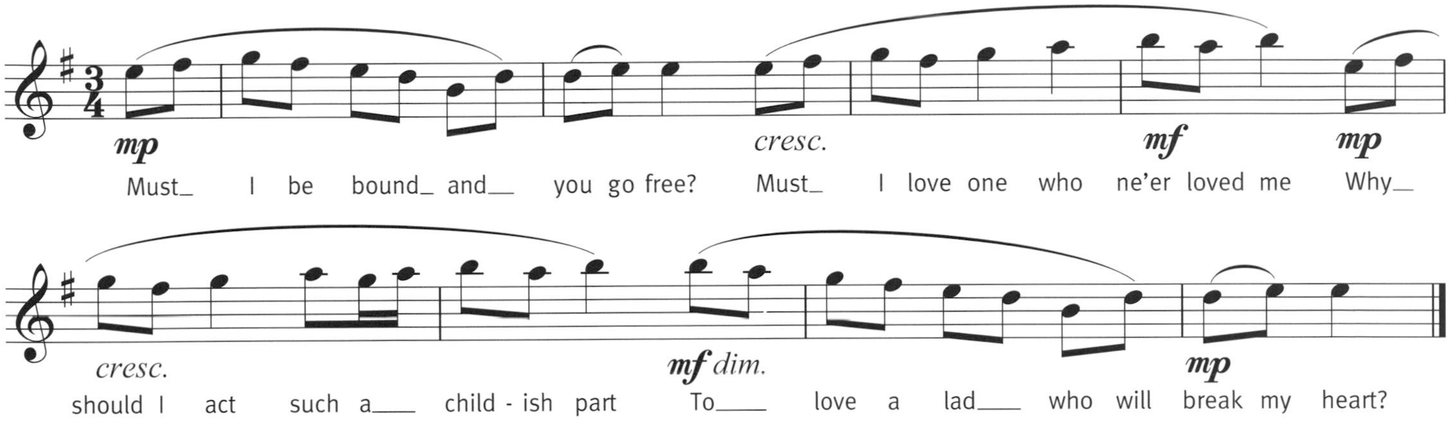

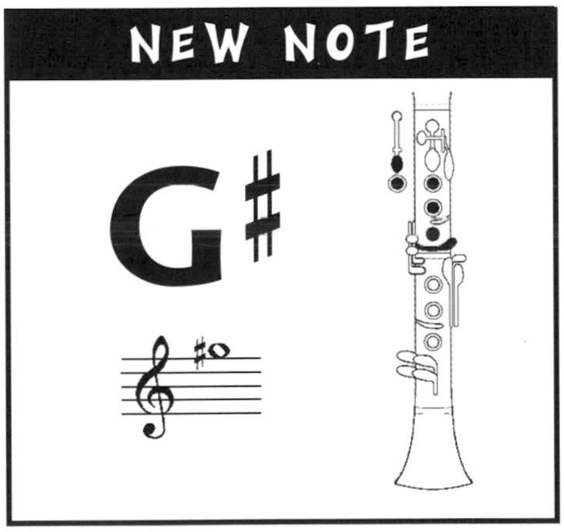

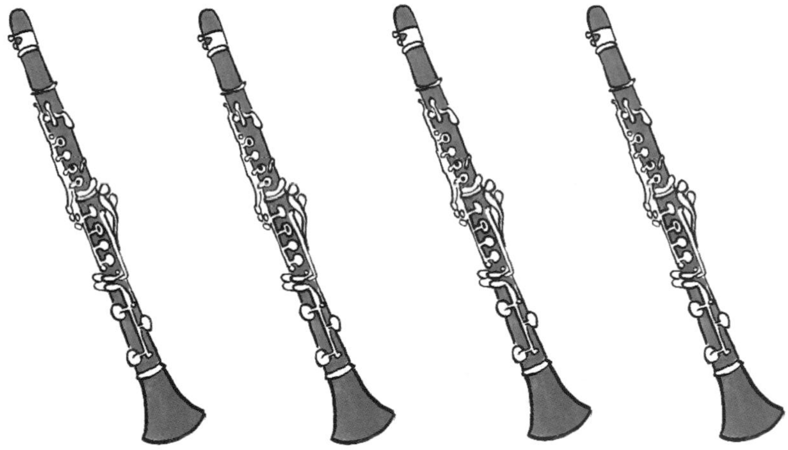

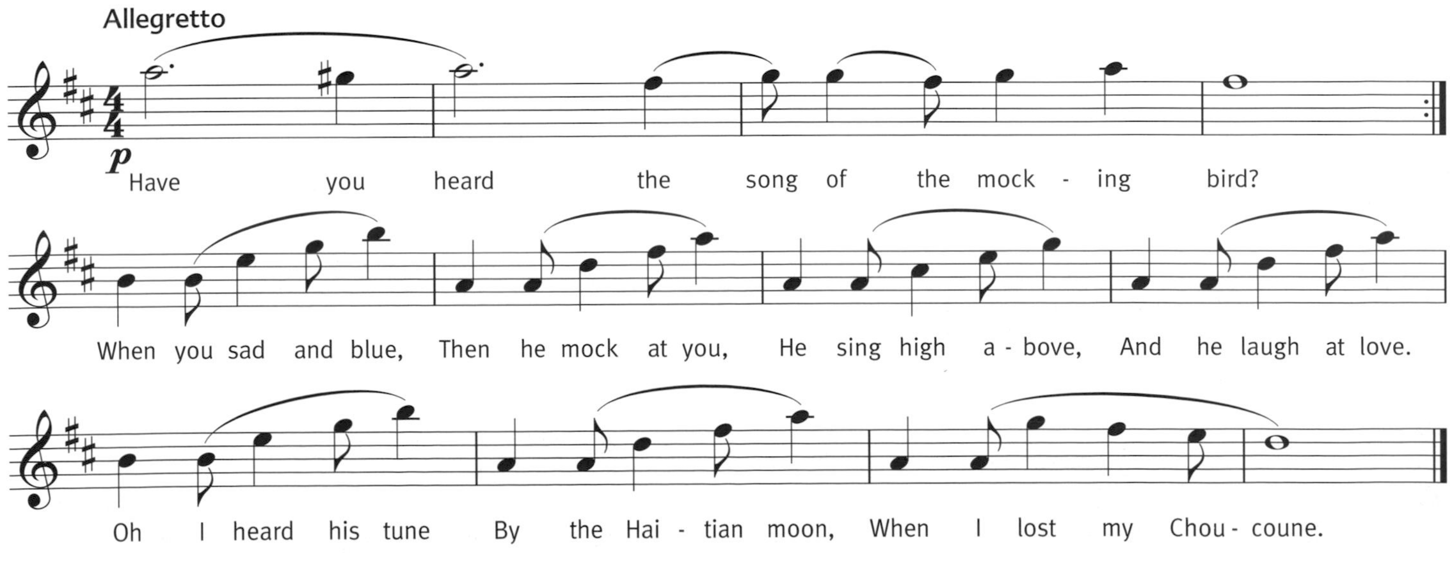

espressivo — expressively

144 THE ASH GROVE 96a first 54 secs

English words: John Oxenford
music: Welsh

Andantino

mf espressivo

The ash grove how___ grace - ful, how plain - ly___ 'tis___ speak - ing, The
o - ver its___ bran - ches the sun - light___ is___ break - ing, A

wind through___ it___ play - ing has lang - uage for me; When
host of___ kind___ fa - ces is gaz - ing on me. The

friends of___ my___ child - hood a - gain are___ be - fore me, Fond me - mo - ries___

f > mf

wa - ken as free - ly I roam, With soft whis - pers___ la - den its

leaves rust - le___ o'er me, The ash grove,_ the___ ash - grove that shel - tered my home.

NEW NOTE

B♭   or

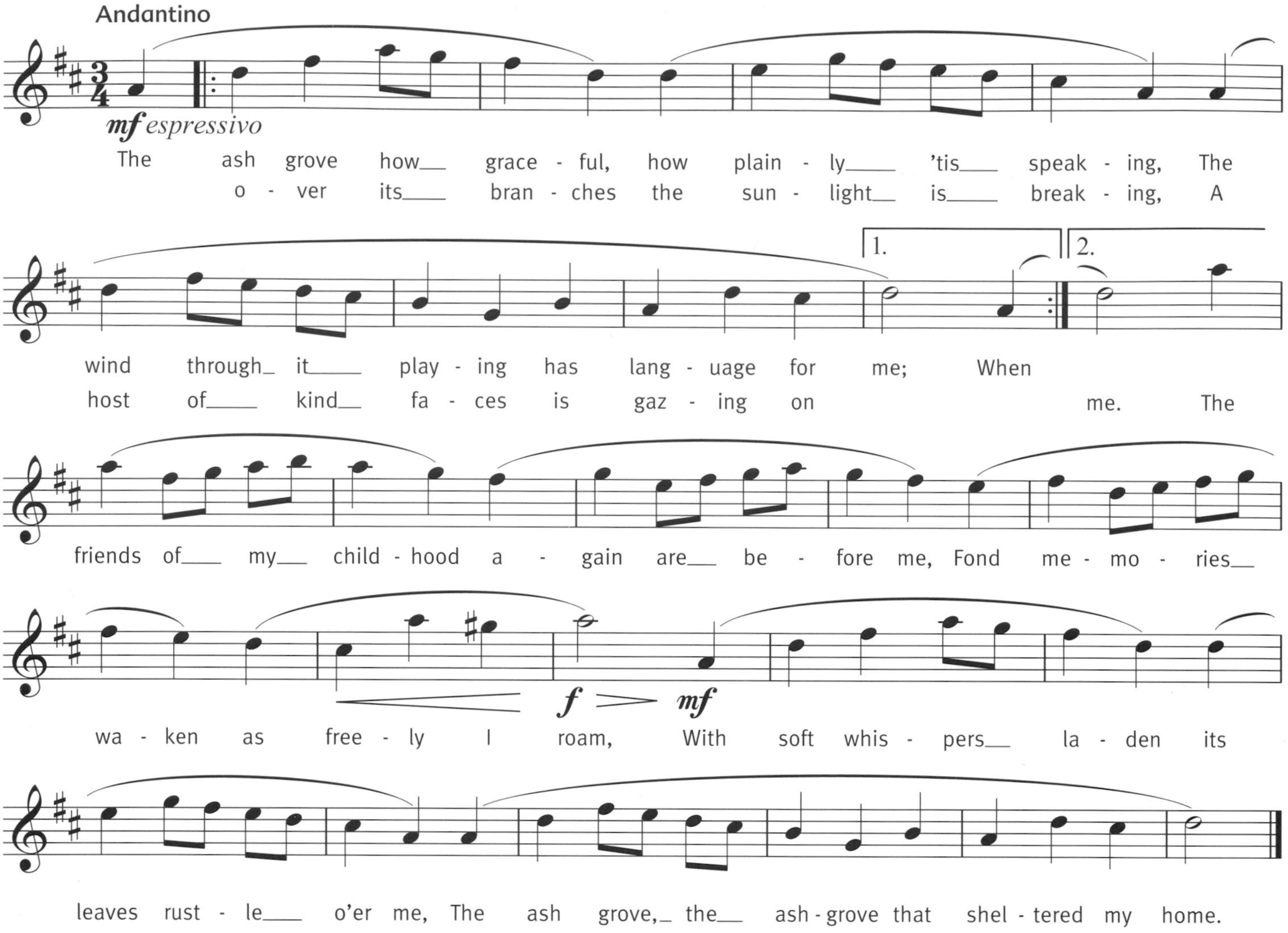

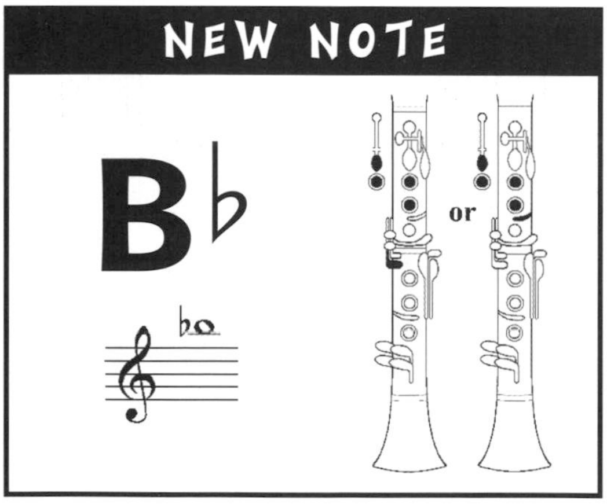

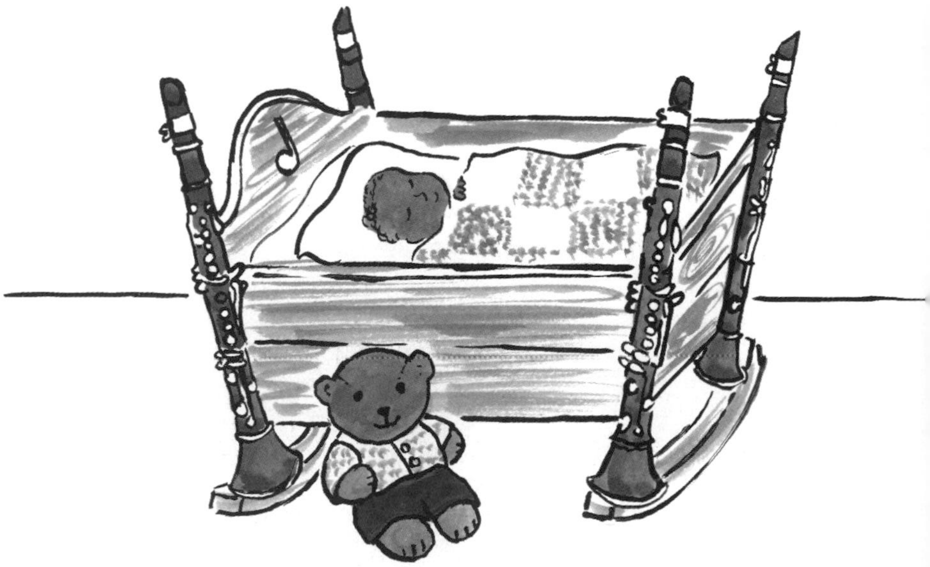

145 SLEEP MY BABY 96b after 54 secs

Yiddish folk song

Adagio

p

Sleep my ba - by, I will croon to you, I will sing a lul - la - by, And when my child you grow to

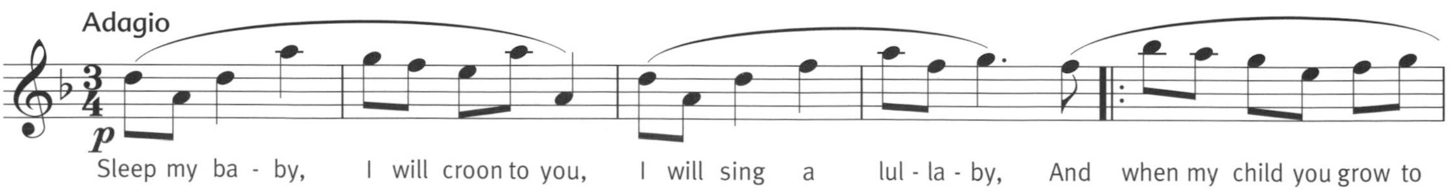

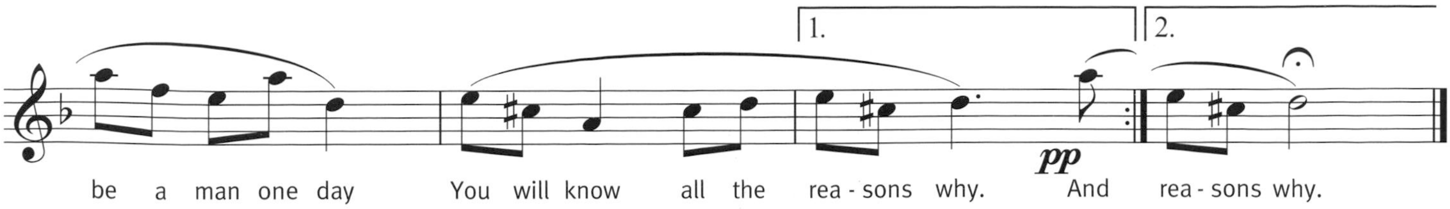

be a man one day You will know all the rea-sons why. And rea-sons why.

146 KHAYANA **97a** first 20 secs

Gujarati

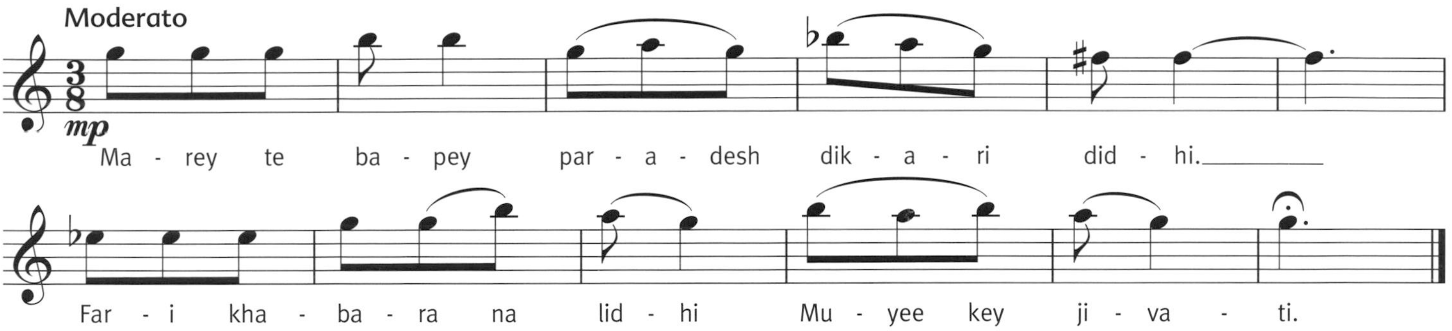

Moderato

mp

Ma - rey te ba - pey par - a - desh dik - a - ri did - hi._____

Far - i kha - ba - ra na lid - hi Mu - yee key ji - va - ti.

147 THE KING OF LOVE
MY SHEPHERD IS (duet)

words: H W Baker
music: Irish
arr. L H Page

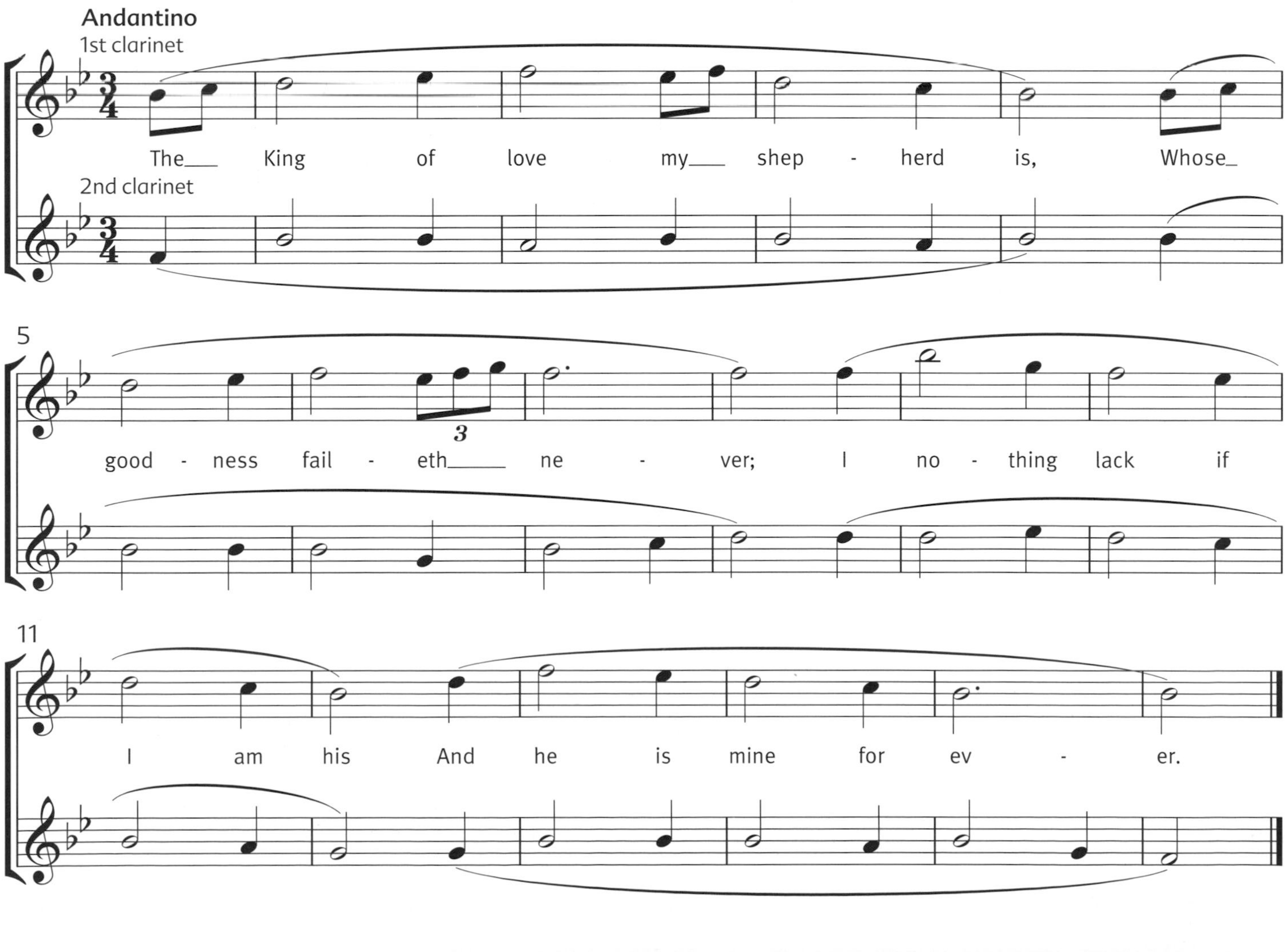

Andantino

1st clarinet

The__ King of love my__ shep - herd is, Whose__

2nd clarinet

good - ness fail - eth___ ne - ver; I no - thing lack if

I am his And he is mine for ev - er.

148 CONSIDER YOURSELF

97b after 20 secs

Lionel Bart

NEW NOTE

C

149 MY GRANDFATHER'S CLOCK

98a first 60 secs

Henry C Work

My grand-fa-ther's clock was too large for the shelf so it stood nine-ty years on the floor, It was

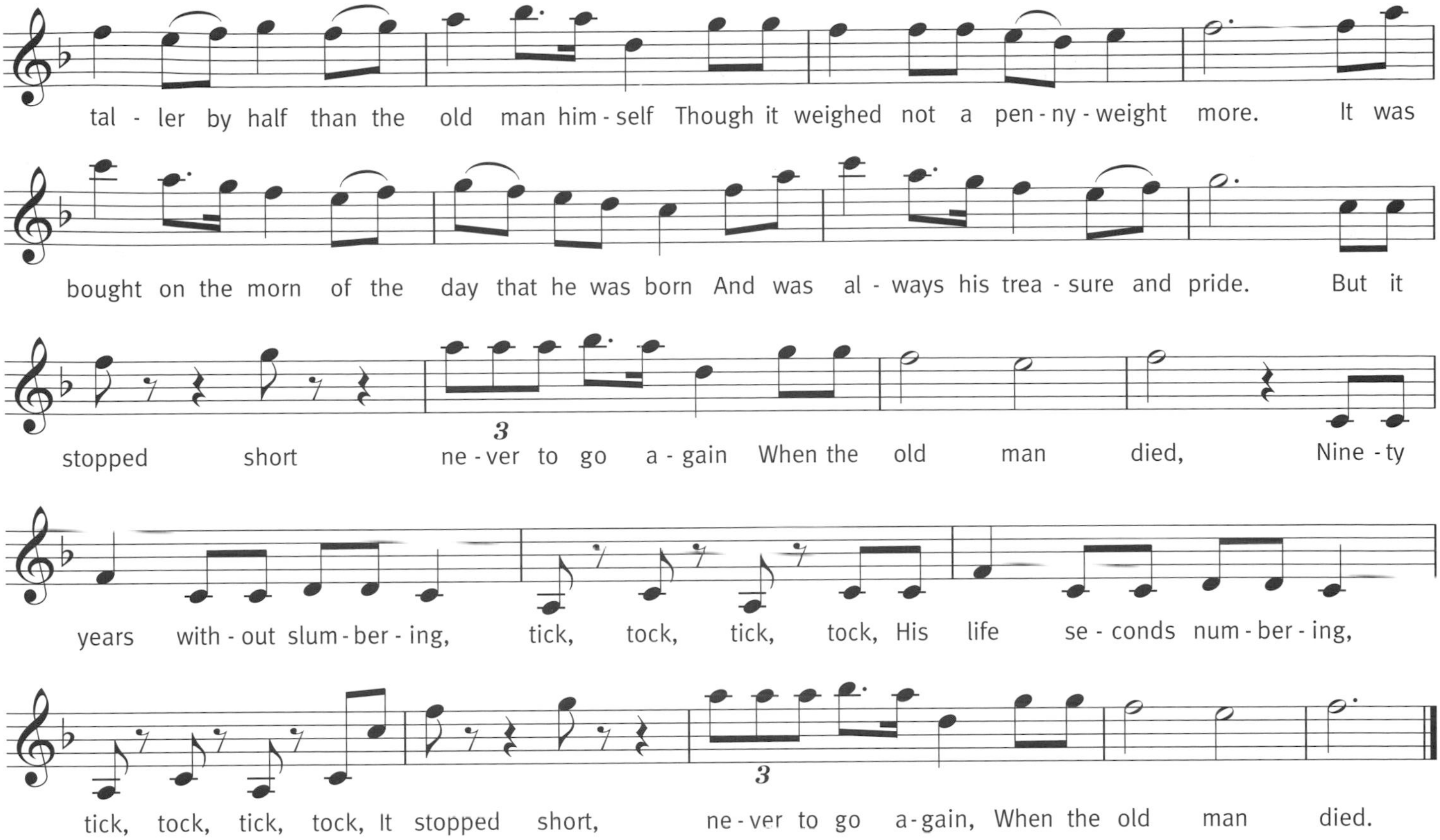

tal - ler by half than the old man him - self Though it weighed not a pen - ny - weight more. It was

bought on the morn of the day that he was born And was al - ways his trea - sure and pride. But it

stopped short ne - ver to go a - gain When the old man died, Nine - ty

years with - out slum - ber - ing, tick, tock, tick, tock, His life se - conds num - ber - ing,

tick, tock, tick, tock, It stopped short, ne - ver to go a - gain, When the old man died.

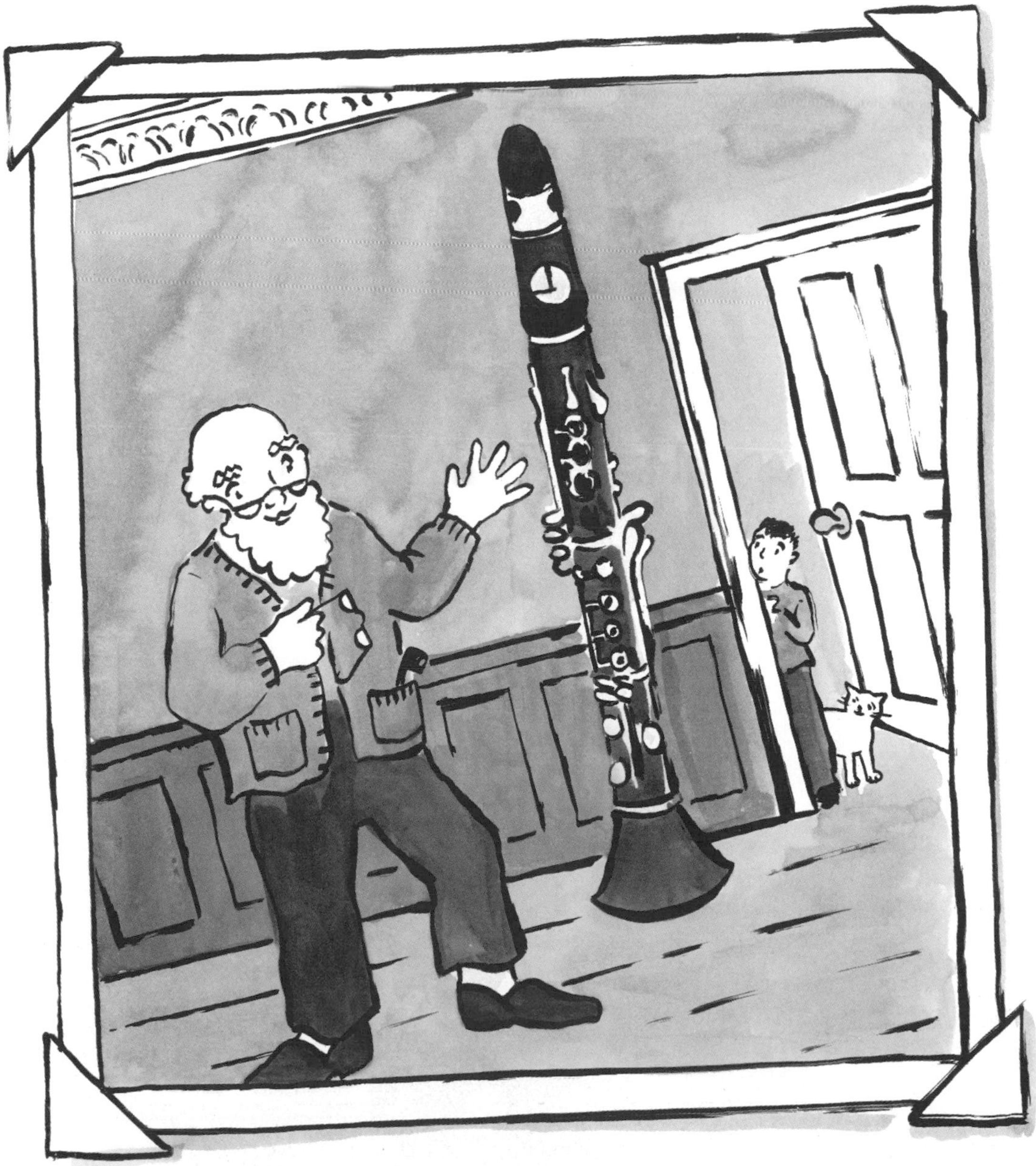

150 MINUET (duet)

Mozart arr. JR

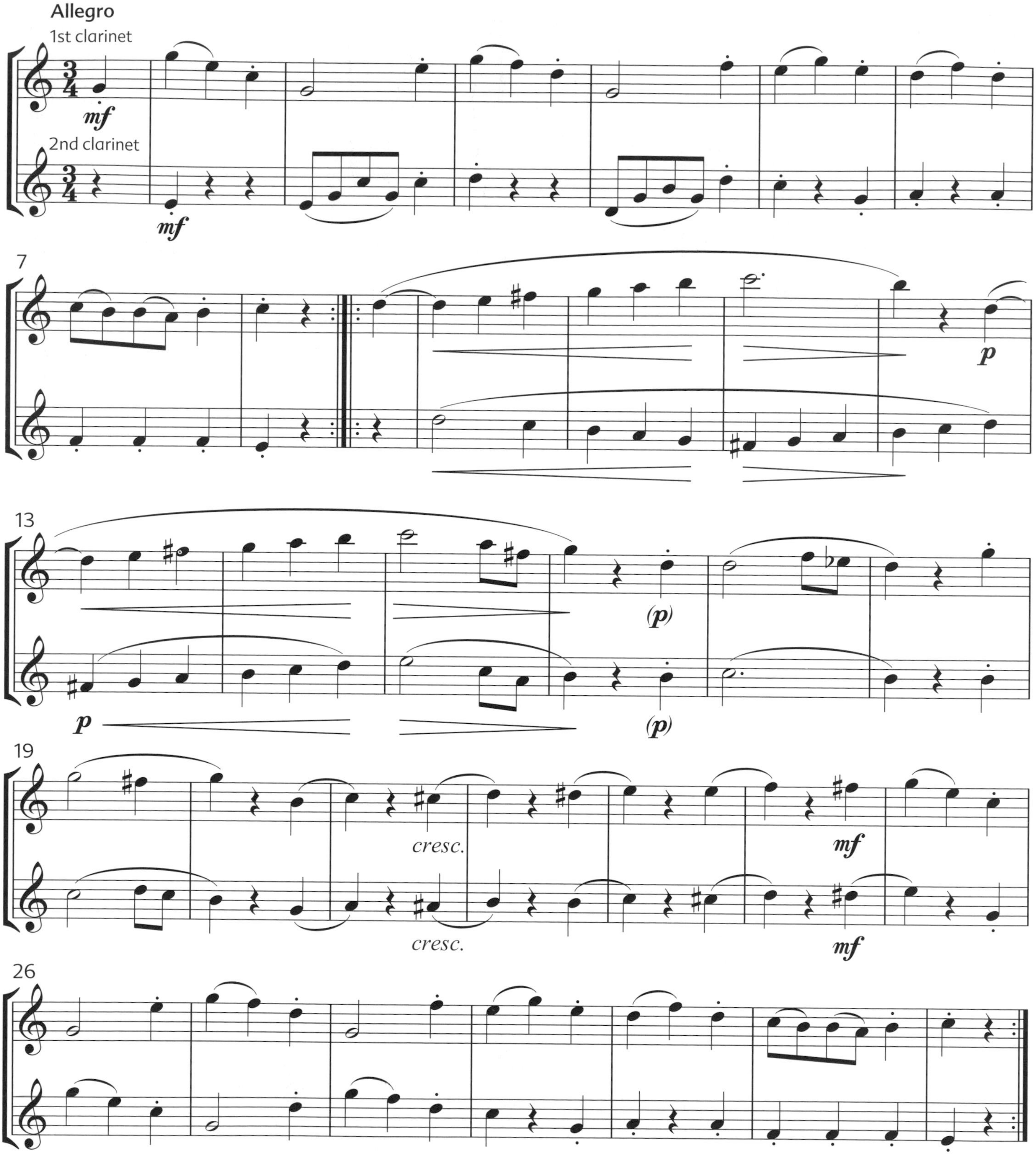

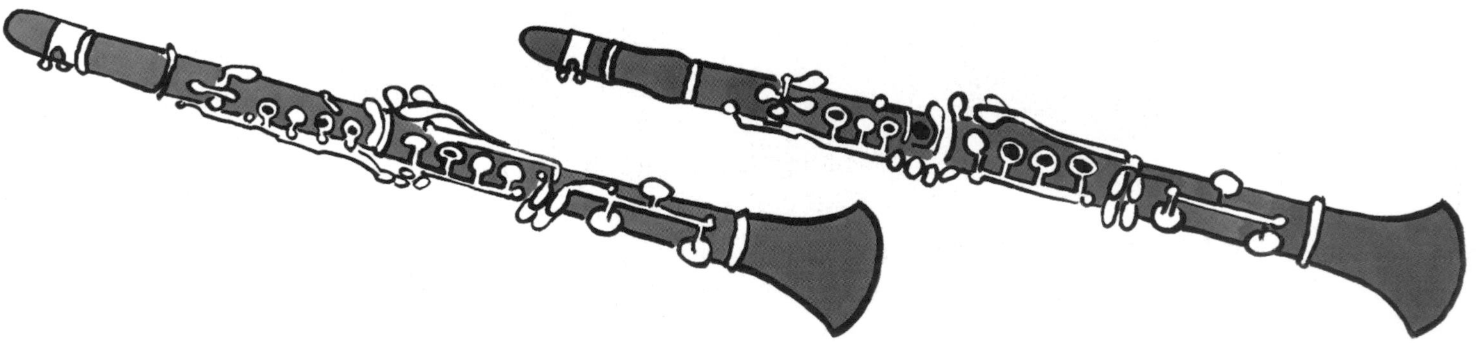

In jazz and blues music, pairs of quavers are played with a triplet feel

151 AMERICAN PATROL 98b after 60 secs

F W Meacham

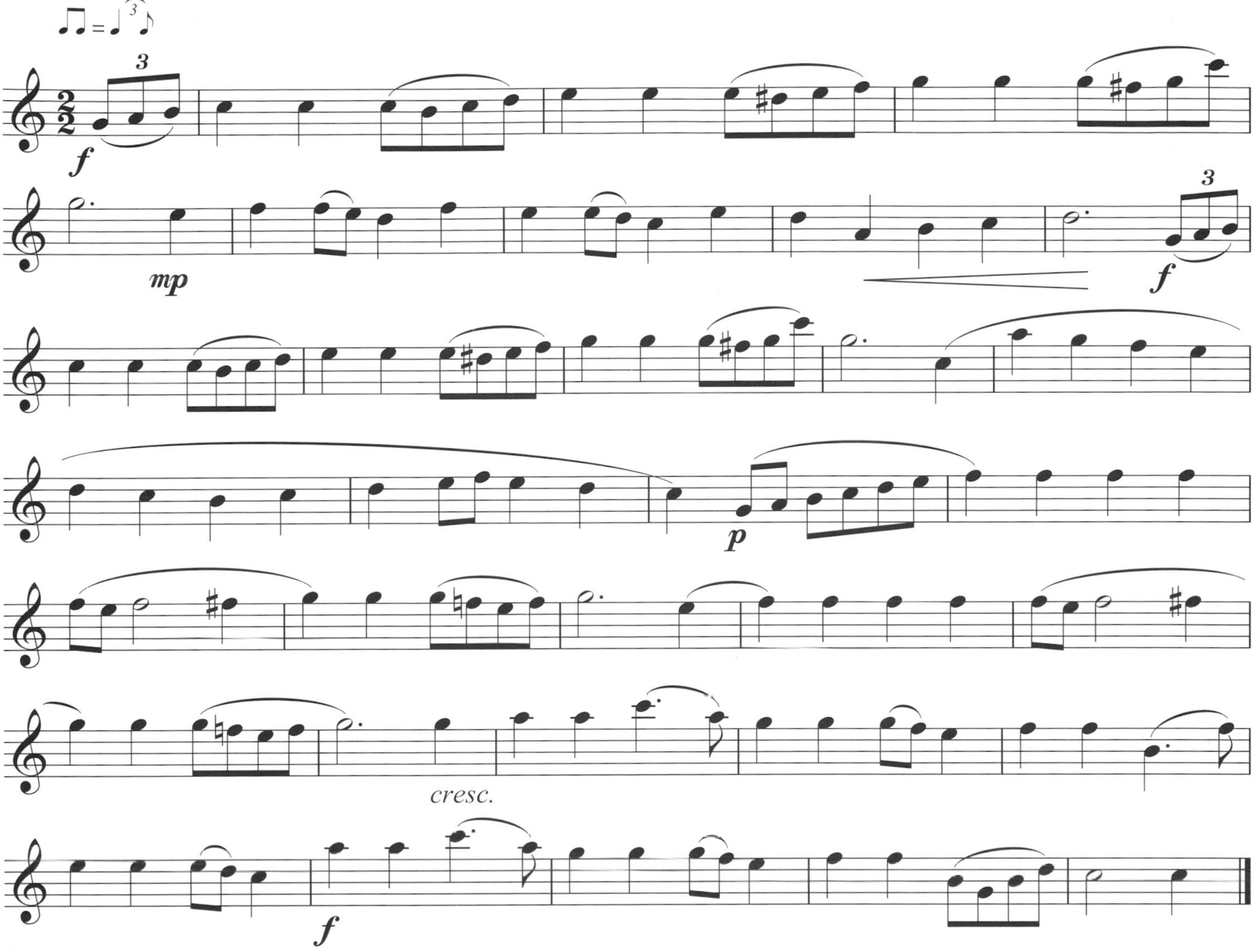

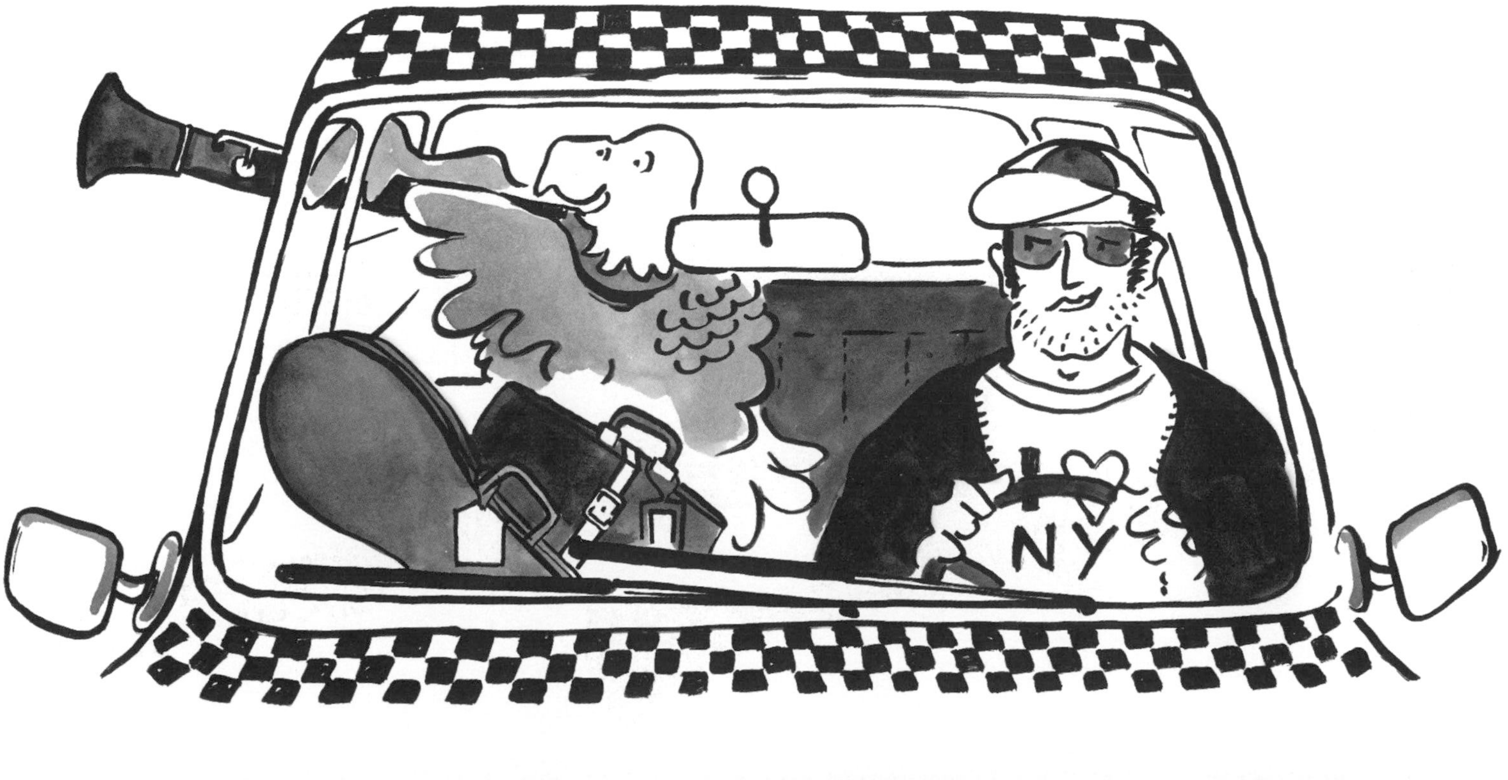

152 DUET (duet)

Ozi arr. JR

Allegro moderato e leggiero

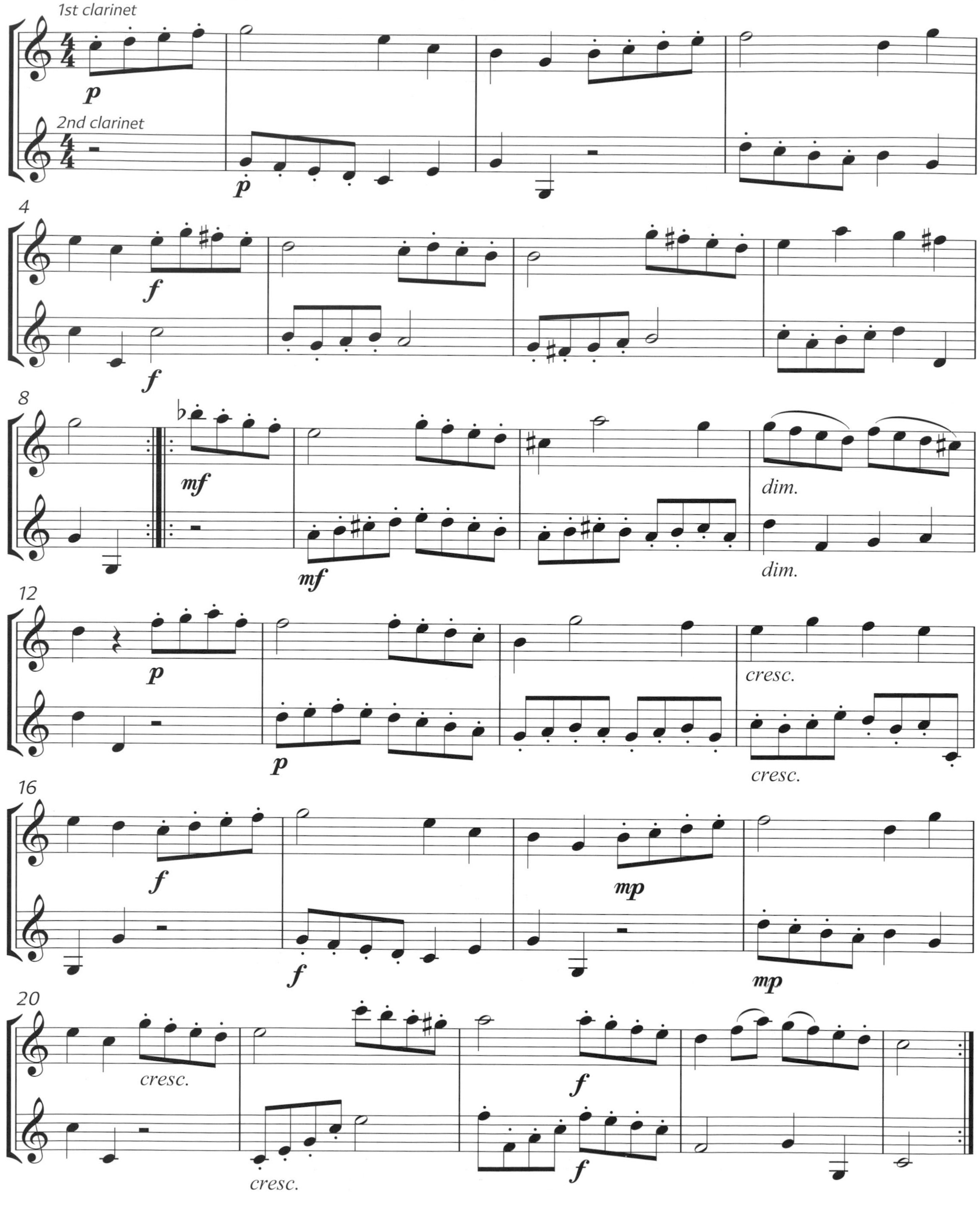

153 CZECH DANCE 99a first 17 secs

traditional

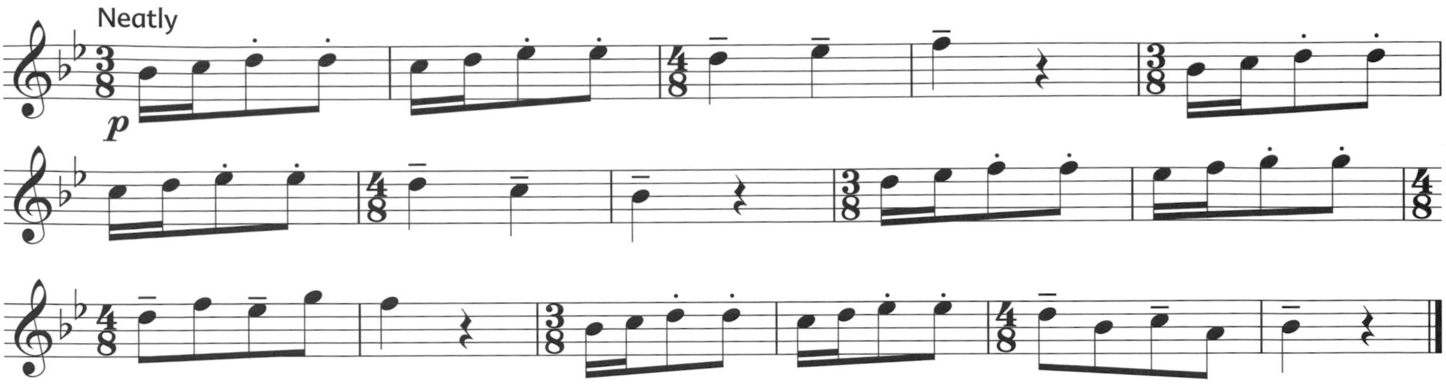

🎵 — semiquaver rest

154 THE ENTERTAINER 99b after 17 secs

Scott Joplin

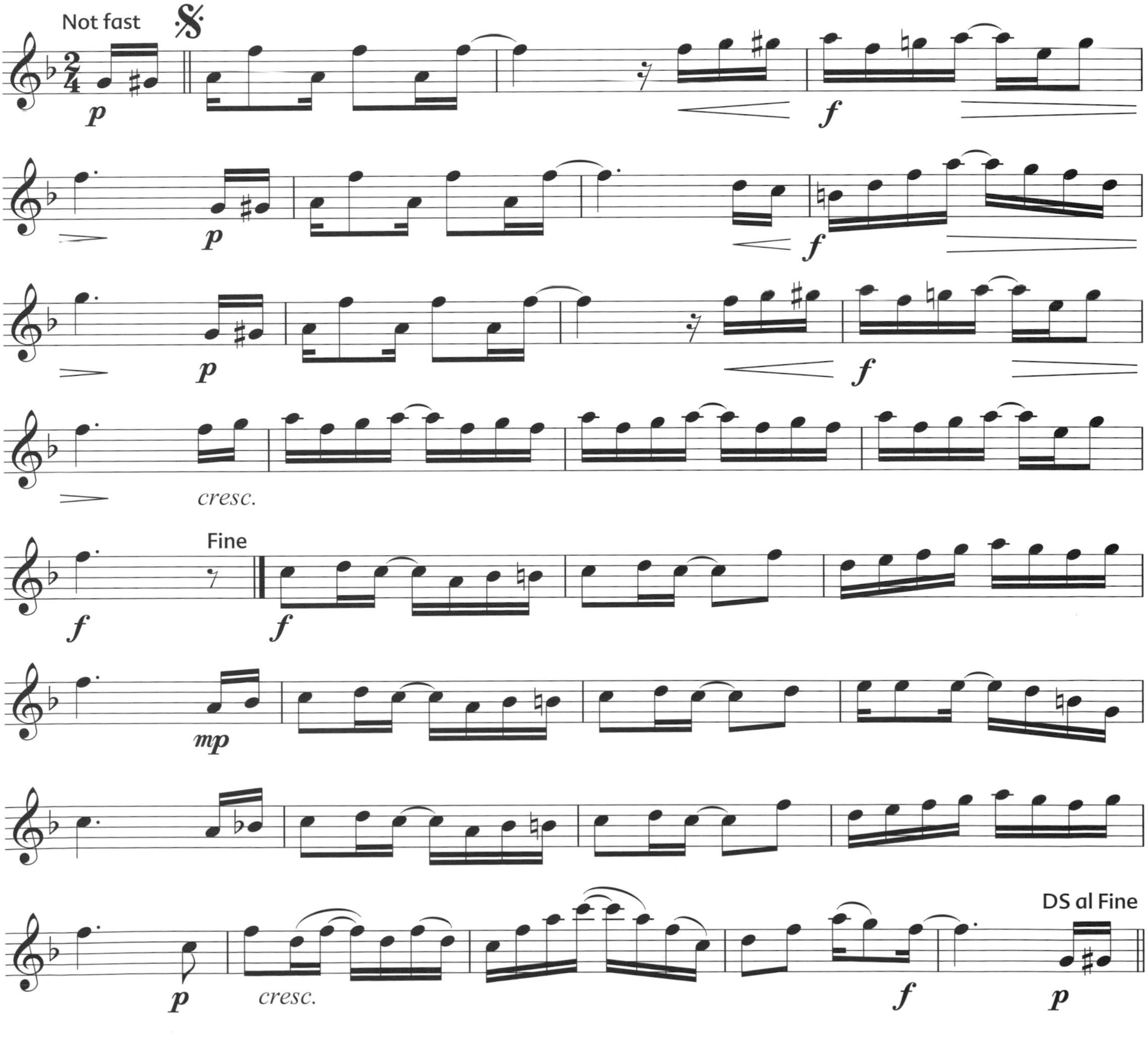

INDEX

Piano accompaniment numbers are shown in brackets. See below for details of Abracadabra Clarinet Piano Accompaniments book.

ABRACADABRA CLARINET PIANO ACCOMPANIMENTS

Over 100 pieces from Abracadabra Clarinet expertly arranged with simple and effective piano accompaniments to give musically rewarding support to the learner right from the start.

ISBN 0 7136 4724 8

For a full list of A&C Black titles, including music for the classroom, song books, musicals, CDs and cassettes, assembly resources and instrumental tutors, contact A&C Black, PO Box 19, St Neots, Cambs PE19 8SF
telephone: 01480 212666 fax: 01480 405014 email: sales@acblack.com

www.acblack.com

ACKNOWLEDGEMENTS

The author and publisher would like to thank the following for their help in the preparation of this book: Roger Abbott, David Fuest, Michael Haslam, Emily Haward, Christian Horn, Chris Hussey, Lynda and Richard Ling, Jocelyn Lucas, Ralph Orlowski, Alison Pinder, Graham Pinder, Sheena Roberts, Michelle Simpson, Helen Williams and Zoe Williams.

The following have kindly granted permission for the reprinting of copyright material:

Amadeo-Brio Music Inc for **Morningtown ride** © 1959 Amadeo-Brio Music Inc. International copyright secured. Administered by Leosong Copyright Service Ltd.

Dorothy Armstrong for **In Paris.**

John Bannister for his adaptation of **Sing this song** © John Bannister.

Boosey & Hawkes Music Publishers for **The Cat Theme** from Peter and the Wolf by Prokofieff © 1937 Hawkes & Son (London) Ltd and for **Two canons** from Mikrokosmos (Bartok arranged Suchoff) © 1940 by Hawkes & Son (London) Ltd. Definitive edition © copyright 1987 by Hawkes & Son (London) Ltd. Reproduced by permission of Boosey & Hawkes Music Publishers Ltd.

Michael Cole for the words of **Ten chimney pots.**

J Curwen & Sons Ltd for **Hills of the north rejoice.** Hymn tune "Little Cornard". Music © Martin Shaw. Exclusively licensed to and reproduced by kind permission of J Curwen & Sons Limited, 8/9 Frith Street, London W1D 3JB. All rights reserved. International Copyright Secured.

Peter Davey for **Off to France in the morning.**

Ted Edwards for **Coal-hole cavalry.**

David Fuest for **Break Dance, Frog in my throat** and **Smooth mover** © 2002 David Fuest.

Noel Gay Music for **Thank U very much.** Words and music by Michael McGear © Copyright 1967 Noel Gay Music Company Limited, 8/9 Frith Street, London W1. Used by permission of Music Sales Ltd. All Rights Reserved. International Copyright Secured.

Ronnie Hazlehurst for **Last of the summer wine** © Ronnie Hazlehurst Ms.

David Higham Associates for the words of **Morning has broken** by Eleanor Farjeon, from The children's bells, published by Oxford University Press

Catherine Johnson for the arrangement of **Portsmouth.**

Lakeview Music Publishing Co Ltd and TRO-Hollis Music Inc for **Oom pah pah** and **Consider yourself**; from Oliver! Words and music by Lionel Bart © copyright 1960 (renewed 1988). Lakeview Music Publishing Co Ltd; London UK; TRO-Hollis Music Inc, New York controls all publications rights for the USA and Canada. Used by permission. All Rights Reserved.

Nick Munns for the arrangement of **Gavotte** (Hook).

Novello & Company Limited for **Bushes and briars.** Collected and arranged by Ralph Vaughn Williams. Reproduced by permission of Novello & Company Limited, 8/9 Frith Street, London W1D 3JB.

Oxford University Press for the words of **Lord of all hopefulness**, words by Jan Struther (1901-53) from Enlarged Songs of Praise 1931 by permission of Oxford University Press; **Hey little bull**, words by A H Green © Oxford University Press 1966; **Andrew mine Jasper mine** from Three Moravian Carols, by permission of Oxford University Press; for the music of **Over the earth is a mat of green**, melody adapted by Herbert Wiseman (1866-1966) from Children Praising, by permission of Oxford University Press and for the words and music of **Susan and Catherine** from The Oxford Book of Carols © Oxford University Press 1964.

Peermusic (UK) Limited for **You are my sunshine**. Words and music by Jimmie Davis & Charles Mitchell © copyright 1949 Peer International Corporation USA. Peermusic (UK) Limited, 8-14 Verulam Street, London WC1. Used by permission of Music Sales Ltd. All Rights Reserved. International Copyright Secured.

Alison Pinder for **Yes indeed, Curious tortoise, Zig-zag, One-legged chicken, Night prowler, Take your partners, Prairie call, Wobbly jelly, Blue Lagoon, EGGY bread, FEED me** and **Donkey in the rain.**

Jonathan Rutland for **Setting out, Salad Days, Cool, Checkmate,** and the arrangements of **Berceuse d'Auvergne, Oh Susanna, Hornpipe, Bourrée, Duo, Minuet** and **Duet.**

Lorna Rutland for **Strolling along** and **Sadness.**

Schroder Music Company/TRO Essex Music Ltd for **Little boxes**, words by Malvina Reynolds © 1962 Schroder Music Co, renewed 1990. Used by permission. All Rights Reserved.

Jane Sebba for **Easy, Earwig crunch, Keep on running, Blue mist,** and the arrangement of **Old Joe Clark.**

Stainer & Bell for **Lullaby of the spinning wheel.** Music by F T Durrant. © Stainer & Bell Ltd.

Sticky songs Ltd for the music of **Ten chimney pots.**

Editions Durand SA, Paris for **The Sorcerer's Apprentice** (extract by Dukas). Reproduced by permission of Editions Durand SA, Paris.

Warner/Chappell Music and Cherry Lane Music for **Puff the magic dragon.** Words and music by Lenny Lipton and Peter Yarrow. Copyright © 1963; renewed 1991 Honalee Melodies (ASCAP) and Silver Dawn Music (ASCAP). Worldwide rights for Honalee Melodies administered by Cherry Lane Music Publishing Company Inc. Worldwide rights for Silver Dawn Music administered by WB Music Corp. (70% Warner/Chappell Music Ltd, London W6 8BS. Reproduced by permission of IMP Ltd, 30% published for the world by Cherry Lane Music Publishing Co Inc). International copyright secured. All rights reserved.

Every effort has been made to trace and acknowledge copyright owners. If any right has been omitted, the publishers offer their apologies and will rectify this in subsequent editions following notification.

ABRACADABRA CLARINET - RECORDING

Clarinet played by Dave Fuest
Piano played by Michael Haslam
Engineered by Laurence Diana at Miloco, London

GLOSSARY OF ITALIAN TERMS

adagio	—	slow
allegretto	—	briskly, not as fast as allegro
allegro	—	fast and lively
allegro moderato	—	moderately fast
andante	—	at a leisurely pace
cantabile	—	in a singing style
crescendo, cresc.	—	gradually becoming louder
da capo, DC	—	from the beginning
dal Segno, DS	—	from the sign
diminuendo, dim.	—	gradually becoming quieter
dolce	—	sweetly
e	—	and
espressivo	—	expressively
forte	—	loud
fortissimo	—	very loud
legato	—	smoothly
leggiero	—	lightly
lento	—	slow
marcato	—	each note stressed
mezzo forte	—	moderately loud
mezzo piano	—	moderately quiet
moderato	—	at a moderate speed
morendo	—	dying away
molto moderato	—	at a moderate pace
pianissimo	—	very quiet
piano	—	quiet
ritardando	—	gradually get slower
sempre	—	always
staccato	—	short and detached

Scales and arpeggios (for Associated Board examinations, grades 1, 2 and 3)

Grade 1

F major (one octave)

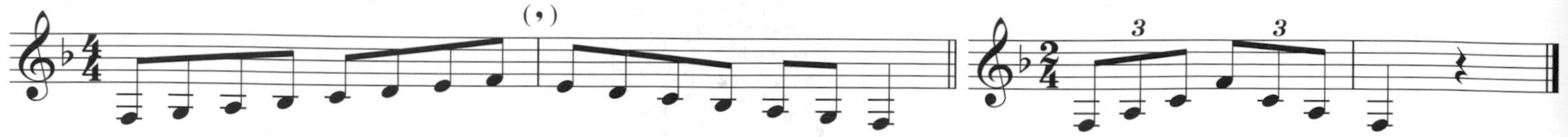

G major (one octave)

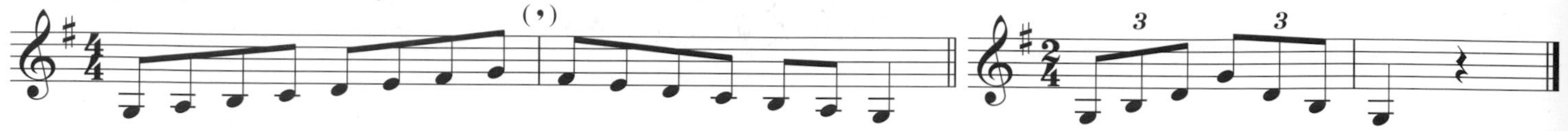

A minor (one octave)

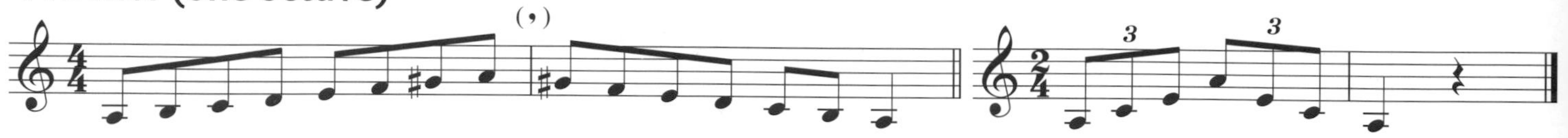

Grade 2

C major (one octave)

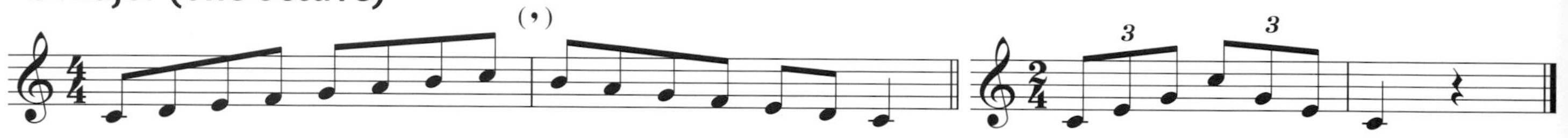

D minor (one octave)

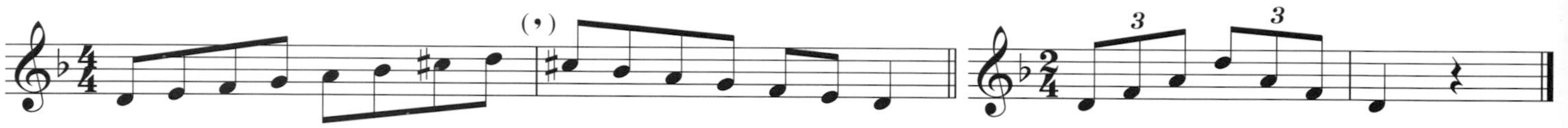

F major (two octaves)

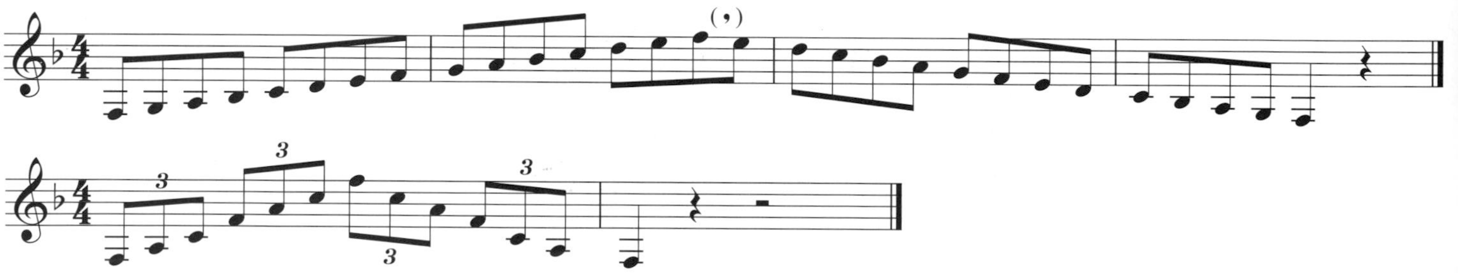

G major (two octaves)

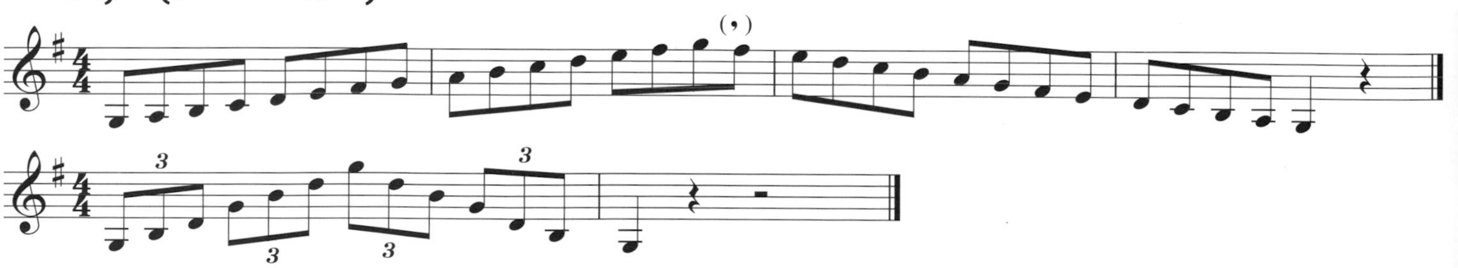

A minor (two octaves)

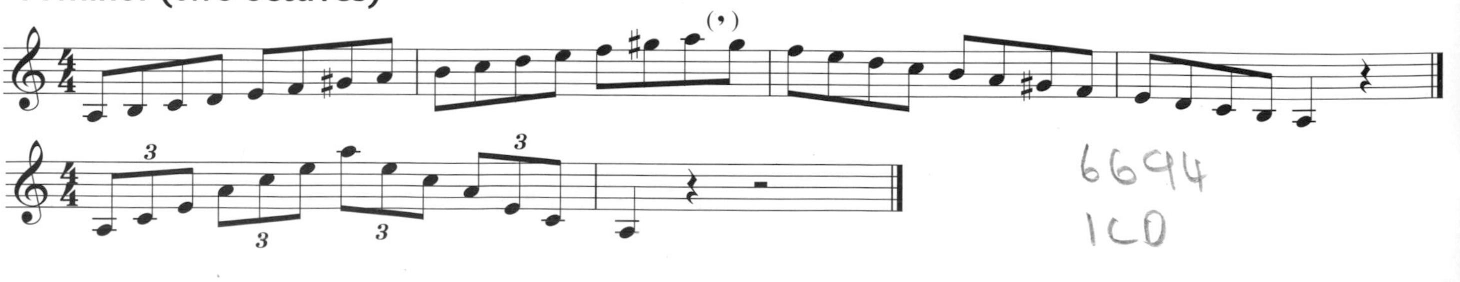